Scions
Of
Smyrna

K. PEARSON BRADLEY

"Be grateful for whoever comes, because each has been sent as a guide from beyond."

Rumi

CONTENTS

ACKNOWLEDGMENTS

It's often said that writing is a solitary act, and in many ways, it is. However, publishing a book, at least in my experience, has been a group effort of immense proportion. You would not be reading this book without the contributions of my developmental editor and brilliant book coach, Emily Tamayo Maher, whom I also consider a friend and mentor. She keeps me on track and motivates me to improve my writing with joy and enthusiasm. DejaVu also inspires me with her cover art, which manages to capture the essence of the story even before I've finished writing it.

My family and friends have been a source of comfort and support while writing this book and transitioning into life as a full-time author, and I have leaned on them heavily while birthing the second book in the Merchant Tides series. Marilyn, Jesse, Ginger, Natalie, Annabel, Audrey, Joelle, Kathie, Lisa L., Lisa M., Stephanie, Debby, Terri, and Mona, thank you. A special note of thanks goes to beta reader, Caroline F., who provided thoughtful comments and cheered me on to the finish line.

I owe a singular debt of gratitude to my dear friends Melanie and Preetika, two of the strongest, smartest, and most compassionate women I know. The many times we've spent contemplating spirituality, drinking wine, discussing the meaning of life, sharing mile-long texts, zooming, staying up late, and traveling together, despite living in different parts of the country, have helped me flavor the female characters in this book with my favorite kind of girl power. You ladies rock!

My brother from another mother, Tony, who gave me the

idea for this series, and who served as the inspiration for Seba's grandfather, Papouli, continues to share his vast knowledge of Greek proverbs, philosophy, food, music, and relationships with me, and has been an integral part of the writing process. He knows all about dancing with the creative muse, and he is never too busy to offer advice when I ask.

I have so much appreciation for those independent authors and bibliophiles who put their ideas and stories on paper and send them into the world. These women write books, reviews, articles, and find all manner of ways to share their knowledge of writing, editing, and publishing, especially: Laura Akers, Emily Dexter, Megan Elder Evans, Laura Lyndhurst, Kristalyn Vetovich, and Rachael Watson. You are my role models.

And finally, to my husband Dave, daughter Kate, and daughter Jane, who brainstorm with me, read drafts, offer lots of helpful insights, and never seem to tire of my obsession with writing. You are the best!

1 FRACAS

Smyrna, Turkey 1766

Sebastian Krizomatis ducked and instinctively raised his arms to protect his head as a splintered wooden stool soared past him. The *Aigokeros* taverna, in the heart of Smyrna's Greek quarter, was a den of chaos. Sebastian winced and inhaled sharply as one of the legs of the stool clipped his left wrist, sending a searing jolt of electricity down his arm. He had injured his wrist several weeks before in an earthquake that rocked the western coast of Turkey and sent huge limestone boulders tumbling into the Aegean Sea. He was lucky to be alive. Somehow, he had made it to the bustling city of Smyrna with one working arm and lots of cuts and bruises. He wanted to inspect his wrist to see if it was broken, but he didn't have time—he was too busy trying to stay alive.

"Seba, stay down!"

It was the voice of his traveling companion, Paolo, who was trading blows with a much smaller man who should have long been beaten. Sebastian noted that the little man fought so ferociously that he was holding his own, at least for the moment. Seba (as Sebastian preferred to be called) had not seen this man at the Aigokeros taverna before, and although Paolo could be overbearing at times, he had never been this violent.

Seba yelled back, "Stop telling me what to do and leave that man alone!"

He jumped up, ignoring the burning pain in his wrist, and reached for Paolo's shoulder, trying to pull Paolo away from the man. "Step off, he's barely conscious! If you keep at it, you're going to kill—"

A glass filled with apricot wine flew over Seba's head, cutting him off midsentence and shattering into a thousand pieces on the wall behind him. Paolo paused his punching fists long enough to shove Seba aside, sending him skidding to the floor past an overturned bench and into a puddle of spilled *raki*. Seba squeezed his eyes shut as his head slammed into the floor with a thud, and when he opened them, the taverna's ceiling was spinning.

Seba stared at the floor to clear his vision, and noticed that Paolo's prostrate victim was curiously well-dressed, with a deep red velvet overcoat that reached almost to his ankles. The cuffs and hem of his coat were embellished with silver and gold embroidery, which matched the elaborate needlework and lace that adorned his silk shirt and bright violet pantaloons. Seba pinched his eyelids together tightly and opened them slowly, hoping that this was all a bad dream.

The Aigokeros was primarily patronized by the working class, so an expensively clothed gentleman in the midst of a barroom brawl was both unexpected and disturbing. Seba shook his head, thinking that Paolo had picked the absolute

2

worst opponent to fight. *Why couldn't he have chosen one of the scrawny pages who sends messages from the ship captains to the warehouses along the wharf?*

Seba loved the Aigokeros; he had eaten there many times since his arrival in Smyrna. It was usually full of lively conversation, deliciously roasted meats and stews, twelve different kinds of fruit wine, and happy customers. But on this sweltering evening in early June, every table in the *kapileo* had been either broken or turned over, and the stools and benches were being launched in the air as weapons. Pandemonium had broken out everywhere, the happy customers transformed into kicking and punching machines, now drawing blood and bruises instead of mugs of beer.

Everything in the Aigokeros was covered in wine, beer, or raki, including the guests. Seba wrinkled his nose in disgust as a plate of smoked redfish catapulted past his temple, and landed on a group of men who had set upon a huge sailor. The cluster of fighters veered sideways, heading straight at Paolo and the small man like a rolling tornado of arms and legs.

"Hands off, bilge rats!"

"You won't see tomorrow, *peiráomai!*"

"Take that, you scourge!"

Seba's head was spinning and he couldn't focus his eyes. The writhing mass of angry sailors rolled toward Paolo and the well-dressed man, who continued to trade blows.

Ignoring the pain in his wrist, Seba reached behind for something to throw at the sailors. Finding nothing, he crawled under the bench that had tripped him, put his feet up underneath the long-planked seat, and jutted his legs out, sending the bench flying into the air toward the sailors, who were shouting insults at each other. Rocking up from

3

the sodden floor, Seba watched the bench hit its target, but only after swiping Paolo behind the ear on its way.

The huge sailor and his attackers were propelled to the right by the bench, which, after clipping Paolo, whacked one of the fighters squarely across the jaw, sending a spurt of blood onto the large sailor, who bellowed in anger and kicked one of his opponents violently between the legs. The man clutched at his groin and was bowled over by the other fighters.

To Seba's relief, Paolo and his opponent were spared. However, Paolo had yelled in pain when the bench glanced off his ear, and blood was now flowing down his neck. Incensed, Paolo had pinned his adversary on the ground, his knee boring into the man's chest, and was pounding his bare-knuckled fists into the man's face. The man's eyes were swollen shut, and his red velvet coat was now stained a blood-stained dark crimson.

I have to do something before Paolo kills him. Wincing and holding his left wrist close to his body, Seba crept out from behind the overturned table and kicked Paolo in the shoulder with the force of a donkey. Paolo lost his balance, and toppled over the man, such that they were crumpled together on the floor like two pickled tosspots.

Paolo looked around to see who had kicked him, and held his hand up to his ear as rivers of blood streamed between his fingers. His eyes widened when they landed on Seba, and he screamed, "Seba, why?"

Seba pointed to the man. "Look at him!" Paolo's chest was heaving, and he looked confused. Seba pushed Paolo out of the way and crouched down next to the small man, staring at his chest to see if it was rising and falling. Seba couldn't tell, so he knelt and leaned in until his ear was directly over the man's disfigured nose. After a moment,

Seba detected a shallow wheezing sound and felt a wisp of air escape the man's mouth, which was nearly hidden under a thick mustache. Seba inhaled the scent of amber, vanilla, and black balsam, which rose up from the man's skin. *He smells rich.*

Everyone Seba had encountered in Smyrna thus far had smelled strongly of body odor and goat droppings. But not this man—with his well-groomed mustache and perfumed skin, he must be someone important.

Seba yelled over the noise, "I thought you were going to kill him. What came over you?"

Paolo blankly stared at the man as if he didn't recognize him or understand what had happened. Seba surveyed the scene around the taverna, where the bedlam continued.

Seba used his right hand to grab the unconscious man's feet and drag him behind an overturned table, where he was less likely to be hit by flying bowls of food. Paolo looked befuddled, his shoulders slumped and his eyes vacant, but he crawled behind the table with Seba and the man.

Paolo said, "I don't think we should wait here for someone else to jump on us."

Seba was staring at the man's shoes, which were made of the softest leather, dark brown with a brass buckle through which a wide flap was inserted and fastened with an iron tongue. Seba had seen shoes like that, many years ago, when he was a young boy. He felt a frisson of electricity pass through his body. This little man wasn't merely rich, he was a ship's officer.

Seba said, "I agree. Let's get him out of here—he needs help."

"So do I." Paolo's feet were splayed out in front of him in a slimy mess of beer, strawberry wine, and olives. The shoulder of his cotton shirt bore a black bootprint where

5

Seba had kicked him, his neck and one side of his head were covered in blood, and his knuckles were cut and bruised.

They both grabbed the man under his armpits, and yanked him through the doorway to the kitchen in several erratic movements, as they remained hunched over to avoid the flying culinary detritus.

Lungs heaving from the exertion, the boys leaned up against the back wall with the man laid out in front of them, unconscious and breathing unevenly.

Seba looked at Paolo. "How did that start? One minute I was raising a bite of grilled *barbouni* to my mouth, and the next, I was thrown over the table like a sack of potatoes."

Paolo shrugged his shoulders, and his eyes flicked back and forth across the taverna's deserted kitchen. Seba stared at the blood beginning to coagulate on Paolo's neck and hoped his friend had not suffered some kind of injury to his brain.

As Seba was contemplating Paolo's potential brain damage, the fog over Paolo lifted, and he said, "I don't know, Seba. I heard a shout, all hell broke loose, and I felt this man's heel kick the side of my head like a mule. I only struck back to defend myself."

"You did more than defend yourself." Seba spit onto the dirt floor and noticed it was tinged with blood. He ran his tongue across his teeth and cringed with pain as the metallic taste filled his mouth. He had bitten his tongue when his head slammed onto the floor just a few minutes before.

"I don't know what happened . . . something snapped inside me, and I couldn't stop." Paolo now looked genuinely remorseful. The day Seba had met Paolo, a few days after the earthquake that injured his wrist, the latter could not stop talking about ghosts, demons, and other creatures that haunted him. At the time, Seba had attributed

Paolo's obsession to an overactive imagination. Now, Seba considered whether a demon had actually taken over Paolo's body and tried to beat the wealthy officer into oblivion.

Seba's thoughts were interrupted by a woman's voice. *"What have you done?"*

Meleia, the owner of the Aigokeros, was standing over Seba and Paolo, her gold-flecked hazel eyes on fire. The muscles in Seba's body tensed, preparing for another assault. He was torn between feeling relief that she was safe and fearing that she might bludgeon him with the rolling pin in her hand. Her long brown hair was wild, curls jutting out from her head in all directions. She stretched both arms outward as she shouted, "Look at my beautiful Aigokeros! It's ruined!"

Meleia waved the wooden rolling pin and pointed it in the direction of the doorway from the kitchen to the dining area. Seba peeked through the kitchen door, and his pulse quickened. There were several men fighting inside, but others had moved out into the street, where dust was being kicked up and carried inside through the open doorway in great brown clouds. Heat shimmered up from the ground, and the sun, though no longer overhead, still burned brightly as it traversed the western sky. The Aigokeros looked like a tempest had spun the wooden tables and chairs into kindling. Shards of plates, cups, and glasses were strewn on the dirt floor, making it dangerous for anyone to pick their way among the splintered furniture. What had once been the most delectable-smelling establishment in Smyrna's Greek quarter was now reduced to a stinking refuse pile.

Meleia's lip was quivering, but Seba couldn't tell if it was from grief or rage. He imagined it was a mix of both, because she was brandishing the rolling pin like a cudgel.

"You know this place is my heart and soul! Do you know how hard it was for me to build this business into a thriving success with my own two hands? I started with nothing, working year after year to create a place where people could enjoy a good meal! Now—now look at it! The Aigokeros has survived earthquakes, fires, floods, and storms, only to be taken down by a hoard of drunken idiots! How could you let this happen?"

Seba knew what it felt like to have everything he had hoped for taken from him in the blink of an eye. He once was part of a happy family on the island of Chios, but it was shattered when the Ottomans captured his father and took him away to Constantinople, where he was forced to build ships for Sultan Mustafa III. That was six long years ago, and Seba's heart had not recovered. He stood up, took a deep breath, and held his hand out slowly, reaching for the rolling pin in Meleia's hand.

"You know we didn't start this fight—you had served us two plates of grilled fish. I told you I was so hungry I could eat an entire sturgeon. I was paying you with the last few coins I brought with me from Chios. Remember?"

Meleia's eyes flashed as she smacked the rolling pin into her opposite palm, causing Seba to jump backwards. "My whole life—brought to ruin in a matter of minutes! Every table, chair, bench, plate, bowl, and cup in this entire restaurant is demolished! How am I going to rebuild it? What am I going to do to survive until that happens? And what will this do to my father?" She was now pacing back and forth and thwacking the rolling pin with such force that Seba thought she might break her own hand.

Then she looked down at the floor and staggered back. The rolling pin fell to the ground, and both of Meleia's hands shot to her mouth as she gasped.

"Oh no! Is he alive?" Meleia's face was drained of color. Then she spoke in a whisper, which was even more terrifying than her shouting. *"What did you two do?"*

Seba could feel the blood thumping in his head as he tried to remain calm. "He's breathing, but he's unconscious. We pulled him into the kitchen to keep him safe."

"How did this happen to him?" Meleia looked scared, an expression that Seba did not recognize in her. Meleia was not afraid of anything, except, it seemed, this injured man lying on her kitchen floor. Seba glared at Paolo. *You and your stupid demons.*

Meleia bent down and put her hand on the man's heart. "His heartbeat is weak, but steady. I know a doctor on Frank Street; she's been a friend of my family for many years. She's French, but she is fluent in Greek, and she turns no one away. You'll need to move quickly, or it will be too late."

Seba looked directly into Meleia's eyes with as much confidence as he could muster, which at the time, wasn't much. "We'll take him. Tell us where to go."

"To Dr. Despina Marguerite Robin. Her office is at the far end of Frank Street."

Seba had never ventured to Frank Street in the short time he had been in Smyrna. That's where the rich merchants from Europe lived and worked. He hoped they wouldn't get lost on their way to the doctor's office. If they did, the little man might not make it.

"Well, what are you waiting for?" Meleia's angry, blazing eyes had returned. "Go—*now!*"

As he looked around for something to carry the man in, Seba caught a glimpse of Meleia's vegetable cart outside the back door of the kitchen. It was half full of carrots, and Seba momentarily envisioned Meleia's wonderful cumin-roasted carrots with turmeric and feta. She wouldn't be cooking them for several days, or maybe weeks, now that her prized taverna was in shambles. Seba spread the carrots out evenly at the bottom of the cart and rushed back into the kitchen, halting inside the door. Paolo lifted the man and placed him gently in the cart, his head and torso resting on the bed of carrots and his legs hanging over the back of the cart.

Seba couldn't help but notice the absurd contrast – minutes before, Paolo had been pulverizing the man with his fists, and now he was holding him as if he were a swaddling a baby. Seba had known when he left his small village on Chios that he would experience new and different sights, but this was beyond his comprehension. As they pushed the cart out the back door of the Aigokeros, Seba glanced over his shoulder to Meleia and said, "You're sure you'll be all right here?"

She looked indignant. "Of course, I will. I can't leave while my taverna is being destroyed by a throng of drunken half-wits. My father will be furious." She reconsidered. "I mean, he would be if he were sober enough to notice." She leaned down and picked up her rolling pin, which she now held like a spear. Seba was reminded of Athena, the Greek goddess of war, who was known to carry a spear and shield and whose symbol was an owl, one of the wisest and fiercest predators on earth. Looking at her now, Seba thought Meleia and Athena could be sisters. Narrowing her eyes, Meleia said, "Go quickly, and tell Dr. Robin that this is Nasir Beyzade Paşa. He must live."

2 TRANSPORT

Seba and Paolo encountered a number of raised eyebrows and angry glares as they pushed the wooden cart containing Nasir Beyzade Paşa down Frank Street. The food scraps were beginning to dry and stick to their clothes, and they were sweating profusely in the heat of the sun that pulsed its golden rays over the Gulf of Smyrna as it lowered slowly toward the horizon. Seba felt like he was on the edge of the earth, looking out over the waterfront past Frank Street, which ran along the crescent shape of the harbor's edge. To the north, mountains rose up beyond the curve of the harbor, and to the west, the dark blue Aegean Sea stretched as far as Seba could see, its crystalline and hypnotic waves undulating beneath the early evening sky.

Apart from the beauty of the evening, the other observation that Seba made was that Frank Street smelled positively opulent. Seba smelled cinnamon, peppercorns, cardamom, anise, and vanilla, wafting on the salt air from the holds of the ships moored in the harbor, as well as from the rows of flat-roofed warehouses that lined the wharf. Seba inhaled deeply, wishing he could bottle that smell, and thinking that was exactly what the rich merchants of Frank Street were selling to their customers in the west.

Seba knew that although the area was called Frank Street, after the French, it was not limited to French merchants. It was inhabited by all manner of wealthy Dutch, French, Scandinavian, and English traders, making their fortunes in Smyrna, far from the watchful eyes of Sultan Mustafa III. Of course, there were Ottoman officials in Smyrna who kept the peace, applied the laws, and managed the Silk Road trade, but the European merchants who were well established in Smyrna enjoyed a freedom that could not be found elsewhere in the empire. As a result, Smyrna's non-European citizens—the Turks, Greeks, Armenians, and Hebrews—shared in the *laissez-faire* environment that extended through the city like a breath of fresh air.

Frank Street's stone-cobbled streets were wide, with large houses and shops, all brightly painted with glass windows framed by bright pink and purple bougainvillea. At this time of the evening, most of the merchants were returning to their well-appointed homes, kissing their children, and settling in to enjoy a nice glass of wine before the evening meal. Although they were dressed very differently from Seba and Paolo, with their western, narrow-legged trousers and fitted velvet jackets, and he could not understand any of the languages they spoke, Seba found the scene to be oddly familiar, even comforting. These foreigners were no different than his family, gathering around the table to fill their bellies and share their stories of the day.

Seba could feel the fresh sea breeze blowing in from the

harbor to his left, and counted no less than twelve ships anchored in the bay, waiting for their chance to load crates full of treasures from the Silk Road. He could hear the sailors calling to each other, and saw several tenders transporting goods and sailors from the ships to the dock, bringing their final deliveries to the warehouses for the evening, and bringing the sailors into the city for a night of carousing. Seba wondered which of these ships had brought the sailors who had just destroyed the Aigokeros.

Frank Street was quite a contrast to the Greek quarter of Smyrna, where the houses were close together and the market stalls so crammed on top of each other that the Aegean Sea breeze could not penetrate. Enymeria Market, the grand bazaar in the Greek quarter, was also brimming with exotic spices, dried peppers, roasted meats, and fish, but felt heavier somehow, as if weighed down by the sheer density of offerings. The same applied to the Turkish quarter, where Seba lodged in the loft above his friend, Buğra's stable. The loft was situated near the bustling Kemeralti Bazaar, the Turkish quarter's labyrinthian tangle of streets teeming with tea houses, coffee shops, and market stalls boasting everything from bay- and gardenia-scented soaps to fresh-caught mussels and clams.

However, in comparing the Greek and Turkish quarters to Frank Street, Seba was reminded of the animal stables of his childhood village of Sessera. His cozy stone home on the island of Chios had housed his donkey, Matilde, and his goats, Myra and Sheba, on the ground floor, and Seba's family lived in the same dwelling, on the floor above the animals. The ground-floor stables for the animals were warm, dry, and safe—but not as nice as where the humans lived. It was the same here in Smyrna; the other neighborhoods, such as the Greek, Turkish, Armenian, and

Jewish quarters, were comfortable, but not as nice as Frank Street.

Those other neighborhoods smelled more of pickled octopus and horse manure than perfumed sea breezes. The air in the narrow dirt streets of the Greek quarter (and the others) hung heavy with the smell of shellfish, tanned leather, tobacco smoke, goats, pigs, chickens, and too many humans occupying the same space. There were always camels and donkeys navigating the unpaved streets, often forcing pedestrians to detour into the crowded stalls and alleys to avoid being trampled. The buzz of numerous dialects pervaded Enymeria and Kemeralti, as vendors dickered with their customers and shop owners barked at young children caught pilfering a piece of fruit or strip of dried meat.

At first, Seba had enjoyed the frenzied hum of the markets. He marveled at the comical jaded skepticism of the ceramics vendors, who tried to sell their wares as artwork, and feigned offense when a savvy housewife refused to pay an "outrageous" price for a common fruit bowl. He laughed at the cats who nonchalantly sat beside the fishmongers' stalls, licking between their pads as if they could care less about the stacks of mullet and bream next door. His favorite sight at the markets, by far, however, was watching the traders unload their wares from the backs of the camels, who strutted slowly down the narrow streets as if they, and not the caravaneers, were in charge. To think that he could reach out and touch the very same creatures that brought the Magi across the desert to visit the Christ Child, was a miracle to Seba. And their eyelashes—they were as long as the fingers on Seba's hands!

It was these days that Seba thanked God for bringing him to Smyrna; if he had stayed on Chios, he would have never witnessed these marvelous miracles of God's creation. However, on other days, the barking dogs, the smell of rotting fish, and the crowds of people elbowing each other to snag the freshest fruit or choicest cuts of meat, became overwhelming. On those days, Seba longed for the open *skinos* terraces of his home on Chios, where he would be living if the Ottomans hadn't stolen his father and robbed him of his legacy.

Seba had left everything he had ever known on the island of Chios: his mother and grandfather, his beloved cat Artemis, all of the people in his village of Sessera, and a plum job as an apprentice to his Uncle Phillip on the village's mastic council. That was because mastic gum, or *mastiha*, was a treasured commodity of the Ottoman empire, cultivated by the few families on Chios who knew how to coax the jewel-like resin from the skinos trees. Seba's mother was descended from those families, and she wanted Seba to carry on the tradition. However, he wanted no part of a tradition of mastiha slavery, where the families broke their backs cultivating mastiha all year long, only to turn it over to the sultan.

No, Seba had a choice when he was a boy: follow his mother's family and work the land for the Ottoman government or follow his father into the shipbuilding trade. Seba had always known he had a choice between the land and the sea, and it was clear to him from a young age that the sea called to him. His mother, though disappointed, supported Seba's choice.

That was until the Ottomans tore his family apart by forcing his father to build ships in the Ottoman capital. His father was abducted, beaten, and taken to Constantinople by the sultan's cousin, Ahmed. Seba's father never had the chance to say goodbye to his family.

Seba chided himself, believing that he should have seen it coming. His father's skill as a maritime engineer had become so well-known that ships were waiting in line at Sessera's shipyard for the great Kostas Krizomatis to make adjustments that would increase their speed and efficiency. His crew of shipwrights were constructing vessels faster than any other shipyard in the Ottoman empire, and the sultan had taken notice. However, the renowned Kostas Krizomatis was not rewarded for his remarkable talent with higher pay, a bigger crew, or a prominent residence for his family on Chios. Instead, he was treated like a commodity, one which the sultan preferred to have under his thumb in Constantinople. When Kostas refused to go without his family, he was beaten and taken away.

Even worse, Seba had been at the shipyard and seen the awful tragedy with his own nine-year-old eyes. He wasn't sure that it had really happened as he remembered it, but he relived the terror every day of his life. When his father realized, albeit too late, that he had no hope of saving himself, he broke free of the guards who were holding him, grabbed Seba in his arms, and threw him overboard, saying, *"I have to do this to save you! I love you, son. I might not be able to save myself, but I will not let the Ottoman vipers steal my son. Follow the dolphins."*

If Seba thought about That Day, as he called it, he could feel the horror and panic as his own father tossed him high into the air and off the side of the ship. Seba remembered flying over the balustrade, fingers grasping for his father. The last thing he saw were Papa's wild eyes, which Seba thought were filling with tears, but he couldn't be sure. He hung in the air for what felt like an eternity, arms outstretched toward his father, and then smacked the water with a loud slap. Immediately, he was kicking his arms and legs to keep his head above the water line. The crew had let out the huge white sails, and the ship picked up speed, taking Seba's father with it.

Kostas Krizomatis had not deserved that fate at the hands of the Ottomans. Although Seba didn't know for sure, he imagined that his father was slaving away in the shipyards of Constantinople, building the Ottoman fleet to maintain the frenetic pace of trade with western Europe. The thought of his father living like a slave made his chest burn with rage.

As the vegetable cart bumped along the cobbled stones of Frank Street, Seba shook his head almost imperceptibly. He would not be stopped in his quest to find his father and set things right. He wasn't quite sure how, but he knew he would never be free until he found his father. This incident at the Aigokeros was a momentary diversion.

Seba glanced at Paolo. The blood was coagulating on his neck, but it mixed with the sweat and little droplets fell on ground, leaving a trail, as the two young men huffed and puffed toward their destination. Seba wondered if Paolo was going to pass out from heat stroke or blood loss before they reached Dr. Robin. His own hands were sweating and slipping on the cart's handles, and his wrist and head throbbed painfully. Fortunately, the European merchants were so wrapped up in their own busy lives that they barely paid any attention to Seba and Paolo.

Finally, Seba and Paolo came to a building with the universal symbol for medicine over its door—a rod with a serpent curled around it. Seba knew from his grandfather, whom he called Papouli, that this was the Rod of Asclepius, the Greek god of medicine and healing. Although Seba's family were Christians, Papouli said that the ancient stories were part of their Greek heritage, and God's love extended to everything, including the pagans.

According to Papouli, the Holy Spirit encompassed all of creation, even the Titans, Olympians, and mythic stories of the past. Seba tended to agree with his grandfather, especially as it related to Asclepius, the god of healing. Asclepius was the son of Apollo, also known for his healing abilities, and was trained by the centaur Chiron. After learning the healing arts from the most wise and just centaur, Asclepius dedicated his life to others by and through the curative art of medicine. Seba, like Papouli, thought that Jesus would be thrilled to know of Asclepius's dedication to those stricken with injuries and illnesses.

Papouli's other primary word of advice to Seba had been gratefulness, and he was particularly fond of a quote from the great Greek philosopher, Epictetus: *"He is a wise man who does not grieve for the things which he has not, but rejoices for those which he has."* Seba thanked God that this injured gentleman was alive, offered a silent plea for healing, and added a tiny request that the doctor might treat his injured wrist. He remembered the words from the Gospel of Matthew: *If you believe, you will receive whatever you ask for in prayer.*

Seba knocked firmly on the door while Paolo used a large cotton canvas sack in the vegetable cart to (unsuccessfully) wipe the blood from his victim's face. A tall woman with a long, straight nose, gray hair, and jewel-framed glasses opened the door. She was elegantly dressed, with a white lace shirt, pale sage silk skirts, coral-colored bodice, and emerald green velvet coat with enormous gold-embroidered cuffs and lapels. Her skirts boasted wide embroidered pockets and white appliqued butterflies around the hem. A pair of tawny calf's leather boots peeked out from beneath the butterflies. Seba had seen others so luxuriously dressed a few times in his life, such as when he ventured onto the merchant ships that had stopped in his father's shipyard on Chios for repairs, and today, when he noticed Nasir Paşa's clothing. Seba had never seen a woman so finely dressed, and the fact that she was a doctor was even more incredible. In Sessera, the village doctor was usually wearing a large canvas apron, often stained with blood, over a cotton shirt and woven canvas trousers.

The woman's dark brown eyes grew wide behind her jewel-encrusted glasses as she surveyed the two young men. It was at that moment that Seba realized how dirty they were in their bloodstained clothes, covered in food scraps, and smelling of stale wine. To her credit, however, the sophisticated woman did not show any sign of disgust. That is, until she glimpsed the unconscious man in the vegetable cart. Her jaw dropped and she shouted "*Mon Dieu!*" before leaping into action, reaching for the handles of the cart, and gesturing for Seba and Paolo to help her whisk it inside.

The woman was speaking quickly, at once seeming to ask questions and give herself the answers, and Seba couldn't tell if she was talking to herself or trying to communicate with them. They rushed through an ostentatiously decorated room with several chairs covered in rich, velvet upholstery and turned down a hallway with gold-framed mirrors on the walls and gorgeously woven wool carpets with a pattern of green and gold palm trees. Seba looked behind him and cringed, noticing that the wheels of the vegetable cart left a trail of dirt on the carpet.

The French woman was speaking at a furious pace as they continued through the house, and when she finally realized that her visitors were not responding to her, she stopped and looked at them. Seba could see that her gaze rested on Paolo's ear, which was bloody, but which seemed to be clotting and turning a dark reddish-brown. An expression of recognition then came over the woman, and she began speaking in perfect Greek.

"My surgical room is in the back of the house, through this hallway. Follow me."

Seba and Paolo followed her to the back of her large home, into a room with wide windows overlooking a formal garden. The room was filled with bottles, salves, strips of cotton, metal instruments, and a large table with a cotton pallet on top. There were several framed documents on the wall, written in a language that Seba did not recognize, but presumed to be French.

"Are you Doctor Despina Marguerite Robin?"

"*Nai.*" Yes.

Seba was relieved, and he watched as the doctor donned a large ecru-colored apron to cover her silk clothing and gathered the metal instruments on the table to begin examining her patient.

"And this is Nasir Beyzade Paşa, is it not? Even though his face is swollen nearly beyond recognition, I would know my friend anywhere. He is the nephew of Captain Paşa, probably the most important man in the entire city of Smyrna. What happened to him? Not those damnable pirates again, I hope! Was he injured on a ship?"

Seba's heart skipped a beat with the mention of a ship. It was exactly as he had thought when he saw the little man's leather shoes. He must be a ship's officer, or some kind of maritime official. If this man worked on ships, did he know anything about Seba's father? And if so, would he live long enough to tell Seba?

20

3 DR. ROBIN

"We don't know anything about a ship." Seba didn't want to tell Dr. Robin about the bar brawl just yet, and luckily, either the response sufficed, or the doctor was too engrossed in the work at hand to inquire further.

Seba asked, "Is there anything we can do to help you?"

"*Oxi.*" No. Again, in Greek. The ease with which the woman moved between French and Greek was a marvel to Seba. The doctor pointed toward the rear of the house. "You don't need to stay here unless you are interested in the practice of medicine. You may wait in my garden. I may need assistance, depending on whether Nasir has internal injuries to his organs or any broken bones, but I need to assess his condition first. I will call for you if I need to set any bones. After I have stabilized him, if I can, then I will speak with you about how this atrocity befell a man who is the heart and soul of honor."

Dr. Robin gathered several jars and bottles from her shelves as she continued, "Nasir is not one to engage in violence—usually he is the one quelling an argument. I can't imagine how he came to be in this state. The incongruity is appalling." The doctor's hands expertly moved along the patient's torso, searching for broken ribs as she continued to lament her friend's condition.

"It is a tragedy of the worst proportions that he suffered such injustice. It does not appear accidental. I imagine that Governor Paşa will want to seek justice for his nephew, once we find out who did this. The governor is very protective of his family, as he should be."

Seba decided right then that he should tell her what happened before she jumped to any conclusions. "There was a brawl at the Aigokeros. I'm afraid Mr. Paşa got caught in the fray."

Dr. Robin exhaled a deep, discontented sigh. "Deliberate violence is more to be quenched than a fire."

Paolo said, "That's from Heraclitus, isn't it? My sisters often quoted his writings."

Seba couldn't have been more shocked if Paolo had picked up the doctor's instruments and performed a successful surgery on her patient. *How does Paolo know about Heraclitus? I didn't even think he could read.*

Seba had learned about Heraclitus from his teacher, Brother Timotheos, at the village school in Sessera. Brother Tim, as Seba called him, was the village priest as well as teacher, and he was like a father to Seba in the dark days after the Ottomans abducted his father. Brother Tim, like Seba's grandfather, believed that the teachings of Jesus and the ancient philosophers were not mutually exclusive.

Dr. Robin's eyes never moved from her patient, but Seba heard her murmur, "Hmm," under her breath, and then she said, "Did they now? Then your sisters were very wise, as we women often are." Her eyes twinkled from behind her glasses and she turned to Seba and asked, "What about you, young man? Are you as learned as your companion here?"

Fortunately, Brother Tim had shared many of Heraclitus's musings with the students of Sessera. Seba said, "I remember learning this one in school: 'No man ever steps in the same river twice, for it's not the same river, and he's not the same man.' My father worked on sailing vessels when I was a boy, and he said he agreed with Heraclitus that everything is always flowing and changing."

"Yes, that is one of my favorites, although my mother always said 'woman' rather than 'man', and I tend to prefer that version. Did you know that Heraclitus lived less than a day's walk from here, in the ancient city of Ephesus?"

Seba raised both eyebrows. He had heard that the ancient city of Ephesus was across the Strait of Chios from his home village of Sessera, but he had no idea that this famous city from the Bible was so close to Smyrna. "No, I didn't. You mean the Apostle Paul taught only a day's walk from here?"

Dr. Robin nodded. "I see that both of you are true Greeks, in that you know your philosophy as well as your Bible history. I've never met a Greek man or woman who didn't." She smiled impishly at them, and Seba realized that he liked Dr. Robin very much. She was obviously very smart, but even more so, she was kind.

The patient, though unconscious, twitched as Dr. Robin touched his shoulder, which Seba could now see was dislocated. The doctor deftly grabbed the man's arm and pulled it away from his body at a ninety-degree angle, and Seba saw the top of the patient's arm bone slide back under his shoulder blade. Seba shuddered and held his wrist close to his belly. The patient, although unconscious, let out a groan.

"I'm so sorry, Nasir. I never thought I would see you like

this." The doctor was speaking tenderly to her patient, as if to a child.

"Are you related?" Paolo asked.

Dr. Robin looked up. "Not by blood, but all of us are related to each other by the bond of humanity, young man." Her hand remained on her patient's shoulder as she continued, "It was your great Greek ancestor, Plotinus, who said, 'It is in virtue of unity that beings are beings.' I wish more of the environs of Smyrna had studied the ancient Greek texts. Maybe then they would refrain from such depravity." She reached for a cotton towel and handed it to Paolo. "Here, take this towel and clean your ear. It looks like it's been split in two. I see that my friend was not the only one caught in the altercation at the Aigokeros. Please wash yourself in the basin in the garden fountain. It's fed by an aquifer, so don't worry over sullying it. You may need stitches, but I have to attend to Nasir first."

Paolo walked past Seba, bumping his shoulder. "Seba, let's go."

But Seba was rooted in place. Hearing the words of Plotinus had jettisoned Seba into the past, and he couldn't move.

Seba recalled one particular day he spent with his father at the shipyard in Sessera, where his father worked long hours. He and his father were sitting in the unfinished hull of a ship in dry dock, enjoying a meal of salt-cured fish, *koulouria* covered in sesame seeds, and newly ripened nectarines from the shipyard's fruit trees. His father took a bite of a bright orange nectarine and, wiping the sweet juice from his chin with the back of his sleeve, said, "Look at the trees that bear these fruits, the birds soaring overhead, the dolphins out in the sea, and the workers on these ships. Did you know that we are all connected? Our Greek ancestor,

Plotinus, said that we may appear separate from each other, but our souls are all connected."

Dr. Robin had said almost the same thing and Seba wondered if it was a sign from God. In his lifetime, he had observed many of these kinds of signs, and today it seemed that he had received two of them, both about his father. One from Nasir Paşa, with his fancy ship's officer shoes, and now, Dr. Robin quoting something that Seba's father had said before he was kidnapped. *God, what are you trying to tell me? If it's a message about my father, I welcome it.*

Seba's thoughts were interrupted by the pressure of Paolo's hands on his shoulders. "Seba, are you going to help me clean this ear or not?"

Seba blinked several times and shook his head. "Wait, what?"

"What's wrong with you? Dr. Robin said to go to the garden." Paolo gave him a shove out the back door of Dr. Robin's expansive home and into the garden, which had been planted with herbs, edible flowers, and citrus trees, in beds of coordinating geometric shapes, surrounded by mosaics on every wall. Birds chirped and sang, calling to one another and flitting among the tree branches, and a beautiful breeze swept across the patio. In the corner of the garden was a very small gurgling fountain, happily providing water for the birds.

It was here that Paolo washed his ear, and the blood trickled into the basin, tinging the water a translucent shade of pink. Seba watched as it ran into a flower bed filled with tulips, irises, and a bright red flower that Seba did not recognize. The deep crimson petals appeared to be the softest velvet, like the fabrics transported by the sailing ships that called on Chios, and the scent that arose when the water touched the heart of them was strong and ambrosial, simultaneously lifting Seba's spirits and imbuing a sense of calm. The doctor's garden, in the bustling city where the Silk Road caravans came to launch their exotic goods by sea to the west, was an oasis, like the Garden of Eden. Seba wondered if it was another sign. After the hellish brawl at the Aigokeros, Dr. Robin's garden was heavenly.

As he turned in a circle, soaking up the magic of the botanical paradise, Seba's mind was flooded with memories of the garden of Nea Moni, the 700-year-old sacred mountaintop monastery on Mount Provateio, in the center of the island of Chios. It was there that Brother Tim, his teacher, priest, and mentor, had shared a plan with him to find his father. Nea Moni's garden was very much like this one. A thin place, as Seba's mother often said, one where the veil between heaven and earth was so diaphanous that the two became one.

"This garden is so peaceful," Seba said as he watched the red- and black-headed buntings hop from branch to branch, flitting between the dark green leaves. Water bubbled in the fountain and the breeze from the Gulf of Smyrna carried the scent of citrus blossoms through the garden. "There is a garden like this at the monastery of Nea Moni, on Chios. It was a garden shared by six hundred monks who lived in the abbey. I visited there many times with my mother. It's difficult to comprehend that this garden belongs to only one doctor."

Disregarding him, Paolo said, "How does it look?" He gestured toward his ear, leaning forward. "Is the blood gone?"

Seba blew air through his teeth. Paolo was literally surrounded by the radiant beauty and enchantment of this glorious garden, but he didn't even notice. Instead, he was too preoccupied with his bloody ear. When Seba first crawled up on the shores of Anatolia, he was thrilled to have met Paolo, who gave him food and water when Seba was barely clinging to life. Paolo traveled with him to Smyrna and introduced Seba to the city. Seba had dismissed Paolo's obsession with ghosts and demons as a quirky personality trait, his bossiness as an overactive desire to help, and his temper as a common characteristic of a Greek boy who had suffered the loss of his family in a tragic fire. Sometimes, however, it was frustrating to be around Paolo, and this was one of those times.

"Yes, it's fine. In fact, it's nothing compared to what you did to that man."

"I told you, I don't know what came over me! If I'm being attacked, I have to fight back. I'm Greek, for heaven's sake."

"Paolo, that was much more than fighting back. It was like you had a demon inside you, clawing to get out. Couldn't you tell that man was half your size and dressed like a ship's officer? And I don't think he attacked you, I think he was thrown on top of you by that monstrously big sailor."

"I only saw his fists coming at me. He certainly didn't fight like a dandy. It was all I could do to keep him off me."

Seba sighed. "Please, don't try to convince yourself that you were the victim. If I hadn't kicked you in the shoulder, that man might be dead. And if he is Captain Paşa's nephew, doesn't that mean he's someone important in the city?"

Paolo sank to the ground and dug his palms into his eyes. "I might as well turn myself in now."

"What do you mean?"

Paolo spread his fingers open just a bit and peered at Seba through the gaps between them. "I forgot that you haven't been in Smyrna very long. Do you know what

'Paşa' means?"

"No, I thought it was the man's name."

"It is, but it's also an honorary title. Captain Paşa is the admiral of the Ottoman navy, and he holds the highest government and military position in Smyrna. Of all the bureaucrats in this city, none is more important than Captain Paşa. That's why he is also referred to as Governor Paşa, because he is in charge of this whole region."

"And you may have killed his nephew?" Seba's voice had risen an octave, but now it became a whisper. "This is bad."

"Stop reminding me, Seba! I know it's bad. Let me think. No one knows what happened except you, me, and Meleia. We can't tell anyone. Maybe I hit him so hard that he won't remember any of it."

Seba was not so sure. "If this man's name is also Paşa, does that mean that he's a government official, too?"

Paolo groaned. "I don't know! Probably. Beyzade is the Turkish title given to descendants of noble households. And the doctor mentioned pirates. Maybe this man patrols the docks, protecting the Ottoman shipments from pirates. I haven't seen him near the barges, though, so maybe he's not that important."

"Do you think we should get out of here right now?" Seba had no chance of finding his father if he was stuck in a prison cell. And if Paolo was in there with him, Seba was sure Paolo would be conversing with the ghosts of every deceased prisoner who had been incarcerated there for the last hundred years, making it even more unbearable.

Paolo said, "I don't know. I need to wash all the blood off my clothes first. And this doctor doesn't seem like she's going to turn us in to Governor Paşa's military police. I think she likes us."

Seba hoped Paolo was right. He stepped up to the fountain. He washed his hands and attempted to clean some of the food scraps from his shirt, which was ruined, along with the trousers he had borrowed from Buğra. He considered immersing himself in the pool beneath the fountain because his whole body reeked with the smell of sour beer. He wondered how he had gotten himself into this mess. *Papa, I wish you were here. You'd know what to do.*

4 IN THE GARDEN

As Seba and Paolo continued to wash their clothes and bodies with the water from the fountain, Dr. Robin emerged from her home and entered the garden, wiping her hands on her apron, which was now smeared with blood.

Dr. Robin cleared her throat. "Now, I would like you young men to tell me exactly what happened to Nasir. Did pirates raid the taverna? I tell you, they're becoming bolder with every day that passes. They used to steal on board the ships and snatch one or two casks of cargo, escaping with their contraband before anyone noticed. It was the cost of doing business for the merchants. Now, however, the pirates are getting greedy, like the traders. One or two casks is no longer enough—they're waging full-scale war on the ships that dock at the harbor. I think Captain Paşa is having a difficult time controlling the rampant thievery."

Dr. Robin pressed her fingers against her temples and continued, "Nasir was trained in hand-to-hand combat by the Ottoman navy, but he is not the type of man to be involved in a physical altercation if he can help it. Unlike most men, he's too smart for that."

Dr. Robin's gaze moved from Seba to Paolo, where it halted on Paolo's bruised and scratched knuckles. She tilted her head and looked thoughtful. "As I said before, it appears that Nasir was not the only one engaged in violence at the taverna, young man."

Thinking that the doctor was beginning to piece together the events of the evening, Seba fought the urge to run through the garden's back gate. Paolo looked at him, and Seba's eyes bored into his friend, carrying the message that he had made this mess and he better clean it up. Fast.

Paolo said innocently, "We managed to avoid the worst of the fighting, and we pulled this man to safety in the midst of the brawl. The taverna's owner, Meleia Kokokis, told us to bring him to you."

Dr. Robin stared at them and said nothing, the awkward silence hanging over all three of them like a cloud. Seba stood stock-still, ready to bolt at a moment's notice. *I don't think she believes us.*

The seconds ticked by and when Seba thought he couldn't contain his anxiety any longer, Dr. Robin broke the silence, saying charitably, "Ah, yes, my dear friend, Meleia Kokokis. She is an extraordinary businesswoman, taking over the family business from her father at such a young age. I don't venture into the Greek quarter very often, but I've tasted her recipes, and they are exquisite, especially the grilled barbouni. She is an excellent cook and a savvy proprietress. To think that her little taverna was a small tent several years ago, and now it is a prosperous establishment—it speaks volumes about her determination. I have known her family for many years. It was a shame when her mother died in childbirth a few years ago. They called for my assistance, but unfortunately, I arrived too late to save Meleia's mother or her little sister."

Seba was fascinated by the way that Dr. Robin could speak so nonchalantly about grilled barbouni and death, as if both were part of her daily routine. Perhaps that particular form of objectivity was a requirement for a physician.

Dr. Robin walked over to a rosemary plant, plucked several stems, and rubbed them on her hands. "Did you know that rosemary has healing properties? I often use it in treatments for my patients, as well as for myself after I have provided medical assistance." She nodded to Paolo. "You might want to rub some on your hands as well. Let me have a look at your ear."

Paolo shook his head. "It's fine."

"Well, it seems to have stopped bleeding, and I don't believe you need the skin sewn together. But you must keep it clean, free of dirt, and don't do anything that will tear the skin apart, or the bleeding will begin again in earnest."

"Yes, doctor." Paolo's eye was twitching, and Seba wondered again about his mental state.

Seba held out his left arm to the doctor. "Do you think it's broken?"

Dr. Robin gently took Seba's arm and manipulated it, pressing gently on the bones that attached his forearm to his left hand. "It's very swollen, and I believe you may have a fracture in your radius." She pointed to the area below Seba's thumb. "You can see that the blood vessels are ruptured right here, which is indicative of a break."

Seba's heart sank. He had wasted time recovering in Smyrna since the earthquake, and now it appeared that his wrist was going to delay his quest for his father even further. He felt a stinging behind his eyes, and willed them not to fill with tears.

"What should I do?"

Dr. Robin said graciously, "I'll set it and wrap it, but you have to keep it protected for the next several weeks to allow the bones to fuse back together."

"Thank you."

Paolo asked, "Is Mr. Paşa going to live?"

"Yes, young man, but he is going to be very uncomfortable for several weeks. I gave him a tincture, and he is sleeping now. He has several broken ribs, but I did not view any evidence of damage to his internal organs. Governor Paşa will be grateful that you brought Nasir to me when you did." Dr. Robin slapped her hands on her apron. "What I don't understand, though, is how Nasir found himself in the midst of conflict in a taverna in the Greek quarter of Smyrna. He almost always dines on Frank Street, or with one of the Ottoman ministers up in the hills above the city. Do you know why he was in the Aigokeros this evening?"

She muttered under her breath, "I hope to God it has nothing to do with my cousin's husband."

Seba's ears perked up. "Excuse me, what did you say?"

"Oh, nothing. Merely a bit of family drama, but nothing for you to concern yourself over. I have my own theory about why Nasir might have gone to the Aigokeros this evening. Have you ever seen him there before?"

"No. We often have dinner there, but we've never seen him before tonight." Seba racked his brain to remember this man, but he knew that if he had ever seen someone in the Aigokeros wearing the clothes of a prestigious member of the Ottoman naval class, he would have remembered it.

Dr. Robin's brow furrowed as she observed their wine-soaked clothes. "I also see that this skirmish caused you to wear your meals rather than eat them. Are you hungry?"

Seba and Paolo looked at each other, both starving, but worried about whether they should leave in case the governor came to check on his nephew. Seba had been trained his whole life to fear the Ottomans, and despite what Dr. Robin said about the honor of this man, Nasir, Seba did not want to meet his uncle. He wished he knew more about the politics of this city, because then maybe he could determine what threats he faced. At this point, he was operating purely on instinct and faith.

Dr. Robin clucked her tongue on the roof of her mouth. "Come now, it's the least I can do for the two young men who saved Nasir's life. Claudine and I have plenty of food, and this is about the time that the Greeks are drinking their fourth coffee of the day, isn't it?" Dr. Robin winked at them.

The doctor's compassionate manner and welcoming words convinced them to stay. Seba looked at Paolo, who nodded in agreement.

Seba said, "Thank you for your kind offer, Dr. Robin. We would be honored to accept."

Paolo added ruefully, "Unfortunately, we never had the chance to taste the grilled barbouni we ordered this evening."

Dr. Robin gasped in mock horror, raising the back of her hand to her forehead. "Another tragedy of utmost proportion—one that must be remedied immediately."

Then she clapped her hands together and grinned. "It's settled. And if we are to dine together, we should be formally introduced. You know that I am Dr. Despina Marguerite Robin. And who might you be?"

Seba felt that sharing his name with the doctor would be safe. Paolo was right – it seemed as if the doctor liked them, although Seba couldn't figure out for the life of him why that would be.

"I'm Sebastian Krizomatis, son of the great shipbuilder, Kostas Krizomatis." He looked at Paolo, who bowed to the doctor. "I am Paolo Partella, very glad to meet you."

Dr. Robin shook their hands, and Seba was relieved that he had washed them in the garden's fountain. "Well, Sebastian and Paolo, I am very pleased to make your acquaintances, and again, I thank you for bringing Nasir to safety, even if it was by way of a vegetable cart full of carrots."

Dr. Robin walked back into the house, and when she returned, she directed Seba and Paolo to the back corner of the garden, under the shade of several cedar trees, where a wrought-iron dining table and four chairs awaited them.

A young woman appeared, rolling a cart not unlike the shape of the vegetable cart, but made of elaborately decorated silver. It boasted two glass shelves—one above the wheels of the cart, loaded with crocks and covered dishes, and another above, bearing bottles of wine and clear glasses also carved with intricate patterns and scrollwork.

The girl placed all of the dishes and bowls on the table, and Seba noticed that they were made of a fine shining material, like polished bone, white in the center, surrounded by a pale pink ground, on which delicate blue and yellow butterflies danced among similarly airy flowers of purple and red. The outside rim of the plates and bowls were gilded in a bright yellow gold, and all of the butterflies and flowers were embossed with fine gold filaments and embellishments. Inside the white center of each plate was a trio of pink and gold flowers, like those that were so fragrant in the garden.

Seba didn't realize he was staring at the center of the plates until Dr. Robin said, "I see you appreciate the beauty of the rose, Sebastian. Yes, they are one of my favorite flowers, which is why this garden is full of them."

"Rose? I've never seen or smelled anything like it." Seba breathed deeply and tried to capture the scent in his lungs.

"I would like to have provided you with a real French feast, but given the late hour and the circumstances involving our friend, Nasir, I've asked Claudine to bring what remains from our midday meal. I believe it should suffice to satisfy your appetites, even if you are not accustomed to our French cuisine. It is the best in the world!" The doctor rubbed her hands together like an excited child.

Seba could not imagine that Dr. Robin's French dishes could compare to his mother's cooking, but given the elaborate serving ware, and his grumbling stomach, he looked forward to finding out.

When the young girl lifted the lids on the beautiful gold-handled serving bowls, complete with pink roses and butterflies, Seba's mouth began to water. The aroma of poultry in thick carmine brown gravy, complete with chunks of tomatoes, carrots, and mushrooms, wafted up and into his nostrils. Claudine set wide matching pink bowls in front of Dr. Robin, Paolo, and Seba and ladled the rich stew into each of them. She then used two large silver spoons to lift a small cooked bird out of the largest crock and place it in Seba's bowl. She did the same for Paolo and Dr. Robin.

Dr. Robin, fork in hand, said, "Have you never eaten quail in wine and tomato sauce?"

Seba shook his head in the negative.

Paolo said, "No, but I can't wait to try it." Seba noticed that Paolo's mouth was actually watering, and he almost laughed.

Dr. Robin continued, "It is one of the delicacies of French cuisine, and fortunately for us in Smyrna, the common ground quail is quite populous in the surrounding hills. Now, you may notice that these spice combinations are not the same as your Greek grandmothers may have used, but I find them to be tantalizing just the same. Thyme, parsley, and allspice create a delectable medley of flavors, and Claudine is the best cook in the city. I hope you like it."

As Dr. Robin spoke, Claudine lifted an embroidered cotton towel from over a large basket, which contained lengths of a yeasty-smelling bread, shaped in the thickness of a man's upper arm, but even longer. She broke one in three parts, giving each part to Seba, Paolo, and Dr. Robin. As she broke them, Seba noticed that the outside was crispy, and the inside was full of holes and smelled like heaven. Seba had never seen bread this shape. He couldn't wait to dip it into the stew.

There were dishes of cold hard-boiled eggs and small sausages spiced with fennel and caraway, as well as hard sheep's milk cheeses, ranging from deep orange to pale yellow, and little glass jars of jellies and marmalades made from bergamot, strawberries, and figs. There were tiny little spoons in each of the small glass jars, which Seba surmised was for spreading the jellies on the cheese and the bread. As if on cue, Dr. Robin grabbed a few pieces of cheese, placed them on a piece of her crusty bread, and took a dollop from each of the little jelly jars to complete the perfect bite. She held her hand up in mid-air, with her stack of bread, cheese, and jam held in place by her thumb, and invited Seba and Paolo to do the same.

They didn't have to be invited twice. Seba tried every different combination of cheese and jam, and saw that Paolo did the same. Then Seba dipped his fork into the bowl with the quail in sauce, and noticed it was so tender that the small fowl fell apart on his fork. Seba had to use all of the restraint he had in his body not to grab the little bird in his hand and shove all the meat into his mouth.

Dr. Robin appeared pleased that her guests were enjoying their French feast. In fact, it was so blissful that Seba began to wonder if they were being detained so they could be interrogated by Governor Paşa. The funny thing was that Seba was so hungry that his stomach said, "Let them arrest us; if they feed us this well in jail, it won't be so bad."

When their bellies were full to bursting, Claudine brought a tray of fruit pastries and little squares covered in a dark glaze that Seba did not recognize. Even though he thought he could not fit another bite of food into his mouth, he really wanted to try one of those dark squares that smelled a bit like coffee and butter.

Dr. Robin pointed to the little squares. "Would you like a piece of salted caramel? These have been expertly glazed in chocolate by Claudine, and I must say that she has single-handedly invented one of the best desserts in all of Asia Minor!"

Seba slowly reached forward and took a little square in his hand. It was sticky, and he noticed flakes of salt on top. "Go ahead, try it, but I'll warn you, if you taste one, you'll be inclined to eat the whole plate."

Seba popped the whole square into his mouth, and the experience was incredible: comforting, sweet, salty, buttery, dark, and creamy. It was as if he was tasting coffee's younger, sweeter relative. As he chewed, Seba noticed that the inside of the little treat became stuck in his teeth, making it difficult to move his jaw. However, he joyfully kept at it as the sugar, salt, and chocolate lit up the insides of his mouth.

"My apologies, my young men! I completely forgot about the coffee. I've found that my Greek friends, like my French ancestors, enjoy a steaming cup of coffee to aid the digestion of a wonderful meal." Dr. Robin's dark eyes sparkled, and she playfully raised her eyebrows up and down.

Seba, working his jaws on the chocolate-covered salted caramel, nodded enthusiastically.

Dr. Robin turned to ask Claudine to bring out the coffee, but she had anticipated the request, and appeared as Dr. Robin began to speak.

"Claudine, you are a wonder. Thank you."

She silently removed all of the plates and bowls from the table, stacking them on the bottom of her elaborately decorated cart. Claudine brought a small pink pot bearing the same flowered and butterflied design that had mesmerized Seba and poured hot black coffee from the pot into the cups. Seba noticed that there were no grounds that came from the pot, and as he inhaled the familiar aroma of rich, dark coffee, he wondered what magic Claudine had performed to remove the grounds while keeping the light brown foam that she poured from the coffee pot into the matching cups. She placed each cup on a small saucer and handed them to Seba, Paolo, and Dr. Robin.

Seba did not reach for his cup until he saw Dr. Robin delicately pinch the thin, gold-plated handle of the cup between her thumb and first finger and raise it to her lips. Seba did the same, noticing how light and fragile the cup felt in his hand. He sipped the coffee, which was rich and smooth. He didn't even miss the honey that his mother usually added to the coffee when she made it over the fire.

"I should eat in the garden more often," Dr. Robin

mused as she looked around the walled enclosure. "It's quite serene, isn't it?"

The serenity was shattered by a commotion coming from inside the house. Claudine, who had disappeared after serving the coffee, now ran back into the garden, calling for the doctor.

"There's a boy whose hand has been severed. He needs attention immediately!"

"*Mon Dieu!*" Dr. Robin jumped out of her chair, clattering the coffee cups, and ran back to her surgery room, Paolo and Seba following close behind.

There were twin boys, about Seba's age, in the room that had earlier been occupied by Nasir. One of the twins was screaming in extreme pain, his identical-looking brother holding his arm in the air and gripping him tightly around the middle because his legs could not support him. The arm in the air was wrapped in a blood-soaked cotton cloth, which was saturated and dripping dark red blobs onto both boys' arms.

Dr. Robin snapped into action, asking Claudine to bring boiling water, and helping the screaming boy onto the table. Dr. Robin poured a liquid from a small brown vial on the shelf down the boy's throat, and then gave him a leather strap that had been hanging on the wall, and told him to bite down as hard as he could. She unwrapped the cloth, and Seba almost lost the entire meal he had just eaten. Through the bloodied stump, he could see the two bones at the end of the boy's wrist, and the arteries were continuing to pump out his life force, which was spurting from the severed limb. Dr. Robin cleaned the site with cloths dipped in the boiling water, and then asked Claudine to bring the fire iron from the kitchen. Seba gasped as he realized what Dr. Robin was about to do. The boy with the bleeding arm was in such

41

shock that he appeared not to have heard the doctor, but his brother's eyes grew wide.

Claudine brought the red-hot iron from the fire, along with a pail of ashes from the hearth, and Dr. Robin said, "I hope the opium worked quickly. The wound needs to be cauterized, or the loss of blood will be fatal. Son, I'll need you to hold your brother as if you are rescuing him from the jaws of death, because you may be doing exactly that."

The brother nodded and squeezed his twin even tighter. The opium must have taken effect, because the injured boy stopped screaming and instead began whimpering like a lost dog.

Dr. Robin used metal tongs to pinch the skin of the boy's wrist together and then touched the iron rod to the edges.

The boy's spine-chilling wail of pain was so loud that Seba jumped back, hitting the wall and knocking several other leather straps onto the floor. Paolo was beside Seba, pressing his back against the wall and inching toward the door. The putrid smell of burning flesh was so overwhelming that Seba put his hand over his mouth and nose, willing the waves of revulsion to stay down. His eyes were burning with the foul stench, and he held his breath until his head began to pound.

Dr. Robin, however, continued to work quickly, and when she was finished with the iron, she plunged the severed limb into the pail of ashes, and as the boy's eyes rolled back in his head, Dr. Robin laid him on the table, where he fell into an unconscious stupor.

The twin brother looked at Dr. Robin pleadingly. "Will he survive?"

"I cannot say. I closed the wound as best I could, but I don't know how much blood was lost before you brought him to me." She offered the boy the scant contents of another brown bottle of opium. "Here, take a bit of this—you've had a shock as well. You're twins, I presume?" The boy drank every drop in the bottle and nodded. "Yes. I feel as if my own hand is gone. It was horrible! My brother and I work as laborers for a local shop owner. My brother was accused of stealing something valuable from our employer, and before he had a chance to explain or defend himself, the owner violently attacked him with a machete, severing his hand at the wrist. He didn't even get a chance to plead his case before the Ottoman tribunal!"

Dr. Robin said, "I'm sorry. I know that severing a hand is a punishment that is used here in Smyrna among some of the older establishments, but it is barbaric and dangerous. I thought that we had moved beyond that savage brutality in this day and age."

"What's going to happen to my brother's hand?"

"I wish I could predict the future, but I'm afraid time will tell. He won't be able to work for a long time, and likely never again as a laborer."

"Well, I'll never go back to that monster anyway. If there is any justice in this world, he will pay for what he has done to my brother. I'd like to see him in irons, but workers like us are rarely treated fairly."

Dr. Robin said grimly, "Let's focus on healing rather than justice. You can stay here with your brother as long as you like, and we will care for him until he recovers."

Dr. Robin turned, surprised to see that Seba and Paolo were in the room. She smiled wryly and said, "I did not intend to end our pleasant meal in this way, but if either of you had the intention of becoming a physician, now you have a clear view of what it entails."

Seba could feel his fractured wrist pounding, and he thought he would never shake the vision of the bones poking out from the other boy's severed arm. He pulled his left arm in toward his stomach, as if protecting a fragile bird. *What kind of monster could do that to someone?*

Dr. Robin led them to a gate at the far end of the garden, and they pushed the vegetable cart over the threshold and out into an ally leading to Frank Street. Before this horrific encounter, Seba's stomach had been full, the birds were singing their evening lullabies to each other, and the gentle breeze was soothing. That delicious meal in the garden had been a dream, and a fleeting one at that. Seba went from hell at the Aigokeros to heaven in the garden, and back to hell again. He hoped he would not hear the boy's shrieks of pain in his dreams. Seba's insides were roiling, churned into a frenzy by the incident with the twins.

Dr. Robin held her hands out, and when Seba and Paolo reciprocated, she took both of their hands in hers. "Thank you both for your service to Nasir. I'm sure he will want to thank you in person when he is feeling better. Shall I tell him to look for you at the Aigokeros?"

Seba and Paolo nodded and thanked Dr. Robin for her hospitality. Dr. Robin pointed to the surgery room. "It may be quite some time before he is able to visit you, but in the meantime, he will have another with whom to share his recovery. God willing, they will heal swiftly."

Seba and Paolo said in unison, "Thank you, again, Dr. Robin."

"Give Miss Kokokis my best, and Godspeed to you both."

5 STREETS OF SMYRNA

Seba and Paolo moved so slowly down Frank Street that they would have appeared to any observers to be vegetable peddlers who had worked long into the evening or sailors who had imbibed one too many mugs of raki. When they reached the pier, they stood there for a long time, watching the stars move across the soft indigo sky and enjoying the cool air that floated in from the Aegean Sea. The sun had set while they were in Dr. Robin's surgery room, taking the day's heat with it. Sea birds floated on the ocean breeze, their long white wings spread out like the sails of a ship, barely visible against the night's dark canopy. Seba and Paolo could hear the water lapping against the wooden pilings and the muted chatter of sailors on board ships that were moored for the night. If it weren't so dangerous, Seba would have climbed into the vegetable cart and slept the whole night by the water's edge.

Within this peaceful setting, Seba found himself longing for the solitude of his home in Sessera and the deep purring of his cat, Artemis. When he was a young boy, Seba had heard of mastiha thieves having their hands cut off at the wrist, or sometimes four fingers of a hand, but he had never experienced the brutality of the act. He squeezed the fingers of his left hand, trying to imagine what it would feel like if they were gone, then nearly jumped out of his skin as he felt the pain that coursed through his fractured wrist. Dr. Robin had expertly set the bone, but Seba's wrist was throbbing, and he had learned the hard way to keep his fingers still.

As they turned away from the harbor, heading northward toward the Aigokeros, Seba looked up into the mountains surrounding Smyrna. The lights from homes twinkled and Seba could just make out the shapes of other buildings dotting the hills as they sloped from the Caravan Bridge down to the sea. Through the candlelight shining in the windows of those homes in the hills, Seba could tell that some of the buildings were several stories high and had walls around them that reminded Seba of the walls around Sessera, built to keep the pirates and raiders from the precious mastiha and to keep the mastiha-growing families inside at night.

Pointing up into the hills, Seba asked, "Is that where Dr. Robin said the wealthy government officials live?"

Paolo nodded. "Yes, and it's very exclusive. I've lived here most of my life, and I have never been inside any of those homes, not even to run an errand for an employer."

"It doesn't even seem like it's part of the city." Seba gestured toward the lights sparkling across the shadowed landscape, some of which seemed to be obscured by a series of stone walls. "Are those small communities within the walls?"

"Ha! No, those are the individual homes of the wealthy merchants and kadis."

"Who are the kadis?"

"They're the Ottoman judges who adjudicate the civil and criminal matters in the city."

"And they're wealthier than the merchants of Frank Street?"

Paolo clicked his tongue against the back of his teeth in mock disapproval. "Yes. You have much to learn. Frank Street is for the people who are involved on a day-to-day basis with the merchant trade of the seas, like the foreign brokers, salespeople, and tariff clerks. In the hills, however, are those who are too important to deal with the day-to-day administration. They have so much money that they pay the brokers and merchants who live and work on Frank Street to do their bidding, and they don't have to hear the raucous noise from the sailors in the port."

Seba was confused. "How many families live in each one of those buildings in the hills?" There had been dozens of families inside Sessera's stone walls, so Seba imagined that several families lived together in these imposing enclaves.

Paolo chuckled. "One family each. That's how rich they are."

"That can't be right. I can see the rooftops of multiple buildings inside those walls. They look like they could support twenty people or more. You mean to say they all belong to one family?"

Paolo put his hand on Seba's shoulder, continuing to push the cart with his other hand. "Yes, my friend, they set themselves apart and build everything to keep their wealth inside. They like to keep the rest of us outside. Certainly, you've seen castles and walled cities?"

Seba let out a groan. "Yes, of course, but castles and walled cities are for communities, not only one family."

Paolo clucked like an exasperated parent. "It's a good

thing you have me to teach you about the world, Seba. Who knows what would happen to you? As I said, those homes are for one official, who probably has one spouse and a few children. See those orange groves? Most of the homes are situated among them, so they can smell the citrus blossoms and walk out their back doors to pick the fruits."

"But why do they need all of that space?" Raised in a community where everyone shared and helped each other, Seba didn't understand the concept of the wealthy landowners in the hills of Smyrna.

"I don't know—why don't you go knock on one of their doors and ask them? I'm sure they'd like to entertain a poor stinking peon from the Greek quarter."

As the word "stinking" came from Paolo's lips, they entered the Greek quarter's bazaar at Enymeria, and the pungent odor of fish became overwhelming. These fish were the ones that hadn't been sold for the day, and they were being held in buckets of seawater, either to be eaten by the fishmongers' families the next day or fed to their animals. Seba squinted his eyes, and his whole face puckered against the smell. He had experienced enough nausea for the day.

Paolo must have been experiencing the same feeling, because he said, "This foul fish smell is making me sick. My nose can't take another assault."

Seba didn't look up from the vegetable cart, but he said peevishly, "Neither one of us would have smelled so much blood, rotting food, or fish guts today if it weren't for you."

Paolo snapped, "And you wouldn't have eaten the best meal of your life if it weren't for me, either. These are the highs and lows of living in a city. You'll get used to it after you've lived here for a time."

Seba stopped pushing the vegetable cart and turned to

48

Paolo. "I don't want to get used to it. I hadn't heard a bird chirp in three weeks until we entered Dr. Robin's garden. I miss the sounds of nature—I can't hear any of them with all the clangor in this city. How can you stand it?"

"It's different for me, Seba. I was born in this city, amid all of these smells and sounds, and there were only a few times when I ventured out to the farmlands to gather wool and angora for my father. It's so quiet out in the farmlands, it makes me feel uncomfortable. It's ghostly quiet."

As Seba was about to protest, Paolo leaned in conspiratorially and whispered, "You can never trust the ghosts."

Seba's mouth twisted as he fought the urge to laugh. It was amazing how Paolo could turn every conversation to the subject of ghosts. *Maybe this constant barrage of noise drowns out his thoughts of ghosts and demons. I bet he can't keep those thoughts at bay when it's quiet. Just like I'm going to hear that boy with the severed hand's screams all night long.*

He drew in a breath all the way from the bottom of his lungs and exhaled slowly. Even though Paolo was the reason why Seba was going to have nightmares about a boy's amputated hand, Seba realized he was tired of fighting. He wanted to deliver the vegetable cart back to Meleia and go to sleep. That is, if he could sleep after the evening's horrors.

Seba extended an olive branch to Paolo out of pure exhaustion. "I thought you were going to trust the ghosts from now on. Remember when you found me at death's door, calling out for help, after I had injured my wrist in that earthquake? You thought I was a ghost, and I thought you were Jesus, because you were whistling a *tripatos*." Seba shook his head as if to dismiss the memory of that day, when he had been on the verge of starvation and exposure.

It seemed a lifetime ago, even though it had been less than a month.

"Ah, yes, it is a great honor to be mistaken for Jesus, even if it was by you, who was delirious from pain and exhaustion."

"Well, in my defense, I had swum the Strait of Chios."

Paolo whistled, showing his admiration for Seba's accomplishment. "Good point. I can't believe you did it. I don't even think Heracles could have done it. Isn't it that channel more than eight miles across?"

Seba nodded. He didn't want to admit it, but he was pleased that he had impressed Paolo, who was older, bigger, stronger, and seemed to have had more life experiences. "I think so, but it felt like much more. I almost gave up; I was so battered and bruised that a part of me wanted to stop fighting and sink to the bottom of the sea. Then I felt something brush against my feet, and when I looked down, a pair of dolphins was pushing me forward. My father had always told me to follow the dolphins—I think it was a sign. It's almost as if he knew that I was going to need the dolphins' help one day. A few minutes later, my arms touched the sand, and the dolphins were gone. I had made it across the channel!"

Paolo shook his head up and down emphatically, his unruly nut-brown hair falling in his eyes. "I bet dolphins can talk to ghosts, too. They're really smart. That's why they are the symbols of Poseidon." He pointed to Seba's arms. "You know, if I hadn't seen your scrapes and cuts with my own eyes, I'm not sure I would have believed you did it. When I worked the barges at Çeşme, we saw boats smashed against the rocks almost daily because of the powerful current. It looks like you were smashed against the rocks, too."

Seba looked down at his arms, which bore the red scars from where he had been gouged by the razor-sharp rocks of the Anatolian shore. He knew that his legs looked worse, and they felt worse, too. But not as bad as his wrist. "I was. You know, there's a little rocky island in the middle of the channel, more like an outcropping of knives, but I had to stop there to catch my breath before I could get all the way across. I was so bloody from the undertow slamming me against the jagged limestone that I couldn't see where I was going. It was a miracle that I survived."

#

Fifteen minutes later, they crossed the threshold of the Aigokeros, where Meleia was sweeping up the broken plates and cups from the alcohol-soaked floor of her taverna with a large broom fashioned from twigs and small tree branches. Looking up from her task, she blew a stray curl away from her face and said, "Look at this place—it's totally destroyed."

Even though Meleia looked exhausted, and her expression was pained, she was beautiful.

In fact, she had dazzled Seba since the very first time he met her. He would never forget that day, one in which he realized he was truly becoming a man.

Paolo and his friend Buğra had been showing Seba the city. Seba was entertained by Paolo and Buğra arguing over the best tavernas in Smyrna. Whereas Paolo was stocky and looked as if he moved huge crates of cargo on and off barges all day long (which he did), Buğra was equally as tall but lean and sinewy, with a posture that suggested his position—working for one of the Ottoman government clerks. They were opposites—Paolo with a huge, curly mop of nut-brown hair that fell into his eyes when he was animated, predisposed to lose his temper at a moment's notice, and Buğra with his close-cropped, pitch-black hair that emphasized his angular features, and who was introverted but always generous. As they discussed all of the tavernas they had sampled in Smyrna since venturing out into the world, Buğra quietly mentioned that his favorite, by far, was one operated by a proprietress whom people either loved or hated. According to Buğra, the food was unsurpassed, the prices were fair, and if you didn't offend the owner, you would enjoy your meal. It was called the Aigokeros.

New to the city at the time, Seba was thrilled to see the wooden sign hanging over the door, which was a white capricorn, or in Greek, *aigokeros*, set against a field of sage green. The aigokeros was a hybrid animal, bearing the head of a large horned goat with a thick, flowing beard and the tail of an enormous fish, with multiple tail fins. It was a creature of Greek mythology that Seba's grandfather had often mentioned, important because she was said to have nursed Zeus in his infancy.

Seba especially loved the capricorn because it was the star sign under which he was born, fifteen years earlier.

"*Amalthea* herself," Buğra said, looking up at the sign over the taverna's door, the first time he and Paolo had brought Seba to this establishment.

Paolo snapped, "No, it's *Pricus*, you dolt. You're Turkish, so it's understandable that you would mix up the ancient Greek stories."

Buğra flinched, then inhaled and exhaled slowly. "I've told you a thousand times, Paolo, my grandmother is Greek, and I know as much about my Greek heritage as anyone. The creature on that sign is definitely Amalthea. And why wouldn't it be? This is a taverna, which means that it is here to feed and sustain us, like Amalthea, the she-goat who nurtured Zeus."

Paolo was undeterred, and he pointed forcefully at the capricorn's head. "She-goats don't have horns. That means this aigokeros is Pricus, the original male sea-goat."

Buğra smiled serenely at Paolo, and Seba got a glimpse of how Buğra must handle the complaints at the Ottoman clerk's office. "Are you certain? How do you know? Amalthea was a beautiful and magical creature, and she could have had any body parts she wanted."

"But Pricus was the first sea-goat and the ruler of time, so that's the sign they'd use to bring in the most business. They would want their customers to be fed any time of day or night. It's definitely Pricus."

Buğra said thoughtfully, "We can ask the proprietress of the Aigokeros. It's her sign, so she can set the record straight."

"All I know," said Seba with a shudder, "is that my mother would make the sign of the cross and shove me in the other direction if she saw me walking into a place signified by a capricorn. She would say it must be run by heathens."

Buğra laughed. "I know how that feels, Seba. My family is Muslim, and even though my grandmother is Greek, my mother, her daughter, does not approve of the ancient Greek tales. She says they are pagan stories that contradict the Qur'an. My mother is especially devoted to Maryam, mother of Isa. One of her favorite verses from the Qur'an, which she taught to me as soon as I could speak, is 3:45: *'When the angels said "O Maryam! Allah gives you the good news with a Word from Him that you will be given a son: his name will be Messiah, Isa, the son of Maryam. He will be noble in this world and the Hereafter; and he will be from those who are very close to Allah.'"* Since I am her firstborn son, I believe my mother feels closer to Maryam when she hears that verse."

Seba's mouth gaped open. That sounded very much like the New Testament of the Bible and the Annunciation. "Are you talking about the Virgin Mary and Jesus?"

Buğra grinned. "Yes, of course. We Muslims share many of the same stories with the Christians. I'm guessing you are a Greek Christian, then?"

Seba managed to nod the affirmative, but his head was spinning. "Wait, I don't understand. You're saying that the Qur'an talks about Mary and Jesus?"

Buğra smiled patiently. "Yes, Seba. We call them Maryam and Isa rather than Mary and Jesus, but they are the same. They are both great prophets of Islam."

"But I thought that Muslims didn't believe in Jesus or Mary."

"That is a tragic misunderstanding, my friend. We adore Maryam, mother of Isa. She is peaceful, loving, and nurturing, a refuge in the storms of life. It is said that she lived not far from here, high on a mountaintop, in the last years of her life. I have journeyed to that mountaintop with my mother, and I can tell you unequivocally that I felt the presence of Maryam in my body, as did my mother. It was a pilgrimage for which I will be forever grateful."

Seba's mouth was still open so wide that Paolo leaned over and tapped the bottom of Seba's chin. "Catching flies, Seba?"

Seba snapped his mouth shut and pushed Paolo's hand away as he said to Buğra, "I had no idea."

Buğra smiled brightly and said, "Yes, and did you know that there is an entire chapter of the Qur'an devoted to Maryam? Well, maybe that is the same in the Christian

Bible, but I can't remember. Do you have a chapter of the Christian Bible named after Mary, Mother of Jesus?"

Seba shook his head, embarrassed. "No, Buğra. The Christian Bible does not have a chapter named after the Virgin Mary. At least not one that I know of."

Seba wondered why that was. He had been taught about the differences between the two religions, but no one had bothered to explain to him the similarities. Maybe there was more to the two religions than he had been taught.

Seba said, "I'd love to know more about your beliefs. I knew the world was bigger than my existence on Chios, and Smyrna is a great city of many cultures, but you're the first person who took the time to explain it to me."

Buğra put his arm around Seba's shoulder. "That is music to my ears, Seba. As someone who straddles both cultures, I've had many similar questions. And it sounds like our mothers have much in common, regardless of the difference in their religious teachings."

Seba looked up, and they were right under the sign. The capricorn's visage was one of welcome, reminding Seba of his grandfather and stories around the hearth. That, along with the mouthwatering aroma of grilled fish, propelled Seba forward.

He put his arms around Buğra and Paulo and smiled. "I think this place is perfect."

The smell of roasted meat, lemon, oregano, and marjoram drifted from the kitchen. The sweaty smell of humanity did not diminish the culinary aroma; rather, it mingled with it to create the atmosphere of a summer festival. There were dishes of cured olives, salty and pungent, and herb-spiced flatbread, toasty with a hint of rosemary. The smell of grape leaves stuffed with vegetables and ground lamb, salt-cured fish, and, of course, the yeasted aroma of beer permeated the entire building.

The proprietress had been standing in the doorway to the kitchen, tall and welcoming, with wavy brown hair, copper-tinged with henna. Her curls were tied up in a knot near the top of her head, giving her the look of world-weary royalty. Her shoulders were broad and muscular, and she carried three mugs of beer in one hand and two plates of food in the other. Her eyes were hazel, but also sharp like a raven's, and flecked with gold. She didn't miss a snippet of conversation or a patron's inquisitive glance around the taverna. If she was not the owner, she was obviously the person in charge.

"Welcome to the Aigokeros! Have a seat anywhere you can find it and tell me your drink of choice!"

Seba had never encountered a woman with such a blend of strength and femininity. It gave her an air that was oddly familiar and reassuring. He liked her immediately.

Paolo said, "This is Meleia Kokokis; she owns this respectable establishment. Which is quite an accomplishment, given that she's only seventeen years old, the same as me. Her taverna, the Aigokeros, is the pearl of the Aegean."

Meleia's eyes narrowed and she frowned at Paolo, as if she'd heard his false flattery too many times to count.

"I mean, her father really owns the place, but he's a drunk—"

Meleia lifted her arm wielding the two plates of food threateningly toward Paolo.

"—and this business wouldn't exist without her."

Meleia relented, and the corner of her mouth turned upward to the slightest degree.

Buğra said, "Three beers and three plates of grilled fish, please."

Meleia nodded and was off, busying herself delivering food and then gathering drinks behind the bar.

"She's amazing," said Seba, dreamy-eyed.

"And she can cook food that fills you up while sending your tastebuds straight to heaven. I can't wait to devour some grape leaves and grilled fish—I've had enough salted meats to last an eternity," said Buğra.

Seba's mouth watered. He hadn't been this hungry on the journey after he swam the Strait of Chios, and the smell of delicious food nearly drove him mad.

Meleia returned faster than Seba thought humanly possible, slapped three mugs of beer onto the table, and said the food would be right out. *She's so confident. And beautiful.*

Seba took the mug in his hand and inhaled deeply. In his childhood home, they drank goat's milk and the clear water from the springs every day, and wine and *tsipouro* were reserved for village celebrations. Things were different in Smyrna, however. Each evening meal included several mugs of ale, wine, or raki, and Seba's body had not yet become accustomed to the new routine.

Meleia was running around, putting food and drinks on tables, clearing them, and talking to the patrons, and she had already filled Seba, Buğra, and Paolo's mugs a second time. Her red-tinted hair was coming loose from the topknot, and while hurrying into the kitchen, she tripped on a stool that someone had kicked over when rising to leave. *She needs some help.*

Seba noticed the fire behind the bar, where Meleia made coffee the traditional way, over a firepit in a copper pan that was filled with sand. She had several copper *cezves* in the sand, obviously making coffee for more than one customer. Seba saw that one of the coffee pots was frothing at the rim, threatening to boil over, and Meleia was in the kitchen. Seba had learned from his mother that the ideal foam for Turkish coffee came from bringing the coffee to the boiling point and then quickly removing it and pouring it into the cup. He had watched his mother make coffee thousands of times, and he knew the process as well as he knew his own name. Feeling uninhibited by Meleia's barley-brewed ale, Seba jumped up, ran behind the bar, and grabbed the wooden handle of the cezve that was almost boiling over. As he attempted to raise it away from the sand and fire, to allow it to cool so it could be poured, he heard a shout.

"What do you think you're doing?"

Startled, Seba whipped around quickly, and because he was holding the red-hot cezve by the wooden dowel, he swung the coffee pot over the fire, sending all of the other copper pots toppling over into the sand like flaming dominoes, and spilling coffee everywhere. As each cezve tumbled sideways, it caused the blistering sand to explode upward, all over Seba, Meleia, and the floor surrounding the firepit. The clanging of copper was so loud that many of the patrons in the Aigokeros stopped talking and looked over at Seba.

A hand reached out and snatched the wooden handle from Seba, but because he didn't want to spill it, and because his reflexes had been slightly dulled by the beer, he continued to hold on.

Meleia's hair had completely escaped the knot on her head, and her red-tinged curls were covered in sand and boiled coffee foam, as was her skirt, the floor, and most of the area behind the bar.

Seba looked down and saw their hands touching on the wooden dowel, and he slowly released his grip. Looking at Meleia, he said, "Why did you yell like that? I was helping you with the coffee. It was about to boil over. I had everything under control until you startled me."

Her eyes were blazing as she yanked the cezve's handle away from him. "Do I look like I need your help? Do you think this bar has run itself for the last three years? No! I've run it by myself, without some wet-behind-the-ears schoolboy going behind my back to bungle it up! I have an entire restaurant full of customers, some of whom are going to have to wait even longer for their coffee, and now I have this mess to clean!"

Seba, bewildered by the turn of events, tried to defend himself. "But the coffee was about to boil over—"

"It didn't, though, did it? Because I was right there to move it off the fire and then put it back for the second boil! That's how you get the flawlessly thick foam, by bringing it to a boil two times."

Seba felt the pink rising in his cheeks. "I've never seen anyone boil coffee two times."

"Exactly—how would a dimwitted juvenile like you know anything about making coffee?"

Seba puffed out his chest and jutted his shoulders back. "I'm not a child, I'm a man. I am fifteen years old, I know how to make coffee, and I swam the Strait of Chios!"

"Well, why don't you swim back, because it seems like you might do better with water than you do with fire." She held the small copper pot out to him. "Here, hold this and *don't move*— I'm going to get my leather gloves so I can clean this mess and start the coffee again." She grabbed the other cezves by their handles and took them back into the kitchen. Seba could hear her muttering under her breath as she stomped away, "Stupid boy, now I have to wash the sand out of all of these copper pots. Just what I need on one of the busiest nights of the week."

"I was trying to help." Seba hoped his voice did not

sound too sulky.

From the kitchen Seba heard the dismissive response. "More like put me out of business."

Seba, now feeling foolish and embarrassed, held the wooden-handled cezve over the sand until Meleia returned. His face was flushed with shame and the effects of alcohol, and he stood stock-still as he watched her gather up the sand with her leather gloves and stoke the fire under the sand until it was blazing again. When she was finished, she faced him as she took the wooden dowel from his hand.

He felt ashamed. "I'm sorry, I didn't know."

Meleia's brow was furrowed, and her face was hot from exertion. "I have a feeling there is a long list of things you don't know. Now get out from behind my bar, and don't ever come back here again."

"I can wash the copper coffee pots for you. Would that help?"

"I doubt it. Your idea of helpful is not the same as mine." She pointed to the coffee foam that was splattered over everything. "Obviously."

"But you're busy, and you need an extra hand, right?"

She looked around and sighed. "Fine, you can wash the pots, but don't touch anything else."

Seba stood there a moment, staring at her face, which was beautiful despite the look of anger she was wearing.

"What are you standing around for? Didn't I just say how busy I am?"

Seba pointed to her head. "Um, you have coffee in your hair." He reached his hand forward and touched his fingers to the hair above her ear, brushing away the foam and sand as she stared at him, incredulous.

Then he turned and ran into the kitchen.

His first day at the Aigokeros had been memorable. Now, at this late hour, as he looked at Meleia, broom in hand, surveying her entire taverna, which was in a shambles, he regretted that he had been the cause of her having to clean up the coffee squalor weeks earlier. Granted, the calamity he had caused was confined to the fire and sand pit behind the bar, and the current disaster was much worse, but Seba felt horrible that someone who worked as hard as Meleia suffered so much. *Don't worry, I'll make it better for you.*

6 PEARL OF THE AEGEAN

A week after the disastrous brawl, Seba, Buğra, and Paolo were back in the Aigokeros, which looked surprisingly good for an establishment that had been nearly demolished the prior week.

Seba's quest for his father was put on hold while he allowed his broken wrist to heal, and even though he wasn't at full physical capacity, he helped Meleia as much as he could. After what he had done with the coffee, he thought it was the least he could offer her.

It had taken Meleia and all of her friends the whole week to clean the place and render it operational, although a faint odor of stale beer remained, and there were several nicks and indentations carved haphazardly across the walls. Today was the first day the taverna had opened since the ruckus that had smashed the Aigokeros to pieces. It was busy, as the people in the neighborhood wanted to show Meleia their support, and also because she made the best *shakshuka* in all of Smyrna.

"Look at these cups and plates—they're even nicer than the ones she had before." Buğra held up a gray ceramic mug that was rimmed at the top with a dark blue stripe. Seba and Paolo did the same, and they touched the mugs together with a celebratory clink. Each was brimming with Meleia's specialty, sprouted barley ale.

Meleia also smoked and grilled all of the meats and fish that she served, and she could make a tantalizing dish out of any vegetable that she discovered in the Enymeria or Kemeralti markets. She often sent the local children into the hills to forage for *chora*, which she served cold in tasty salads or roasted and used as a topping for her stewed dishes. All of her specialties were on display for this grand re-opening, but the one that made Paolo happy was the barley ale.

"And the drunkards didn't ruin her amphorae full of fermenting barley, or we wouldn't have anything to drink for a few more weeks." Paolo swilled down half of his mug in one gulp.

Rather than being offended by Meleia's name-calling on the day they met and the fact that she thought him a boy, Seba couldn't help but be mesmerized and impressed by her. For one thing, she was one of the smartest people Seba had ever met. She showed him how she brewed her own ale and how the cats that prowled the Aigokeros kept the mice away from the wheat and barley that served as the basis for her brews.

Meleia's two best mousers were a formidable pair: a black female with a white spot on her chest, called Desta, and an orange, black, and white female called Ryma. The felines were always on duty at Meleia's taverna, and despite their busy jobs, they were often found brushing up against Meleia's legs or looking cute while sitting on the wooden barrels of grain and ale surrounding the bar. Seba noticed how she spoke sweetly to her lithesome friends while scratching them softly behind the ears. Sometimes he could hear them purring from across the taverna, especially if they were situated in a patch of late-afternoon sun. Seba even caught Meleia putting out bits of fish on little plates and dishes of goat's milk for them in the kitchen. Seba wouldn't have believed she had such a tender heart if he hadn't seen it with his own eyes.

Paolo and Buğra often argued over which cat caught the most mice. Or, rather, Paolo argued, and Buğra explained his opinion. There was a subtle difference that Seba noticed, and he realized that he preferred Buğra's methods to Paolo's bullying.

Paolo said, not surprisingly, "Desta is bigger, so she catches the bigger mice. That's why she's the better mouser."

Buğra replied, "You make a good point, but I've watched them hunt. Ryma is smaller and faster, almost twitching, so she gets the jump on the rodents. She's always prowling."

"Are you insinuating that Desta is slow? That's ridiculous! Her size is deceiving—that's how she lures her prey into a false sense of security. Then she pounces!"

Seba said, "I think you're both forgetting that they catch the most mice when they work together."

Buğra and Paolo raised their mugs in appreciation, saying together, "Fair point, fair point."

Seba laughed, understanding that everyone had a favorite feline. His favorite was back in Sessera, named Artemis, because she was the best hunter in the village. "I'm glad they're both so good at their jobs that we don't have to see any mice or rats in this taverna."

Seba looked over to Meleia, who was standing behind the bar, conversing in French with a sailor who worked the trade route from Smyrna to Marseilles.

Being in the Greek quarter, Seba expected the customers of the Aigokeros to be only Greek, but he often heard other languages being spoken, usually Turkish, Armenian, and Hebrew. English, French, and Dutch sailors who appreciated good food also patronized the Aigokeros, and Seba was amazed to hear Meleia conversing with all of them, including this Frenchman.

When the sailor paid his bill and left, Seba walked to the bar, sat down on a newly constructed wooden stool, and said, "How many languages do you speak?"

"I don't know, a few. It's not difficult if you hear them all day, every day."

"More than a few, I think. I've heard you speak at least six different languages here in the taverna over the last few weeks, and I'm sure you know more. It's amazing."

Meleia did not look up from her task of cleaning the glasses behind the bar. "I think it's amazing that you've decided to keep to your side of the bar and not try to help me anymore."

Seba felt the heat rise from his neck to his cheeks, which he knew were turning red. "I've apologized a hundred times, haven't I? I'll say it again—I'm sorry. I watched my mother make coffee my whole life, and next to you, she's probably the best cook I know. If she wasn't aware of boiling the coffee two times to get the best foam, how was I supposed to know?"

Meleia's expression looked skeptical. "You are an unusual sort of person, Sebastian. Most boys I know wouldn't apologize if their lives depended on it."

"I've also told you a hundred times, I'm fifteen years old, and I'm not a boy. I'm a man." He stroked the recent proliferation of hair on his chin for effect. The treasured

66

growth, sable-colored like the curly mop on his head, had begun to appear in the last year and was incontrovertible proof that he was no longer a child.

Meleia laughed, and Seba couldn't discern if she was laughing at him or the patchy stubble on his face. Shrugging her shoulders and changing the subject, she said, "Anyone can speak another language—all it takes is a little practice."

"Can you teach me?" *Please say yes, please say yes.*

Meleia put down the cloth she was using to clean some of her new mugs and narrowed her eyes. "Why would you want to learn a new language? You don't seem like the merchant or sailor type. I mean, Paolo told me the story about the Strait of Chios and your heroic swim, but swimming and sailing are not the same thing."

"What is that supposed to mean?" Seba's voice lifted a bit higher than he intended, and he corrected, continuing in a deep baritone, "I'm descended from the great shipbuilders of ancient Greece, who built vessels so strong and fast that they travel to the far corners of the earth."

Meleia held her hands up in mock protest. "Settle down, I mean you don't have the rowdy temperament of most of the sailors swarming this city."

Seba didn't know whether to be offended or flattered, but Meleia was smiling, so he decided to tell her the truth. "I'm looking for my father, and I learned that a textile shop owner named Stavros Alkeidis trades silks and velvets with the French merchants. Stavros's brother told me to ask him for help. I was thinking that if I knew how to speak a little French, Stavros might be more willing to assist me. I was bruised and battered from swimming the Strait of Chios, and I broke my wrist in the brawl, so I've been trying to learn as much about the city and its merchant business until I'm well enough to present myself to the shop owner. Now that you're back in business, I can plan my meeting with him."

Meleia slammed her hand on the bar, and the cleaning cloth she was using fell to the ground. "You're going to ask Stavros Alkeidis for help? Are you crazy?"

Seba was amazed how Meleia could go from laughing and helpful to thrumming with anger in a fraction of a second. "No, I'm not crazy. I know his younger brother, Timotheos. He's a priest in my village of Sessera, trained at Nea Moni's monastery, and he is one of the most kind, caring, and intelligent people I ever met. He gave me a letter of introduction so Stavros would help me. Why would that be crazy?"

Meleia frowned, her eyes sparking like a wildfire, but she took a deep breath before she spoke. "Do you know anything about Stavros Alkeidis?"

"I told you everything I know."

Meleia reached down behind the bar to retrieve the towel and resumed cleaning. "Fine, I can teach you a few French words to help you find your father, but you'll have to do something for me in exchange."

That was easy.

"Anything." Seba heart was starting to pound at the thought of spending more time with Meleia than he had this week while they were cleaning up the taverna. *Maybe she wants to spend more time with me, too.*

"Stay away from Stavros Alkeidis."

Seba stood up, his eyes even with Meleia's, as they were approximately the same height.

"Anything but that. I told you that I need him to help me find my father."

"You can find some other way to locate your father. You have no idea what you're getting into, do you?" Meleia began attacking the mug with the cloth, gripping it so tightly that Seba thought it was going to explode into shards of dust and clay. "I guess you're going to have to learn French by yourself. I'm not going to help you ruin your life." She turned on her heel and stomped into the kitchen.

Shaking his head in disbelief, Seba slowly walked back to the table, where Paolo and Buğra sat wide-eyed and open-mouthed.

Paolo said, "What did you do to her? Haven't we told you not to poke the hornet's nest? It's the Aigokeros's opening day after a week of cleanup. You were already on shaky ground after the coffee incident, and now you send her stomping off into the kitchen? What if she spits in our food?"

Seba knew that Paolo was only kidding, or possibly being dramatic. Meleia would never spit in anyone's food. *Or would she?*

"I don't know. I was asking her to teach me French, and at first, she said yes, but then she changed her mind." Seba didn't want to tell Paolo and Buğra what Meleia said about Stavros. He didn't need Paolo or anyone else mucking up his chance to find his father.

Buğra looked concerned. "Maybe you should go apologize." He raised his mug and took a long draught. "We haven't gotten our food yet."

Seba thought that was a good idea, so he walked into the kitchen, where Meleia was preparing several plates of grilled lamb that she had sliced from the spit that was turning over the fire behind the taverna.

Seba said quietly, "The only connection that I had before I came to Smyrna was a letter of introduction to Stavros Alkeidis. I don't feel like I can throw that away. I need your help."

"It seems like you always need my help, doesn't it?" Meleia's voice wasn't angry, merely tired.

"Is there something I need to know about Stavros? It would help me if I were prepared, especially since I've never met him before, and I haven't been in Smyrna very long."

"Wait here. Let me serve these plates, and then I'll tell you why you should stay as far away as Stavros Alkeidis as you can get." Meleia grabbed all three plates, layered them up her forearm, and darted out of the kitchen.

Seba surveyed the kitchen, which was clean, bright, organized, and smelled amazing, like Meleia. There was a stew of beef and cabbage spiced with cumin, coriander, and smoked paprika, bubbling away happily on the stove, and a stack of *dolmas* almost a foot high, the tender grape leaves filled with rice, sultanas, parsley, and mint. Seba knew they would all be gone within the hour.

When Meleia returned, she said, "You can never repeat this story. Do you promise?"

Seba nodded.

"Remember when Paolo made that crack about my father being a drunk? It was the very first night you came into the Aigokeros."

Seba nodded again, and his heart skipped. *She remembers the first night I came into her restaurant.*

"Stavros Alkeidis is the reason my father is a drunk."

Seba, who had been sitting on a stool in the kitchen, with his leg on the lowest wooden crossbar, almost tumbled over as his foot slipped off the stool and onto the floor. "How can that be?"

"Stop interrupting me, and I'll tell you."

Seba crossed his arms over his chest and leaned back. "I won't say another word."

Meleia continued, "The Aigokeros did not always operate in this location. My family has operated a taverna in this city under a different name, the Sea Lion, for many generations, but the original taverna burned to the ground in a fire that ravaged the city six years ago. Everything my father worked for was gone. We had no resources to rebuild the business, and the fire burned most of the lumber in Smyrna. The wealthy European merchants were cutting down the new trees and milling the planks for their warehouses before anyone in the Greek quarter could get our hands on them.

"However, the great Stavros Alkeidis offered to come to the rescue. He agreed to loan my father the money to rebuild the Sea Lion and get him access to the lumber, under two conditions: first, that my father promise to work for Stavros for several hours a week in exchange for the loan, and second, that the new restaurant be named 'the Spider.' I hated that name—who would want to eat at a restaurant called the Spider? Anyway, there was some back-and-forth about the interest rate being charged on the loan, but my father believed that the deal was fair, and he took Stavros's money. He began rebuilding the taverna in the northeast section of the Greek quarter, where it had operated for hundreds of years. However, instead of allowing my father to rebuild the restaurant back to its former status, Stavros kept creating more work for my father to do at his factory. It was backbreaking labor—tasks like moving heavy tapestries, velvets, pallets of fabrics, and making the indigo dye, which is a brutal and difficult process.

"Sometimes my father would come home from the factory breathing so shallowly that I thought he was going to die. He said it was the fumes from the indigo-dyeing process. It was eating away at his lungs. Whenever my father protested that he didn't have time to work on the restaurant because he was spending too much time in the workshop, Stavros told him that if he would help in the factory a little longer, then Stavros would send some 'laborers' to help my father rebuild the taverna. More like henchmen, if you ask me. It's well known that Stavros surrounds himself with several big men that he calls his 'laborers,' whom he says he also needs to keep around for security to protect his precious silk tapestries. In my opinion, those thugs are no different than the pirates who raid the ships in the harbor on a weekly basis. In fact, they might actually be the very same pirates. I've heard stories from the sailors who come in here, saying that Stavros's thugs skulk around the waterfront, looking for easy targets to plunder."

Seba noticed that Meleia's eyes shined with a slight wetness, and her voice intensified as she went on. "The restaurant construction was at a standstill—we had no money to buy any of the produce, meats, or fish, and we had no supplies for making beer or wine. We didn't even have a roof so we could keep people dry who may have wanted to come in and smoke a pipe after work. I noticed that my father was coming home later and later from Stavros's workshop, his eyes glassy and smelling of alcohol. His temper would spark if I mentioned anything about the slow progress on rebuilding the restaurant. In a moment of frustration, after we had argued for the hundredth time, I asked him to show me the terms of the loan, and when he did, it made me physically sick. For every month that the construction of the new taverna was delayed, the interest rate of the loan was increased. Stavros was purposely keeping my father away from rebuilding the restaurant to increase the interest rate, so my father would never be able to pay back the loan, and that was even if we managed to rebuild the restaurant at all.

"By that time, my father was a shell of himself. I couldn't imagine how a strong person like that could have been reduced to a drunken, shriveled, broken husk. Immediately, I told everyone who was working at the restaurant to stop everything. I told them that my father was sick, and that we could not reopen the Sea Lion; I refused to call it the Spider. We would find some other way to support ourselves. My father's body was so beaten down from long hours and his mind was so addled from abuse of alcohol that he couldn't go to Stavros's workshop anymore.

"It was the worst time of my life, and I will be eternally grateful for Buğra's support. He was amazing—he offered to meet with Stavros and give him the news that my father defaulted on the loan and there were no assets available to repay it. My father wasn't even able to continue working in the factory to pay the default. We returned every piece of wood that had been provided to rebuild the restaurant, and Stavros kept the wages my father had earned at the factory, as payment of the loan."

Meleia's hands were curled so tightly in two fists that all her fingers had turned white. Seba could feel the anger coiled up inside her. "That fiend made my father into a slave, and he broke him—physically broke another human being! I wouldn't have believed it possible if I hadn't seen it for myself. Now, my father drinks all night, sleeps all day, and barely knows the difference between the two."

Seba forgot his promise not to say another word and asked, "But how did you build this place, then?"

Meleia didn't seem to notice Seba's broken promise not to interrupt. The veins in her forearms receded slightly as she relaxed her fingers a bit. She inhaled slowly, filling her

73

lungs as if to give herself strength.

"To this day, Stavros does not know that it was me. I negotiated to purchase this property, again, with the help of Buğra's family, who, being Turkish dragomen, have certain privileges within the Ottoman government. I used the name of my mother's family—Kokokis—instead of my father's name, because I didn't want Stavros to know. When I first opened, this place was four wooden posts and a large piece of canvas—it miraculously appeared on my doorstep one morning, and I'm certain it was a ship's sail that someone left as a gift. I couldn't use the old restaurant name, so I chose the Aigokeros, because it represented a mix of land and sea, like this beautiful city. I've never told anyone this, but I also thought that maybe if I had a she-goat as my taverna's symbol, it would nurse my father back to health, like Amalthea nursed Zeus."

Seba interrupted, "I knew Buğra was right!"

Meleia narrowed her eyes. "What?"

"Oh, nothing—Paolo and Buğra were arguing over whether the aigokeros on your sign was Amalthea or Pricus. Of course, Paolo said it was Pricus because he wanted it to be a big masculine goat, but Buğra said he thought your taverna was named after Amalthea, the first she-goat."

Meleia tilted her head. "My mother used to say, 'It is to one's honor to avoid strife, but every fool is quick to quarrel.' I think Paolo could use the same advice."

Seba nodded. "I agree. And I'm sorry, I interrupted you. I really want to know what happened next."

Meleia smiled. "I put out a few nets in the marshy area near Frank Street, gathered enough fish to smoke in one batch, and smoked one large quantity of mullet or bream every three days. I sold the smoked fish, along with any wild greens and other chora I could find in the hills. I picked apples, mashed them up, and fermented them in the sun. That was the menu of the Aigokeros. I was implacable; I never slept, and I barely stopped to eat my own cooking. I would not let that monster ruin my family's legacy. He had broken my father, but he was not going to break me.

"I was astonished by the number of people who donated their time and resources on our behalf. Sometimes I would come to the restaurant and find construction materials or a spit. One time, someone had even built a fire ring in the back so I could begin to roast fish and meats in earnest, as we had done before. It took several years, and we finally had a new sign made—the one that hangs over the door today. I thought that bringing the taverna back to the family's original success would snap my father out of his torpor. I guess I was wrong; once a man is lost, sometimes he forgets that he wants to be found."

Seba, worried for Meleia, said, "Does Stavros know that it was you who saved the restaurant?"

Meleia shook her head. "I've never met him, and I don't think he knows who I am. He broke my father's spirit, profited from an egregiously unfair loan, and employed my father as slave labor without pay for almost a year. I'm sure he thinks it was some kind of savvy business arrangement for him. He probably moved on to his next victim without a care."

Meleia slammed her hand on the wooden sink. "Which is why you should have nothing to do with him."

Seba said, "I'm sorry that happened to your family and your father." He held his arms open wide inviting her into an embrace, and to his surprise, Meleia stepped into his arms.

She thinks she doesn't need any help, but she does.

Seba could have stayed there for an eternity, but after a

moment, Meleia said, "I have to get back to work." She broke from the embrace and held her finger in front of Seba's nose. "And remember, do not breathe a word of this story to anyone."

Seba agreed.

He returned to the table and said to Paolo and Buğra, "I apologized, so no one is spitting in anyone's food."

"Are you sure?" Paolo appeared unconvinced.

Seba's eyes darted toward the kitchen, where he could see Meleia's skirts swishing in and out of his view as she maneuvered around the kitchen. "Yes, I'm certain."

7 MR. FLORIDA

Before Seba, Paolo, and Buğra could finish their spit-free meals, they heard a commotion at the Aigokeros's front door.

Several pale-complexioned men entered the taverna together, looking well-fed and well-dressed. Their leader was of average height and, like the European merchants Seba had passed on Frank Street, had the protruding rounded midsection that was common within the ranks of Smyrna's affluent. The gentleman's clothes were mostly silk, with a bit of tightly woven cotton, in bright shades of indigo and vermilion. His boots were coal-black leather, so shiny that Seba could see the reflection of the taverna's ceiling rafters in them. A brass buckle and several brass buttons decorated his boots and his bright blue overcoat. His face was round, with a bulbous nose and weak chin sandwiched between a thick set of jowls. His face was completely clean-shaven.

The man's expression was animated and jolly, and some

of the men in the taverna seemed to recognize him. They called out to him in Greek, and he responded in the same excellent Greek as Dr. Robin, so natural that Seba couldn't detect an accent.

"Back with more stories of adventure, Dr. Turnbull?"

"I heard they set the janissaries on you in Methoni!"

"Does Governor Paşa know you're here?"

"Where is Maria Gracia de Robin, your beautiful wife? I hope you didn't leave her in England!"

"Have you visited her cousin, Dr. Robin, since you've been in town?"

"I thought you would have already been on your way to East Florida!"

The English gentleman, who Seba noticed had been addressed as a doctor, held his hands up.

"In due time, my dear friends. Yes, I've been to visit my wife's cousin, Dr. Despina Marguerite Robin, this very afternoon. She tells me that the Aigokeros boasts the best Greek food in all of Smyrna, which is high praise indeed. And I understand that the good doctor has donated the handsome blue-striped stoneware I see here, as a gift to the owner, whose business was ravaged by a riotous group of ruffians last week."

Walking through the taverna as if he, and not Meleia, was the owner, he patted his midsection, a mischievous look on his face. "I am here to taste for myself the delicacies of this famed establishment, whose reputation is well known on Frank Street among all of the merchant class."

The customers in the taverna murmured approvingly, and it was clear that they believed Meleia's fare to be as good, if not better, than anything available on Frank Street. Seba was disappointed to see that Meleia was in the kitchen when this man and his entourage arrived, so she missed the gentleman's exuberant entrance and paean to Meleia's talent with food. Seba believed she would have been pleased to hear that her taverna had garnered such a favorable reputation on Frank Street.

Dr. Turnbull continued, "And yet, my visit is not solely for the purpose of satisfying my appetite with the magic of olive oil, lemons, and oregano. I have come also to inquire whether any of you strapping young denizens of the Mediterranean would like to join me on a grand adventure across the seas."

The patrons responded with more murmurings and Seba remembered the words of Dr. Robin when they were in her garden. She had whispered something under her breath about Nasir being in the Aigokeros because of her cousin. *Is this English gentleman the reason why Nasir Paşa was in the taverna last week?*

The Englishman took a seat with some Greek workers who had ordered several beers. One offered his mug to Dr. Turnbull, who gracefully accepted it and quaffed it in one confident motion. Looking breezily at the people seated around him, Dr. Turnbull said, "I see from your dirt-covered clothes and tired expressions that you all have toiled all day in the workshops and on the docks, my friends. Tanning leather, dyeing indigo, weaving fabrics, carrying cargo from caravan to ship and back again. You're breaking your backs, aren't you? I'll wager you might be interested in an opportunity to better yourselves."

The patrons' assent hummed through the taverna.

"Do you wish to make a name and a new life for you and your family?" Sporadic clapping followed and Seba noticed by the looks on the patrons' faces that they were carefully considering the man's words. One by one, the taverna-goers slowly meandered over to Dr. Turnbull's table, bringing their mugs of wine and ale with them. Seba wondered how an Englishman knew so much about the lives of Greek workers in Smyrna. Maybe it was his Greek wife, Maria Gracia, who had taught him so much about the Hellenic inhabitants of Smyrna. It also seemed to Seba that this Englishman exhibited an uncanny familiarity with the city that was unusual for a European visitor.

"Are you strong enough to accept a challenge with a great reward waiting at its completion?"

Turnbull certainly knew his audience; asking the Greeks if they were strong enough was the equivalent of throwing the gauntlet for a Frenchman. The men raised their fists, yelling that of course they were strong enough—they were Greek, for heaven's sake!

Seeing his audience grow, Turnbull held his mug above his head with one hand and using his other hand for balance, he climbed carefully onto the bench where he had been sitting. "This adventure is for only the strong of body and constitution! There will be difficulties, as there are with any worthwhile undertaking, but the opportunities are limitless!" He raised his hands as if he were a performer or musician, and the Englishman's antics reminded Seba of his grandfather Papouli's monologues in the village square of Sessera.

"I am here to help us both. I need to gather workers for my East Florida enterprise, and being that my beautiful wife, Maria Gracia de Robin, was born and raised in this vibrant city, I am certain that my enterprise cannot fail if it is supported by the valiant Greek men and women of Smyrna."

Seba was impressed—this man had all of Papouli's qualities for whipping a group of people into a frenzy. And he was offering the opportunity for advancement in life, an escape from the struggles of a lowly Greek worker in a city full of wealthy French, Dutch, and English traders.

Dr. Turnbull continued, "In Florida the beach sands are as white as the clouds, and the sun shines hot and bright every day. The oysters are as wide across as a man's forearm, and the fish are so plentiful that they practically jump into your nets. Wild pigs, one of the few blessings left by Spain's abysmal failure on East Florida's sunny shores, roam freely and are yours for the taking. Deer, pheasant, turkey, and other wild game will be offering themselves to you with little or no effort on your part. For those of you who don't fancy the taste of meat—" (here he paused as the crowd screamed and laughed at that outrageous statement) "—there are fruits of all shapes, sizes, and sweetness: fragrant oranges and grapefruits, tart lemons and limes, grapes like bits of candy, red ripe strawberries and raspberries, blackberries, blueberries, and cherry-sized tomatoes growing in bunches by the hundreds; peaches, apricots, pears, and plums—so much of God's bounty, growing nearly the whole year as a result of the mild and gentle climate."

Seba, Paolo, and Buğra had remained in their seats, although Seba realized that Paolo was under the doctor's spell when Paolo said, "It sounds like the Garden of Eden, sir."

"An apt description, my young man. I couldn't have said it better myself. A strong, virile Greek such as yourself would all but guarantee the success of our business venture in East Florida."

Paolo sat up taller, raised his mug of ale, and beamed at the man's approbation.

Buğra's face was inscrutable. He asked, "How do you know so much about this place on the other side of the world?"

"A fine question, my young man. As you may have guessed from my dress, I am from the English Isles — Scotland, to be exact, although our kingdoms were united by the Acts of Union under the crown of Queen Anne more than fifty years ago. Not that the politics of the west should concern any of the citizens of Smyrna."

Realizing he had gotten off track, Dr. Turnbull cleared his throat. "Ahem, in any case, I have traveled across the Atlantic Ocean many times to the New World — a beautiful sandy coast as far as the eye can see, broad hammocks of vast forests intersected by gentle streams and rivers, and a climate that beckons all who step foot on its shores to luxuriate in its abundance."

Seba asked, "What kind of ships carry you to this New World?" He was thinking about his father.

"Why, you, young man, must be a budding scientist, not unlike myself, who was interested in the mechanics of the world as a young boy. It is, in fact, the reason I became a medical doctor. Graduated from the University of Edinburgh at the age of thirteen. I know, it sounds quite remarkable, but the weather in Scotland is particularly suited for studying indoors, especially in winter." He winked.

Seba tilted his head. For a physician, this Englishman did not seem to have the same ability to focus as the elegant and refined Dr. Robin. "I was asking about the ships, sir."

The doctor took a long pull on his mug, swallowed, and said, "Impatient, are you? That is the mark of a true Greek — a fact my wife, who is also Greek, never ceases to remind me of. I find that it's helpful to understand the *why* before you get to the *what*. *Why* am I creating this venture in East Florida? Well, because my analytical mind, expanded and refined at the University of Edinburgh, perceives the opportunity as most auspicious, because the area is mostly undiscovered land that is ripe for fine young entrepreneurs such as yourselves to move up in the world and create your own legacies of fame and fortune. *What* ships will be taking us to East Florida? Well, I have negotiated with the most elite captains in the world to lease the fastest ships that can hold the most cargo, which in this case will be people and the supplies we need to begin our enterprise. In fact, I have come from Constantinople, where I surveyed the very best in maritime vessels from all over the world. I have sailed with Dutch, English, Greek, Turkish, and Danish captains, all of whom pilot snows, brigs, and schooners that are more than capable of navigating the six-week voyage from Gibraltar to East Florida. That, and the favorable North Atlantic currents that propel us west toward the New World, make the journey swift and sure!"

Seba's heart was racing, and he could feel the blood flooding upward into his face. "Did you meet any shipbuilders in Constantinople?"

"Yes, of course, my young man. There are many wonderful shipbuilders in Constantinople." Dr. Turnbull frowned. "Well, there were until that horrific earthquake caused a tsunami that decimated the whole harbor. I was fortunate to be out in the Sea of Marmara when the earthquake and swell occurred, but I have since heard from other captains and sailors here in Smyrna that the port in Constantinople is no more."

Seba could feel the room swimming around him, and grabbed the table to steady himself.

"Are you ill, young man? I hope you do not have relatives in Constantinople, or at least ones that live near the harbor. It was a nasty business, trying to find those who were lost in the great wave."

Seba didn't have a chance to respond, however, because the next thing he heard was Meleia's angry voice, speaking in that clipped language that Seba remembered from the day he spent on the English ship, the *Delight*, with his father many years before.

"Get out! You are not going to dupe my customers into some Godforsaken misadventure on the other side of the earth!" She was holding a towel in her hand, and she snapped it so that it made a cracking sound, punctuating her indignation.

The man responded to her in Greek, so Seba and the others could understand his position, even if they didn't know what Meleia was saying. "My dear woman, you are mistaken. I am offering an opportunity, a chance of a lifetime, for these men and women to better themselves, to create a legacy for their families, to—"

Meleia, who had switched to Greek, said evenly, "They have established their legacies quite well right here, and without the help of a greedy Englishman who says he is here to help them but whose real motivation is to profit off the backs of their hard work."

Dr. Turnbull, possibly accustomed to irritable patients, stepped off the bench and walked calmly over to Meleia, who was standing in front of her bar with her hands on her hips. It looked like a fighting stance to Seba, one he had often seen his boyhood friend, Thaddeus, take when confronted by his archrival, Nikos. Seba noticed that Dr. Turnbull didn't get too close, however. Meleia was like a wild cat, waiting for the exact moment to pounce.

"My dear Miss Kokokis, I am a physician, like our shared friend and my esteemed cousin, Dr. Robin. I know your families have been close for generations, and now that I have married into that family, I do not want to disrupt the peace. You see how these people who are not in the merchant class or the gentry, or successful business owners such as yourself, are treated by their employers. Why shouldn't they have an opportunity for a good life, as we have?"

Meleia smiled, but the inside corners of her eyebrows turned down, so that her appearance was that of the cat who had spotted an unsuspecting mouse. "Oh, and you are the savior to bring these poor souls to the land flowing with milk and honey, is that it?"

Seba could barely concentrate on the verbal altercation. He was thinking of the day of the earthquake, the day that he had climbed up the rocks of the Anatolian coast after swimming the Strait of Chios. He had given up everything he had known to search for his father, and barely survived the journey. It couldn't have been all for nothing. *Maybe this Dr. Turnbull is mistaken about the great wave; he seems a bit absentminded.*

As Seba's mind drifted back to the present, he observed that the doctor continued in vain to defend himself against Meleia's sharp words. "Yes, my dear, if my circumstances allow me to offer this opportunity to those who are less fortunate, then I shall be like Moses leading the Hebrews to the promised land."

"And you are doing this as a service to your fellow brothers and sisters, with nothing to gain for yourself, like Moses, who forsook his place of honor beside Pharaoh in order to liberate the oppressed?"

Dr. Turnbull's cheeks reddened slightly. "Yes, of course, my dear, it is a labor of love that comes from my heart and soul, a gift from me and my beloved Maria Gracia to her Greek kindred. We are using our considerable resources to make this opportunity available to the citizens of Smyrna."

"Oh, how noble!" Meleia held the towel to her heart and bowed deeply. "All in the name of charity? With no glory for yourself, I presume?"

Dr. Turnbull's cheeks were now leaning more toward scarlet, and although he was covering it well, Seba perceived that he was becoming uncomfortable.

"Of course, if the East Florida enterprise is successful, then we will all profit from the work in the New World."

Meleia, knowing she had him cornered, sprang on him. She bounded onto the bench that he had previously occupied, and stated loudly, "My friends and cousins, do not trust this man! 'Mr. Florida' wants to use you to make a profit in the New World, like the merchants of Frank Street make a profit from silk, velvet, leather, spices, and other treasures from this land. He tells you that you are strong Greek men and women, descended from the blood of the Olympians—which you are—but in the next breath, he likens you to slaves, without cheer or choice. You are not a commodity, like leather or silk; you are living, breathing beings made in the image of God. Don't be taken in! Don't let this man make you less than your Creator has ordained!"

"My dear woman—"

"Stop calling me that! I am not your 'dear.'"

"My apologies, Madam Proprietress; forgive my insolence. I assure you that I intend to work side by side with my associates who join me in this venture, such that we will profit together as a community that strives collectively to bring the bounty of East Florida back to this land through the maritime trade. I have no wish to profit from anyone or anything without investing my whole being as well."

Meleia laughed haughtily and pointed her towel in the

direction of his bulging midsection. "You look like you have not invested hard work into anything other than feeding that corpulent belly of yours, and I, for one, don't believe a word of this tripe you are trying to serve my customers."

"My dear—excuse me, I meant to say, er, Madam Proprietress—you cut me to the quick with your harsh judgments! Might I request that you interview my wife, Maria Gracia de Robin, and her family, who will verify my honor and integrity, and who will promptly disavow you of your misgivings with regard to my enterprise? She is Greek, and her family settled in this area many generations ago. If you don't believe me, please interview her."

"The only person I'm going to interview is Governor Paşa. I imagine he has much to say about your honor and integrity, and he would be happy to share his views on your so called 'opportunity' with the fine young citizens of Smyrna. As admiral of the Ottoman navy, I imagine he knows much of your operations on the seas. I have heard rumors of the Ottoman government's displeasure with your activities in this area. In fact, I heard they tried to arrest you in Gytheo. I can't imagine they wouldn't do the same here in Smyrna." Meleia snapped the towel, and this time the English gentlemen jumped, as if the crack in the air might summon Governor Paşa with its loud pop.

Dr. Turnbull looked behind him to see if Governor Paşa had magically appeared, and Meleia jumped off the bench and slipped behind the bar, taking a bottle from the shelf.

Dr. Turnbull, trying to save a shred of dignity after being dressed down by a young woman whom he had obviously never confronted, said officiously, "Not everyone is cut out for the adventure of a lifetime. Some let their fears and prejudices stand in the way of progress and a successful business endeavor."

Seba, who knew that Meleia was now wielding a thick bottle of some kind of liquid, probably wine, felt the hairs on the back of his neck stand up. Meleia couldn't afford another brawl; she had barely cleaned up from the last one.

Meleia jumped out from behind the bar and came face to face with Dr. Turnbull. They were almost the same height, and despite his fancy dress and obvious wealth, it was clear which of the two had the upper hand.

"I am not afraid of anything, and, like every person in this restaurant, I don't need anyone else's help to create a successful business or make a name for myself. If you do not leave my establishment by my count of three, you will be carried out."

"My dear—pardon me, Madam Proprietress—I can see that my presence here has upset you. If only you would give me the opportunity—"

"One."

"—to explain more of my honest intention to do no harm to—"

"Two." Meleia raised the bottle over her head, preparing to strike.

"Look at the late hour! Gentlemen, I promised the owner of the Grey Heron that I would stop by his establishment this evening before I retired to my in-law's residence, so I apologize that I must bid you *kalinixta* for the evening." Turnbull hesitated, putting his hands in his pockets in an attempt to appear unhurried, as if it were his own decision to leave at this very moment.

"Three." Meleia drew the hand holding the bottle back behind her ear, as if winding up for a great toss. Dr. Turnbull ran unceremoniously out the front door, his companions trailing behind him, and had passed the threshold of the Aigokeros as the bottle exploded on the doorway four inches from his head. Seba smelled the bright scent of strawberry wine as shards of glass fell to the floor. Paolo glowered at Meleia as if she had committed a crime.

Meleia then turned to Buğra as if nothing had happened, and said, "Buğra, would you mind asking after Captain Paşa's military guard? I believe they are on orders to escort this Englishman to his ship if he stirs up trouble here. You probably know better than I do where they would be. Tell them that 'Mr. Florida' is skulking to the Grey Heron to steal citizens of Smyrna out from under the nose of the empire."

Buğra nodded and rose quickly from his seat, sloshing his ale on the table. "Our office was notified of Dr. Turnbull's presence when he anchored in the harbor several days ago. You're correct that they were told to report any suspicious behavior. I'll inform them of his whereabouts."

As Buğra hastened toward the door, Paolo called, "Don't worry, Buğra, I'll finish your drink for you." Buğra grinned and waved before slipping out into the street.

Meleia had stirred the crowd even more than the Englishman. They were clapping each other on the back and congratulating themselves for their fortunate Greek heritage, as Meleia had reminded them. A young leather tanner raised his mug and ordered drinks for everyone in the Aigokeros, and another began humming and dancing a tripatos. It appeared that Dr. Turnbull's invitation had the opposite effect than he intended — these citizens didn't feel downtrodden or enslaved; they reveled in their strong Greek heritage, spurred on by the inspiring words of Meleia Kokokis. As the customers drifted back to their tables and benches, Meleia brought another pitcher of ale to Paolo and Seba.

She slammed the pitcher on their table, causing them to reach for their mugs to keep them from catapulting onto the floor. "That man is a menace. He's been hanging around the Greek quarter for the last few days, but this is the first time he was bold enough to step through the door of the Aigokeros. I trust he won't be foolish enough to do that again."

Paolo, holding his mug in one hand and Buğra's in the other, said, "Why did you do that? I thought he was making good sense. Why am I busting my hindquarters every day carrying cargo to and from the docks to the barges, dodging camel and mule dung and who knows what else? We deserve to be treated better. And why shouldn't I be able to travel across the seas to a place where the fish jump out of the sea and onto my plate?"

Meleia scoffed. "You didn't believe the man's lies, did you, Paolo? Because that's all they were—lies."

"How do you know? Have you ever been to East Florida?" Paolo looked like a sulking child who was denied his dessert.

"No, and that's the point. I don't need to go anywhere; my home is here. He's trying to convince you that the grass is greener in some other place, but he's a charlatan. Trust me, those merchants don't do anything out of the goodness of their hearts. 'Mr. Florida' is selling something, and if I were you, I wouldn't buy it."

"Maybe I don't like it here anymore. No one pays a fair wage. Do you know how much my back hurts after carrying cargo on the barges day in and day out? And we're not the only ones who are suffering. Seba and I saw a boy whose hand had been severed at the wrist by his boss, for a crime he didn't even commit." Paolo held his hands up in front of his face. "I like both of these hands, and I don't need someone maiming me for something I didn't do. I'm ready for a change, and I need to do something to raise my place in this world."

Meleia stared at Paolo, one eyebrow raised much higher than the other. It was a disconcerting, yet humorous look. "Or maybe you nearly killed a member of the Ottoman empire's ruling class last week, and you're looking for an easy escape."

Seba marveled at Meleia's sharp mind and even sharper tongue. He himself was more worried about Constantinople, however, where he believed his father was, or had been before the earthquake. If the capital had suffered a catastrophe, what happened to his father? He couldn't bring himself to consider the fact that he had finally taken action to find his father, and now he might be dead.

Seba folded his arms across his chest. "Meleia, you didn't have to chase him away. I wanted to ask him more questions about Constantinople." Thinking of their earlier conversation about Stavros, and feeling frustrated, he said peevishly, "It seems like you have a bias against successful men."

Seba regretted his words as soon as he saw the fire crackling behind Meleia's eyes. Her hand had remained on the pitcher of ale, and Seba tensed his muscles, preparing to duck in the event she decided to fling it at him.

"Oh, does it?" Meleia released her grip on the pitcher and put her hands on her hips. She stared at Seba so long that he squirmed in his seat. Her head was cocked slightly to one side, and Seba was afraid to look directly into those fiery hazel eyes, so he focused his attention on the loose curls that had fallen from the scarf she had knotted on her crown.

"Oh, so now you're a man of the world, are you? You've lived in Smyrna for what, all of three weeks? But you think you know better than I do?"

Seba gulped, understanding that he had poked the hornet's nest, as Buğra warned him not to do. He treated her questions as rhetorical, not requiring a response. However, he could hear his grandfather's words in his head, remembering an incident from his childhood when he had run away from a girl named Xenia who was causing him trouble. His grandfather had said, "Don't ever let me catch you backing away from a conversation with a girl." Those words rekindled Seba's strength, and he returned Meleia's gaze. He tried to match her one raised eyebrow, but he had never been able to move his eyebrows independently, so he wasn't sure if it had worked this time. In any case, he was determined not to be bullied by anyone, even the most beautiful and high-spirited woman he had ever met. But before he could say anything, she continued her tirade, and what she said caused all that bravado to drain out of him.

"As a matter of fact, 'Mr. Man of the World,' why don't we go visit Stavros Alkeidis right now? Let's find out how *you* handle a successful businessman. You said he was going to help you find your father. You won't need to speak with that idiot English doctor after you meet the great Stavros Alkeidis. You can give him your letter, and we'll watch his reaction. I'd like to see that with my own eyes. Then we'll have a little discussion about which one of us knows more about the world than the other."

8 THE INTERVIEW

Before he knew what was happening, Seba found himself being dragged by Meleia down the street toward the large textile workshop that was at the intersection of the Greek quarter and Frank Street.

Meleia was muttering to herself, and Seba though he heard the phrase "stupid men" once or twice. He chose to remain silent, focusing instead on the fact that she was holding his hand.

As they passed several restaurants and businesses, Seba realized that he and Paolo had come this way more than a week ago, returning from Dr. Robin's house. Seba and Meleia alighted at the Alkeidis Tapestry Workshop, a huge storefront with a warehouse behind it that housed all of the fabrics, as well as a covered area where indigo dye was being extracted from the leaves of the shrub-like indigo plants that blanketed the Anatolian landscape. The front of the workshop had a large glass window adjacent to the entry door, inside which hung an enormous silk tapestry, intricately woven with vines, flowers, and a pastoral scene that included a lake, flocks of sheep, and several people reclining by the water. Upon his arrival in Smyrna, Seba had stood before the window, drinking in the beauty of the artwork, and contemplating what he would say when he met the famed Stavros Alkeidis, the man who was going to help him find his father.

"This is a bad idea. I don't even have the letter with me—Buğra's letting me stay in his loft until I leave to find my father—that's where the letter is right now."

"You said you wanted to find your father, and Stavros Alkeidis was your great chance. There is no time like the present." Meleia had his left forearm in a death grip, sending pain shooting into his wrist, which was tightly bandaged, and still tender.

"But what if that Turnbull character has information about my father? I'll go to the Grey Heron and ask him right now. You should go back to the Aigokeros. It's your opening day after the cleanup and now all the patrons are riled up from this evening's excitement. They need you."

Meleia raised one eyebrow, and Seba thought it was not the same one she had raised when she gave Paolo that withering look in the Aigokeros. *I need to learn how to do that.*

"Paolo knows how to keep an eye on the taverna for a short time. He's kicked a few unruly patrons out of my restaurant over the years. He's actually very good at security."

"Even after what happened with Nasir Paşa?" Seba was reaching for anything. He wasn't ready to meet Stavros Alkeidis; he needed time to plan what he was going to say. He had swum the Strait of Chios on the promise that this man could help him, and he didn't want to ruin his chances by being unprepared.

Meleia didn't slow down for an instant. "Why don't you keep your nose out of my business?" Turning away from the workshop's entrance, she said, "Let's go to Buğra's loft and get your letter."

Seba tried to pull Meleia in the opposite direction, to no avail. He was distracted by the warmth of her hand on his forearm, and he was so confused. Part of him wanted to run to the Grey Heron and find Dr. Turnbull, and another part of him wanted to go back to the Aigokeros and forget about Dr. Turnbull, but the part of him that was winning right now was enjoying being so close to Meleia. *She seems concerned—she must really care about me.*

Seba said desperately, "It's getting late. I don't even think the workshop is open. Stavros Alkeidis probably isn't here right now anyway. Why don't we go back to the Aigokeros and devise a plan? I need to organize my thoughts so I don't say the wrong thing. We can call on Stavros Alkeidis another time."

Ignoring him, Meleia led Seba briskly through the streets of the Greek quarter, to the loft above Buğra's stable in the Turkish quarter. She stood outside and gave Seba a look so imperious that he felt he had no choice but to go inside and retrieve Brother Tim's letter of introduction.

Buğra's donkeys and horses snorted as Seba climbed the ladder to the loft. He retrieved the letter from a leather bag that had been given to him by Stavros's brother, Timotheos, along with a velvet pouch that was bulging with mastiha, also known as the Tears of Chios. That pouch had been given to Seba by his uncle, and it was his prized possession. The Tears of Chios were little pebbles of mastic gum from the skinos trees, and they were the most valuable resource in the Ottoman empire because of their medicinal value, their exotic flavor, and their rarity in the world. Mastiha was a magical resin that dripped from the limbs of the skinos trees several times a year, and those trees could only be grown on the island of Chios, which was under Ottoman rule. Seba's Uncle Phillip was the leader of the mastic council in his village of Sessera and was one of the few people permitted to be in possession of a pouch of such a large quantity of mastic gum. He had given the pouch to Seba as a gift, and it was a precious treasure that Seba kept hidden under his straw mattress. He hadn't even told Paolo about it.

Up in the loft, Seba popped one of the little mastic jewels in his mouth and tasted the fresh, minty, piney, and ambrosial flavor on his tongue. Seba chewed it purposefully, praying that its magical medicinal powers would give him strength. He folded Brother Tim's letter and put it in the pocket of his trousers and gently returned the velvet pouch of mastiha to its hiding place.

As soon as he emerged from the stable with the letter, Meleia seized his forearm and renewed her blistering pace all the way to Stavros's workshop. They passed the window with the intricately woven tapestry again, and Meleia stopped at the front door, releasing Seba's arm and placing her hands on her hips.

They held each other's gaze, both expecting the other to move first.

Finally, Meleia said with an exasperated tone, "Well, are you going to knock or not?"

Seba scowled at her. "This was your idea, not mine. You dragged me all the way over here and nearly yanked my arm out of its socket. If you're so interested, why don't you knock?"

Meleia took a step back, put one hand under her chin and tilted her head, as if pondering an important thought. "How is your father going to feel, knowing that his only son was too scared to do what it took to find him?"

Seba felt his whole body flood with a mixture of shame and anger. His indignation temporarily alleviated his fear. He took a step toward the door and banged on it with more intensity than he had intended.

Almost a minute passed with no response, and Seba was about to turn away when a young woman opened the door. She was short and slight, her thick dark hair pulled back in a series of interlocking braids that ringed her head. She wore loose, cream-colored cotton trousers gathered at the ankle, and a pale olive-green jacket with gold-embroidered split sleeves over a lavender blouse. Her silk jacket was cinched at the waist by a bright yellow sash embroidered with tiny purple tulips. Her ankle-high boots were made of camel leather that was dyed a brilliant pomegranate red, topped with gold silk tassels that fastened them tightly around her calves. Her eyes were coffee-colored and intelligent. Seba gasped—other than a scar running across the top of her right temple, the resemblance to Brother Tim was unmistakable.

"Can I help you? Do you have business with the shop? Unfortunately, our brokers have left for the evening, but I can show you some of our tapestries if you are interested." The well-dressed woman looked from Seba to Meleia and back again. "Mr. and Mrs. . . . ?"

"Wh-what?" Seba stammered.

Meleia stood there smiling, letting him wallow in his embarrassment. Seba said, blushing a deep red, "Uh, no—"

The young woman blinked slowly. "You don't have business with the shop?"

Seba sputtered, "Uh, um, no, not that—I meant no, we're not married."

97

A hint of a smile flickered in the woman's eyes, although her gaze remained professional. "My apologies. Then what can I do for you at this late hour?"

Seba was staring at the woman. He blurted out, "You look just like him."

The woman's smile now spread from her eyes to her mouth, although it carried an air of accommodation. "I'm sorry. Like whom?"

"Brother Timotheos, the priest from my—I mean, a priest that I know from Nea Moni." Seba reached into his pocket and held up the crumpled paper like a prize. "I have a letter from him."

The woman's smile now enveloped her whole face, and this time it was genuine. "Well, of course I look like him; he's my brother. You say you're from Nea Moni? That's wonderful." She looked at the rumpled paper in Seba's hand. "And you have a letter—is this an order for additional velvet çatmas for the sanctuary? The monk who was here last month said that he might want to supplement the monastery's order. The Festival of Saint John will be held in a few weeks, and they requested additional velvets for their celebration."

Meleia was smiling as well, and again Seba was reminded of the cat. However, unlike the savvy smile she wore when confronting Dr. Turnbull (like a cat about to pounce), this smile recalled the cat while it was playing with its prey, fully engaged and entertained. It was extremely disconcerting to Seba, who felt uncannily like the mouse at the moment. Meleia jabbed him in the ribs. "Go on, tell her your story."

Seba's gaze shifted from Meleia on his left to this perceptive woman on his right, and he felt that he had a new appreciation for Meleia's best mousers, Desta and Ryma.

He took a deep breath and said to the woman, "We're not buying any çatmas, and we don't work with the monastery."

The woman held one finger to her cheek, and Seba got the distinct feeling that she perceived much more than she revealed. "I didn't think so, but in our business, you can never be sure who the brokers are, or who they're representing. Our purchasers sometimes like to maintain their anonymity. You don't look like the usual brokers we deal with from Chios, and forgive me for saying so, but you would not likely be mistaken for a monk from Nea Moni."

Meleia laughed, and Seba felt the heat gathering in his chest. He imagined what he must look like—thin, scruffy beard, wild sable-colored hair, a fractured wrist bandaged tightly and secured to his shoulder with a sling, and Buğra's clothes and boots, which were a bit too small for him.

He tried to banish his embarrassment and instead concentrate on the gracious woman who reminded him of Brother Tim. "You're right. I'm not a monk. But your brother—the monk—sent me here to see his brother—I mean your brother—Stavros."

The woman looked at the letter as if Seba were presenting her with a gift. It reminded him of the time he invited Brother Tim to a meal of grilled barbouni, and the monk had nearly exploded with happiness. Their expressions were exactly the same. The woman clapped her hands together, saying, "A letter and an interesting story? What a delightful diversion. Timotheos always was a good storyteller and full of surprises." A frown passed across her face, then was gone. "In fact, I haven't seen him since my father died."

Meleia raised both eyebrows at Seba this time, as if to say, "What did I tell you?"

The woman held her hands to her heart. "My goodness, where are my manners? We haven't even introduced ourselves."

She spread her arms and gestured inside. "My name is Eleni Alkeidis—please come in."

Meleia jabbed Seba in the ribs again, and he coughed. "I'm Sebastian Krizomatis, and this is-"

"Sebastian's friend, Meleia Kokokis," Meleia finished. She obviously didn't trust Seba to speak for her.

Seba and Meleia followed Eleni into the workshop, where men and women were seated in rows on little tufted stools, large wooden looms before them. Each weaver's workspace bore curtains of silk and cotton threads hanging from the tops of their looms, and there were piles of every color of silk and cotton surrounding them like children seated around a teacher. The workers, who ranged in age from grandparents to adolescents, moved silently, their hands whipping back and forth between the vertical lines of thread. Each one had a painting of a beautiful design pinned to the side of their loom, and Seba could tell what the finished piece would be from the little painting on each loom. The patterns were intricate and so complicated that Seba could not believe how the weavers could keep track of them. And so many colors! One woman, seated at a loom that rose to the height of twelve feet, must have had more than fifty different colors of silk thread on her tapestry. Despite the late hour, there were hundreds of lanterns lining the floors around the looms, providing light for the workers even after the sun had dipped below the horizon.

They walked past the weaving area and down a hallway, which also contained many flickering lanterns. The hallway intersected with another passageway at the back of the workshop, with a door to the right and another to the left.

From behind the door to the right, Seba could hear the sound of raised male voices arguing.

Eleni waved her hand in the direction of the door to the right, while leading Meleia and Seba to the passageway on the left. "That's my other brother, Stavros. He's always been the loud one, even when we were children. Why don't you join me in my office and tell me about Timotheos while we wait?"

She ushered them quickly in the opposite direction, but Seba could not help but overhear a few snippets of the argument coming from behind the door on the right.

"He didn't even do it!"

"Do you think me a fool? I caught him with the silks in his hand."

"He was putting them back! He is a loyal employee!"

"He was caught, and he will never work in this city again!"

"You didn't have to cut off his ha—"

Eleni hurriedly shooed them into her office and shut the door. It was a small, square room that looked exactly like Brother Tim's room in the schoolhouse at Sessera. There were bookshelves on three of the walls, overflowing with leather-bound tomes, an illuminated Bible, the Qur'an, maps, books with silk and cotton swatches peeking out from them, sketchbooks, portfolios of painted flowers and animals, and wooden models of ships. There were expensive-looking illuminated manuscripts and botanical detailed paintings and drawings of vines and flowers. To Seba, it appeared that Eleni had much in common with her younger brother, Timotheos.

What drew his attention and caused him to gasp, however, was on a large wooden table in the middle of the room. It bore a series of different sized colored glass cylinders, a syphon, and a water pump submerged in an enormous amphora of water adjacent to the table.

"Is that a *clepsydra*?" Seba was incredulous.

Eleni laughed at Seba's enthusiasm. "Yes, it is, and I must say, Sebastian Krizomatis, that you are the only visitor who has ever recognized this invention of Ctesibius." She smiled fondly at the water clock. "And if I wasn't sure of your connection to my brother Timotheos before, I certainly am now. In fact, he built this very clepsydra when we were children. He was so proud of himself when he could tell my father what time it was, regardless of whether the sun was shining. He taught me how to operate it, and now I love to use it when I'm here at the workshop."

Seba beamed. "He showed me how it worked when I was eight years old. It was like magic! I'll never forget that day."

"Yes, my brother was quite the scientist. He always had his head in a book." Eleni's eyes had a faraway look, as if remembering her childhood. "My father was so proud of him."

"He gave me a book once. It was called *The Clouds*."

Eleni giggled. "Ah, yes, that wonderful play written by the great Greek playwright, Aristophanes. Timotheos could not get enough of him. He called Aristophanes our Father of Comedy."

Seba couldn't believe his luck. A few moments before, when Meleia was dragging him down the streets of the Greek quarter, his feet felt like heavy boulders. Now his whole body felt light and effervescent, as if he might bubble up to the ceiling.

"I remember thinking that his head was so big because it housed an extra-large brain."

Eleni's mirthful laugh was exactly like Brother Tim's,

and it made Seba feel warm and comfortable, just like his village home on Chios. Gasping for breath between chortled laughter, Eleni said, "We used to tease him because his head was so large and bulbous. He was always good-natured about it, though." She pointed to her head. "He said he never wanted to run out of room up here for all the things that God wanted him to learn."

Seba said brightly, "Good-natured is a fitting description for Brother Tim. He is one of the smartest and kindest people I know, which is why I trusted him when he told me to come here and ask for help."

Eleni laughter turned to a sad smile. "I haven't seen my brother in many years. He occasionally sends letters to me — we were always close — but when the monks of Nea Moni visit Smyrna, he never seems to be with them. Too busy teaching the young acolytes, I suppose. He always was fascinated with the teachings of Jesus and the workings of the world. A true Greek scholar, I always called him when we were children. It was clear to me from a young age that he would enter the church, although Stavros tried to lure him into business with us."

Meleia glanced at Seba and raised an eyebrow. He was certain that it was not the same eyebrow she had raised a moment before. *I have to ask her to teach me how to do that.*

Ignoring Meleia's unspoken "I told you so," Seba said to Eleni, "Brother Tim often told me that I could do anything. He said God was too big to fit in a box created by our expectations, and we were made in the Creator's image. Your brother taught me not to limit myself, because God is limitless, a flowing fountain of unconditional love."

Eleni laughed. "Yes, I could envision those words coming from that big head of his. He was interested in every part of God's creation, from the lowliest insect to the stars

in the sky. He used to say, 'Everything is of God, even the —
'"

"—'scientists and mathematicians.'" Seba finished Eleni's sentence.

Eleni's eyes sparkled like Brother Tim's when he was amused, and Seba thought he detected the first hint of a tear in them. "You know, Sebastian, you have a gentle soul that reminds me of him. I almost feel as if my brother is here with us."

Seba nodded his thanks, recalling the day that Brother Tim said those words to him, years ago on the roof of the village classroom, before he had demonstrated the workings of the ancient Greek water clock, the clepsydra. And Brother Tim was the one who convinced Seba that he had the courage and strength to swim the Strait of Chios on his quest to find his father.

Someone knocked on Eleni's door, but before she could open it, a boy rushed into her office and said, "You know what he did to my brother was wrong! How could you let this happen to Michalis and my family? He's my twin – I feel like my own han—"

Eleni interrupted, "Mattheios, let's talk outside in the hallway." Turning to Meleia and Seba, she said, "Please wait here for a moment."

Seba and Meleia strained to hear Eleni's conversation with the boy, but could only catch a few words.

Meleia said, "Did that boy say 'cut off his hand'?"

Seba felt his delicious meal from the Aigokeros turn sour and rise up into his throat. He nodded. "I never told you what happened when we took Nasir Paşa to the doctor."

"What does that have to do with cutting off someone's hand?"

"Well, when Paolo and I were leaving the doctor's office,

someone was brought in with a severed wrist. His hand had been cut off, he was bleeding like a slaughtered pig, and the doctor fused his flesh together with a hot iron from the—"

Meleia raised her palm within inches of Seba's face. "I know how physicians treat a severed hand; I don't need to hear the details. What of it?"

"The doctor called the person who did it barbaric. She said the shop owner didn't follow the protocol of reporting the theft to the Ottoman tribunal. Dr. Robin explained that whenever there is a dispute between an employer and his workers, it should be decided by the kadi, but this shop owner never gave the employee a chance to tell his story. He meted out the punishment without investigating the circumstances and bypassed Smyrna's judicial process."

"That's a strange coincidence—two amputations in the same week?"

Seba frowned and shook his head.

"Seba, what is it?"

"The boy we saw was the same one who was in the doctor's office. That means his employer is—"

The door opened, and Eleni said, "Stavros is ready to see you now."

Seba's stomach lurched as he contemplated the man he was about to meet. *What if Meleia is right about Stavros? Did he cut off a boy's hand without giving him a fair chance to defend himself? What kind of monster does something like that?*

Eleni tapped on Stavros's door, calling out, "Stavros, we have visitors! One says he has a letter for you from Timotheos."

A low raspy voice full of authority and power replied, "Timotheos who?"

A laugh caught in Eleni's throat. "Your brother, Timotheos Alkeidis."

Seba heard shuffling, and then the door was opened by the biggest man Seba had ever seen. He was a foot taller than Seba, and his shoulders were almost as wide as the doorway. He had a full beard, and Seba could see thick, wiry hair sticking out of the collar of his shirt. Another man, also very tall, but not as wide as the man who opened the door, was standing in the middle of the room.

A third man, standing in front of a large mahogany desk, spoke. "Thank you, Hector and Marco. I appreciate your being here. As you can see from what just happened, I need your protection from unwanted intrusions. Now, if you wouldn't mind waiting at the back door, I'll meet you when we're finished here."

The man was handsome, of medium height and build, with short, black hair graying at the temples, and dark eyes peering out beneath thick eyebrows. He was dressed impeccably, and covered from head to toe in silk. His indigo silk coat shimmered over a well-cut white shirt, both of which were worn over a pair of red silk pantaloons and a luxurious pair of brown goatskin boots. On his first finger, he wore a ring that appeared to be made of hundreds of thin gold filaments woven together. On his other hand he wore an enormous onyx gem ring that had streaks of silver running through it, like the strands of a web. While searching the man for a resemblance to Brother Tim, Seba realized that he had never even noticed the clothes Brother Tim wore. He only noticed Brother Tim, the person. This man, however, put so much energy into his outward appearance that Seba couldn't see past his clothes to recognize the person underneath them. Seba wondered if that was purposeful.

After the two burly men had exited the office, the man held out his hand and said cordially, "I am Stavros Alkeidis.

Welcome to my workshop. I trust my sister, Eleni, has made you comfortable and shown you the most pleasing hospitality?"

Meleia said, "Yes, she's been wonderful."

Stavros looked quizzically at Meleia, and Seba froze, hoping that Stavros did not recognize her. Meleia said, "I'm Meleia Kokokis, owner of the Aigokeros," and held out her hand. Stavros shook it, and Seba watched the battle of wills, as each tried to overpower the other's grip.

Stavros, presumably more concerned about appearances than his opponent, released his hand first, saying, "It is my pleasure to make your acquaintance, Meleia. Your establishment's reputation is one of the best in the city. It has such an interesting name. I was once involved with a restaurant." He frowned. "Unfortunately, it was not a successful venture. I suppose it was a message for me to maintain my loyalty to the business my father began, rather than venturing into new territory."

Meleia looked defiant but remained silent. Stavros then turned his attention to Seba, who shifted uncomfortably. "And you are?"

"Sebastian Krizomatis, son of Kostas Krizomatis, the greatest shipbuilder in the Ottoman empire."

Stavros chuckled. "Well, that is quite a bold statement, young man. I can't say that I recognize the name, but the sultan likes to maintain his best ships' engineers at the capital in Constantinople. Smyrna's fame is growing, however, so you never know what may happen here as the merchant trade flourishes." He slowly spun the gold ring, the one that looked like strands of golden sugar, around his finger. "My sister tells me that Timotheos has sent you with a message to share with us?"

Seba took a deep breath and launched into his plea. He

hoped that the Holy Spirit would assist him in making a good impression. He also hoped that he wasn't about to bare his soul to a monster who had severed an innocent employee's hand. "It's a bit of a long story, but the Ottomans have taken my father to Constantinople because he was a great shipbuilder on Chios, and Sultan Mustafa III wanted him to build ships for the Ottoman fleet at the capital. I was too young to go with my father, but now that I have become a man, I need to find him. I know I'm meant to work on these ships and on the seas. Unfortunately, my circumstances did not allow me to bring any money or resources from Chios. Your brother told me that you were very wealthy and influential and knew everyone in the merchant trade, from Constantinople to the western regions of Europe. He said if anyone could find my father and help me connect with him again, it would be you."

"Ah, yes, Timotheos has a penchant for putting me to work. I imagine he is relaxing on Chios, reading books and nibbling *baklava,* while we work our fingers to the bone here in the city. A very bold request indeed, given the circumstances. He couldn't be bothered to help us build this business, but he has no qualms about asking us for favors." Stavros spun the interwoven golden strands of the ring around forcefully, as if pouring his irritation into the band around his finger.

Seba took a step back. This was not the response he expected. "I don't know anything about any favors or charity. Maybe you should read the letter." He pulled the folded paper from his pocket and handed it to Stavros, who pulled a magnifying glass from a drawer in his desk and held it over the letter to read it. After a minute, he placed the letter on his desk.

"Have you read the contents of this letter?"

"No, he gave it to me already sealed in a leather pouch, and I trust him with my life. He is the reason that I was able to journey all the way from Chios to Smyrna."

"Your life, you say? That's quite a statement of loyalty. One I've come to expect from my little silkworms here at the shop."

"Silkworms?"

Stavros laughed. "That's what I call our employees here. It's a term of endearment I've coined for their contributions to our textile factory."

Seba said earnestly, "Yes, I'm loyal. I wouldn't be here without the help of Brother Tim."

Stavros narrowed his eyes. "And how did you travel here?"

Seba thought that a man like Stavros might be impressed with his heroic feat, so he took a gamble and told the truth.

"I swam the Strait of Chios."

Stavros had bushy eyebrows, like his brother, and they raised sky-high. Eleni looked surprised as well.

"Don't you mean rowed across the Strait of Chios?"

Seba stood a bit taller and said defiantly, "No, sir. I swam."

"An impressive feat of strength and perseverance, if it is true."

Seba snapped, "It's true, and I have the scars to show it." He pulled up his trousers with his right hand. The cuts and scrapes of the sharp rocks in the Strait of Chios had healed into red raised lines that crisscrossed both legs. Then he pulled his left arm from the sling, showing similar scabs all the way to his elbow.

"And is that how you injured your wrist?"

Seba gulped. He thought it best not to mention the brawl at the taverna, lest Stavros think poorly of him. "I injured it in the earthquake which shook the ground after I climbed out of the water and onto the western shores of Turkey."

"This letter says that you have many skills, including an excellent mind for mathematics, the discretion to consider your actions before you speak, a deep integrity, and a passion for justice. That is high praise coming from my brother, who, according to his own words, has lofty standards."

Seba was shocked—he had no idea that Brother Tim felt this way about him. He felt a warmth moving up from his insides and seeping into his limbs. He didn't understand Stavros's irritation with the mention of his brother, but the accolades made him feel important. A glimmer of hope surged inside his body.

Stavros continued, "Unfortunately, I do not know of your father or his whereabouts, but Timotheos is correct that I have a few connections in the merchant trade. I know many Ottoman ship captains, as well as those from France, Scandinavia, and the Dutch Republic. I may be able to help you."

Seba's heart leapt. "I don't know how to thank you, sir."

"I do." Stavros swirled the gold ring around his finger. "If you want me to help you, I will require something in exchange."

9 THE AGREEMENT

Stavros stepped out from behind his desk and looked intently at Seba.

"Before I enter into any agreement, I'll need to determine whether my brother's analysis of your character and aptitude is correct. I will not tolerate liars or thieves in my business. We'll find out if you are who you say you are. The Ottoman tax collectors and inspectors are ruthless and unforgiving, making sure that we pay every piece of silver that the trade tariff requires. They do not make exceptions, and neither do we. In this line of work, justice is swift and severe, which is why I depend on my associates, Hector and Marco, to make sure things run smoothly."

Seba glanced sideways at Meleia, who shot him a knowing look.

Stavros opened the door of his office and gestured for everyone to follow him to the warehouse, which was behind the shop and connected by a covered walkway. "I know someone who may be able to assist us."

Seba's heart was thumping in his chest. *I knew it was going too well. Why did I let Meleia drag me here? I'm not ready for a test. This was a bad idea.*

As the four of them walked toward the textile warehouse, Seba caught a glimpse of the women's expressions. Meleia's was one of wariness, a furrowed forehead atop determined eyes, but Eleni's demeanor had changed. Minutes before, she had been smiling and laughing brightly as they spoke of Timotheos, but now the corners of her mouth turned downward, and two vertical wrinkles appeared between her eyebrows. Seba wondered if she was thinking about her former employee, whose brother had accosted her in the hallway. *Did Stavros actually sever an employee's hand himself? He seems a bit too refined for such violence. Or maybe it was one of his henchmen—Hector or Marco. They seem like the opposite of refined.* Seba's only conclusion was that there was something missing from the account that he didn't understand. He knew the Ottoman government enforced its rules with violence, but he had never known any business owners to act that way.

Seba couldn't concern himself with the twin boys, however, because it appeared that his chance of finding his father depended on this test. He needed help. Seba had been told from a young age that the heroism of his Greek ancestors flowed in his blood. He hoped that was true this evening, and as he contemplated the great Greek heroes, he was given a sign.

"Will you be joining us, Eleni?"

"Even the wild horses of Mongolia couldn't stop me from this entertainment, brother."

When Eleni mentioned horses, Seba thought of one of his favorite stories of the labors of Heracles—the Augean stables. His father had told him the story many times, and

112

he loved it because it spoke not only of the raw strength of Heracles but even more so of his cleverness. The version told by Seba's father went something like this:

King Eurystheus held a personnel vendetta against Heracles and did everything in his power to humiliate the honorable Greek hero. All twelve labors assigned to Heracles by Eurystheus had seemed hopelessly futile, grueling, and absurd, and yet, each time Heracles prevailed. His belief in himself never wavered, and that is something we can all learn from, Seba. Another ruler, King Augeas, was so immensely wealthy that his stables housed 1,000 immortal cattle, along with a host of earthborn cows, bulls, sheep, goats, and horses. Unfortunately, King Augeas could not find anyone to clean his stables, and the animals' dung had grown over the course of thirty years, so that now the task of cleaning the Augean stables was impossible.

King Eurystheus had the devilish notion to assign Heracles the task of cleaning the Augean stables in one day, knowing that it would be both disgusting, humiliating, and utterly hopeless. Eurystheus wanted to see Heracles waist-deep in the animals' excrement, toiling away with no expectation of completing the job. Heracles knew that in order to succeed, he needed to use his brains in addition to his extraordinary strength.

It so happened that King Augeas was unaware of Eurystheus's demeaning task, so Heracles went to King Augeas separately, and made him an offer. He proposed to clean the stables in one day if King Augeas would pay him one-tenth of the immortal herd. King Augeas was so thrilled at the prospect of fresh, unsullied stables, and knowing nothing of the labor assigned by Eurystheus, he readily accepted Heracles's offer. Heracles then used his strength to push the riverbeds of two nearby rivers, the Alpheus and Peneus, from their paths, directing them toward the Augean stables. The water rushed through the animals' shelter, taking the muck and filth with it. This happened in a matter of a few hours.

When he was satisfied that the stables were tidy and bright, Heracles returned the riverbeds to their original routes, but being kind and compassionate, he left a small babbling brook beside the stables for the gentle creatures. When the herds returned from the pastures, they were greeted with fresh hay, warm oats, and cold water, all thanks to Heracles, who had successfully cleaned the Augean stables in one day, much to the pleasure of King Augeas and his grateful animals.

Seba knew he didn't have the strength of Heracles, especially with his arm in a sling, but he hoped he might be able to call on a bit of Heracles's resourcefulness.

Eleni, Meleia and Seba followed Stavros into a warehouse that smelled of fresh cotton, wool, and silk, all stacked high on pallets and wound tightly on giant wooden spools. A small man was hunched over the cotton spools, as if inspecting them. Seba was astonished that the workshop seemed as busy this evening as he expected it to be during the day. *Does anyone sleep in this city? At least on Chios, our work was finished at sunset.*

Stavros said, "Excuse us, Nasir, but I am hoping that you can help us with a little examination in aid of my business."

The small man turned around, and Seba's breath caught in his throat. The skin around the man's eyes was swollen and was a sickly purple and green color, the exact shading of one-week-old bruises. His right arm was wrapped loosely in a cotton sling that was tied around his opposite shoulder, and his left arm rested on an intricately-carved wooden cane of Anatolian black pine. Under his red velvet, knee-length coat, Seba observed that the man's ribs were wrapped tightly in cotton bandages. He was wearing the same buttery leather shoes that he had worn when Seba and Paolo transported him to Dr. Robin in a vegetable cart.

The man bowed very low, putting pressure on his cane,

and grimaced slightly. His breathing was labored and a bit wheezy, as if each breath pained him, but his voice was clear. "It would be my honor to assist you, Stavros. As you know, I work with my uncle to inspect your beautiful fabrics as well as other goods that are transported by sailing ships, and although I have been delayed ever so slightly in my duties" (he nodded to his injured arm), "I am pleased to report that everything in your warehouse is of exceptional quality, as I knew it would be. My uncle, and the sultan himself, are very proud of the extraordinarily fine silks from this workshop that are sold throughout the world. I wish the job of keeping pirates away from the precious cargo was as easy as inspecting the goods."

The man tilted his head and looked at Eleni and Stavros's companions, his gaze moving from Meleia to Seba's face before resting on Seba's left arm. Seba exhaled in relief as he saw that the man did not recognize him.

Stavros bowed to the man. "Thank you, Nasir, and I agree completely. It is becoming more and more difficult to protect our exports from those who seek to profit from our hard work. Eleni and I would like to introduce you to our two new acquaintances—Meleia and Sebastian. Meleia and Sebastian, this is Nasir Beyzade Paşa."

Nasir's face momentarily clouded when he heard the name Meleia, as if remembering the incident in her restaurant, but he recovered quickly.

"Ah, yes, the proprietress of the Aigokeros. I am chagrined to say that on my very first outing to your acclaimed establishment, circumstances prevented me from savoring the dishes which have made you famous throughout the city. I was" (he cleared his throat ceremoniously) "regrettably incapacitated."

In response, Meleia stood proudly and remained

composed. "I sincerely apologize for the events that occurred in my taverna last week. In the many years that my family has been feeding our Smyrnean neighbors, we have never suffered a catastrophe of such large proportions. It is with the sincerest remorse that I offer to make amends and compensate you for the senseless and pernicious violence of that evening. It would be my honor and privilege to offer restitution for your injuries. In fact, today we have reopened. Is there anything I can offer you as compensation?"

Seba was impressed with Meleia's sudden formality. Her likeness to a cat was uncanny – graceful, as fierce as a huntress, playful, and able to adapt to any situation.

Nasir Paşa seemed likewise impressed with Meleia's offer. "That is very kind of you, dear. There is no need for compensation. I can feel the love and care that you put into feeding your customers, and I imagine that you suffered as much as I did that evening. I am pleased to learn that you are back in business."

"Thank you, sir. It would not have been possible without the generous donation of Dr. Despina Marguerite Robin, who replaced all of our tableware, mugs, and glasses. My family owes her a debt of gratitude."

Nasir looked surprised. "Then we have something else in common, because she is the person who has nursed me back to health over the last week. I am told that but for the quick actions of two young men who were dining at your establishment that evening, I might have died. The good doctor has not only treated my wounds, but her cook, Claudine, has fed me so well that I may need an entirely new wardrobe."

Everyone laughed as Nasir tapped his trim midsection with the top of his cane. Seba observed that Stavros was shifting his weight from his right to left foot and back again, his impatience palpable. However, Seba noticed that he did not interrupt the nephew of Governor Paşa.

Watching Stavros send nearly imperceptible signals that he, and not Nasir, was in charge, Seba marveled that he was so different from Brother Timotheos. Although the two brothers resembled each other in physical appearance, Stavros's persona emitted an air of cunning and shrewdness that was the opposite of Timotheos, who was equally intelligent, but more open and honest. Seba guessed that Timotheos joined the monastery because he was more interested in seeking Godliness than participating in the competition of business. Seba had heard multiple times since entering Smyrna that the merchants and exporters were obsessed with selling more goods than their competitors or fetching the highest price from their customers. It reminded Seba of his father's stories of the battles of ancient Greece, except there were far more than two armies in this fight.

Stavros said, "Sebastian and I are contemplating entering into a contract, whereby I share my resources with him to help him on a quest, of sorts, and he shares his abilities with me in return. My brother, Timotheos, whom I've not spoken to in many years, seems to think that young Sebastian can be an asset to me, but I'll admit that it's an unusual request from someone who hasn't deigned to visit our family workshop, despite being born into this family and given every opportunity through the sacrifices of our mother and father, may they rest in peace."

Seba could feel his stomach juices gurgling and he put his hand on his abdomen to quiet them. Brother Tim had never mentioned that he was estranged from his brother, Stavros. As Seba tried to remember exactly what Brother

Tim had said, he realized that he had never mentioned that they were particularly close, either. It was too late to do anything about it now. Seba would have to manage the best he could, keeping in mind that there was no love lost, at least in Stavros's mind, between the Alkeidis brothers.

Stavros continued, "In order for me to vet those abilities, however, I was wondering if you might ask him a few questions about seafaring. Your experience on the seas is legendary, and this young man claims to have learned from one of the best shipbuilders in the empire."

Nasir bowed again. "It would be my pleasure, Stavros. What a treat to engage in a discussion of one of my favorite topics in the world. I couldn't be happier to oblige you!"

Hearing Nasir speak so eloquently, with such humility, made Seba feel sick to his stomach for what Paolo had done to him. It was hard to believe that the damaged body Seba had jostled and bumped down Frank Street in a vegetable cart last week belonged to this genteel man. It was also hard to believe that he was an Ottoman official. Seba had spent most of his life hating the Ottomans for what they had done to his family. For some reason, though, he could not bring himself to hate Nasir, who had the affable demeanor of a spritely satyr.

Turning to Seba, Nasir asked, "Can you explain to me the importance of the angle of the hull as it rises up from the keel, with regard to its effect on the speed of a merchant ship?"

Seba closed his eyes and the vision of a sunny day, many years ago, appeared in his mind. His father was speaking at the shipyard, something about difference between the block coefficient of fineness and the prismatic coefficient. He searched that vision and said, "The sharper the angle of the hull rising up from the keel, the faster the ship's speed."

And before Nasir could respond, Seba added, "But the sharp angle may also affect the amount of cargo that can be carried, so each of those factors must be weighed in fashioning a vessel that can carry the biggest load, endure the force of wind and tide, and move from port to port with the greatest speed."

Nasir tapped his cane rapidly on the ground, mimicking the sound of clapping, as he was unable to put his hands together. His entire face lit up with surprise and delight, and the purple and green bruises around his eyes crinkled in amusement.

"I couldn't have said it better myself, young Sebastian. Excellent response."

Stavros made the slightest growling sound, and Seba couldn't determine if it was from pleasure, indigestion, or resentment. Seba was emboldened by Nasir's response, however, so he disregarded Stavros's reaction.

Nasir said, "There is an island very near to Smyrna, whose trees serve as the best material for the main masts of the Ottoman fleet. Do you know the island and the type of tree? And if so, do you know why these trees are considered the best material?"

This time Seba didn't need to envision the day. There had been so many ships limping with broken masts into the shipyard in Sessera throughout Seba's childhood that he knew the answer to this question immediately. He said brightly, "Chian pine is the best material for the masts of ships in the Ottoman fleet, as well as any other ships on the sea. This is because the pine is tall, straight, strong, and yet includes enough flexibility to protect it from breaking in rough seas. There are some that say that the pine trees from the island of Samos, also near here, provide the same features, but my father always told me that pine trees from the island of Chios are the best."

This time Nasir leaned on his cane and did a little dance with both feet. It reminded Seba of the times that his grandfather, Papouli, tapped his toes to the tripatos. It was a sign of genuine glee, and Seba's chest swelled with pride.

"Yes! It is exactly as you say, and you must have some experience with sailors from both Chios and Samos, because I have witnessed the arguments that break out when they try to prove which pine trees serve as the best masts! Ah, it brings back memories of traveling to those islands. Such pleasant remembrances of my early days on the seas." Nasir was truly enjoying this conversation, and Seba was in awe, remembering the condition this man had been in one week prior. Seba envisioned spending a pleasant afternoon with Nasir in Dr. Robin's garden, drinking coffee and hearing the stories of a true sailor, philosopher, and gentleman. He wished his father could meet this man. Seba knew they would be fast friends.

The indeterminate growling sound rumbled again from within Stavros before he said stiffly, "Thank you, Nasir."

This time, it was clear to Seba that the grumbling signaled displeasure, and Seba guessed it was because Nasir was overshadowing Stavros's position as the most important person in the room.

"Sebastian, it appears that my brother was telling the truth about your talents. You may be able to provide value to my workshop, because the faster my fabrics travel to France on these ships, the faster my profits are generated. This benefits not only me but also every person employed in this factory.

"Nasir has been invaluable to us in sharing his knowledge of the European merchant trade and protecting our precious cargo from pirates, but he has many businesses to oversee, and he can only spare so much time with us. As chief regent under his uncle, Captain Paşa, his primary responsibility is to ensure that the trade tariffs due the Ottoman government are properly paid before the goods are transported. We are grateful for the time he is at our disposal, even though it is not as often as we'd like. Perhaps your knowledge might assist us during the times when Nasir is otherwise engaged. The more we know about the ships and the routes to our European customers, the more advantages we have over our competitors. I'm sure you have noticed that we are not the only textile workshop in Smyrna."

Stavros looked at his sister. "In the past year, however, we have become the most successful, and it is my humble opinion that Eleni's intricate designs are the primary reason why our products are in such high demand. Her loyalty to our family business is invaluable. That, and the loyalty of our little silkworms, have made this business a thriving success." Stavros smiled slyly at Meleia and Seba and said, "There is one more skill that is very important to my business, and if you are to assist me, I need to know that you have this proficiency."

Seba, feeling confident from his successful answers to Nasir's questions, looked into Stavros's impenetrable dark eyes and said, "Whatever it is, I can do it."

"Being conversant in French is a requirement in this business. Nasir, would you mind asking my new friend a few questions in French?"

Seba, whose whole body had been inflated with self-assurance, felt his shoulders sag as the blood drained from his face. He stole a glance at Meleia, whose countenance was indiscernible.

Nasir asked, in flowing French, *"Quel est le produit le plus*

121

populaire importé de Marseille à Smyrne, pour le commerce avec l'Orient?"

Seba's jaw tightened, as he envisioned the dream of finding his father dissipating like smoke from an extinguished candle. He heard "Smyrna" and "Marseilles," and he surmised that the question had to do with trade between the two cities, but that was as far as he got. He felt his stomach churn as he frantically tried to think of how to respond.

Seba's head whipped around as he heard Meleia reply in French, *"C'est le corail rouge de la mer Méditerranée, qui est amené par des navires à Smyrne, où il est transporté par des caravanes de chameaux gérées par des commerçants arméniens, vers l'est à travers l'empire ottoman. C'est l'une des rares importations d'Europe qui génère des revenus pour les commerçants de l'est."*

Stavros looked smug, and again Seba was reminded of the cat who had feasted on a bird that it sliced from the air with its claws. He knew that Seba did not understand, so he said, "Very impressive. Indeed, the most popular import from Marseille is the red coral of the Mediterranean Sea, which is imported through Smyrna, and transported by Armenian camel caravans eastward through the Ottoman empire. And yes, it is a rare European import that generates income here."

Seba was also impressed, not only with Meleia's apparent proficiency in the French language, but also with the fact that she knew about red coral imported through Smyrna from Marseilles. Seba's disappointment at her refusal to teach him French was made even more painful in this exchange with Stavros, who directed his words to Meleia. "I believe you already have a job, my dear, and you would not be able to assist your friend Sebastian if he should work for me in exchange for the use of my resources on his quest."

Seba wished that he could melt on the spot and seep into the dirt floor of the warehouse. He appreciated Meleia's efforts, but if Stavros was only willing to help Seba in exchange for his ability to converse with the workshop's brokers and purchasers in French, then this whole interaction with Stavros was a waste of time.

Meleia quickly responded, "I'm teaching him French, and he's a quick study. You can see how smart he is. He'll be conversant within the week. I will vouch for him."

Seba could have hugged her right then and there.

Stavros's smile widened, as if this was exactly what he had planned. "Very well, then I suppose our pending business transaction will be a great success. Sebastian, please meet me in my office tomorrow morning at nine a.m., and we will begin what I expect will be a very lucrative relationship."

#

Walking through the narrow streets of Enymeria Market back to the Aigokeros from Stavros's workshop, Seba said, "Do you think I did the right thing by accepting his offer?" Meleia glared icily at him without breaking her stride. "You are unbelievable. Less than an hour ago, you accused me of hating successful men and dismissed everything I said. But now my opinion has suddenly become important? You have no shame, do you, Sebastian Krizomatis?"

Seba recoiled as if slapped. "You're the one who's unbelievable—you dragged me here, haranguing me the whole time about Stavros being the devil, and then when you were about to be proved right, you stepped in and practically accepted the offer for me!"

Meleia's scowl eased a bit, but she said nothing.

Seba continued, "I know his brother so well, and it's difficult to believe that Stavros is some kind of conniving demon. The man we met doesn't seem like a butcher who would brutally sever an employee's hand over a misunderstanding about a piece of cloth. He seems like a serious-minded businessman, passionate about the success of his workshop. I can tell that he's arrogant, and he likes to feel important, but I know many people like that, and it's certainly not a crime."

"I guess you have to witness the beast in action, Seba. He is exactly as I described him to you, and his obsession with loyalty and success colors everything he does."

"Then why are you helping me?"

"Have you ever heard the axiom about keeping your enemies close?"

"No."

"Most people put their energy into understanding their friends, which is admirable. What I've learned, though, is that it is much more practical to put your energy into understanding your enemies. And the only way to do that is to keep them close—by talking to them, observing how they interact with others, learning their vulnerabilities, and ascertaining their motives."

Seba was nonplussed. "Why would I want to do that?"

"So you can defend and protect yourself. That's what I did to save my family's business, although it was by reading Stavros's one-sided contracts and watching how he treated my father, rather than working face-to-face with him. In your case, however, you were sent to him, and I can see that you're not as stupid as I thought you were, so if you remain vigilant, you may be successful, too."

Seba smiled at the compliment, but it quickly faded when Meleia said, "Even though you should never make coffee again as long as you live."

Seba bristled, but Meleia was smiling now, and she looked radiant against the backdrop of the starry sky and the gentle June evening.

Meleia continued, "It seems to me that you'll have to engage with the enemy in order to locate your father. I'll do my best to help you." She gathered all of the curls that had fallen out of her bun and reassembled her top knot in the bright pink scarf. In the light of the rising moon, she looked like a goddess. *Aphrodite.*

The spell was broken by an unexpected burst of sound and fury.

"Did you call me Aphrodite?" Meleia kicked Seba in the shin, sending a wave of pain up his leg and into his groin.

Did I say that out loud? Seba hopped on one leg, his working hand covering the emerging pink lump on his lower leg as his sling slipped off his opposite shoulder.

Meleia hissed, "Aphrodite? I take it back—you really are stupid. I'm giving you advice about how to protect yourself from that fiend, and all you can think about is Aphrodite?" Her eyes were glowing with anger, and her cheeks were flushed. "You've signed on to work with that knife-wielding monster. He could tear you to shreds in an instant, and you have no idea what you're doing. You need to be on your guard! I'm only doing this so I can keep watch over you, and so you can tell me what's going on in that factory. That way I can protect you from him." She stomped her foot. "Does that sound like Aphrodite to you?"

Meleia's reaction was similar to that of his mother when she thought Seba was stumbling into something foolish. It was the same reaction that had earned her the name given to her by his grandfather, Papouli: "five feet of fury." Meleia was taller than Mama, and in his mind, Seba dubbed her "five and a half feet of fury." He was wise enough to keep that moniker to himself, especially since his shin was throbbing where she had kicked it.

He said angrily, "You're imagining things. I did *not* call you Aphrodite. And even if I had, I'd take it back because you're more like Medusa right now anyway. And by the way, I don't need protection from Stavros. He's going to use his contacts to help me find my father, and I'm going to help him get his fabrics on the fastest ships leaving Smyrna for France. Then I'll be on my way to Constantinople. It's that simple."

Meleia scoffed. "No, you're the one who's simple. I don't care how much you know about the coefficient of fineness, hulls, keels, masts, or sails. That man is a vulture, and if you think that you are entering into fair dealings with him, you couldn't be more wrong."

10 LEARNING FRENCH

Despite their argument, Meleia kept her word and agreed to teach Seba the basics of conversing in French. He vowed never to mention Aphrodite again, and he kept his mouth shut whenever he wasn't conjugating verbs or practicing pronunciation. He actually found the French lessons entertaining and learned many French words derived from Greek, like *ambroisie* (ambrosia) and *philanthropie* (philanthropy). Seba didn't know if it was all of the instruments that Papouli had taught him to play, or whether he had an ear for sounds, but even Meleia commented on how quickly he was able to mimic the accent and spit out short sentences that were passable in French. He fantasized about sneaking aboard a French ship headed for Constantinople to reclaim his father, trading barbs with the French sailors, and rescuing Kostas Krizomatis like Orpheus rescued Eurydice—using his charming voice to disarm her guards and extricate her from the underworld.

Seba loved learning French, but the lessons were not all

butterflies and sunshine. A few times, when Seba was enthralled by the lilt of Meleia's voice (and probably looking at her like an adoring sheepdog), she would abruptly stop talking, and say, "Stop."

"Stop what?"

"Looking at me like that."

"I'm appreciating your French accent." Seba knew she didn't believe it, but he often tried to salvage a small speck of dignity.

"Well, try to appreciate it with a different expression. I'm not—"

"I know who you're not; you don't have to say it." *Aphrodite.*

Meleia had an uncanny ability to seem to know what Seba was thinking, even when he didn't realize it himself. She was also whip-smart, direct, and the slightest bit frightening, if Seba was being honest. He found it best to focus on her fierceness rather than the curls that fell out of her scarf or the gold flecks in her eyes.

One evening, after a successful lesson in which Seba accomplished a full French language conversation with Meleia about purchasing silks, he was feeling extremely pleased with himself and enjoying a hot cup of strong Turkish coffee at the bar. Every time he drank coffee at the Aigokeros, he remembered how beautiful and angry Meleia had looked as he wiped the spilled coffee from her hair the first day they met. Today she was wearing a lavender-colored scarf, and she looked like an angel as she wiped down the bar. *She's perfect.*

"Did he make you sign a contract?"

Seba choked on the Turkish coffee he was sipping, and some of it dribbled down through his beard. *Why does she always do this to me?*

"No, I told you, it was a handshake. I've only been there a few days. Why can't you trust that I know what I'm doing? This is not charity or a loan like your father bargained; it's an entirely different situation. I am helping Stavros with his business, and he is using his merchant contacts to ascertain my father's whereabouts. He said the earthquake and the flooding of Constantinople's harbor have disrupted the shipping routes, and information is hard to come by. If only I had gotten here a few weeks sooner, maybe then I could have boarded a ship to Constantinople, but now the caravans are rerouting through Bursa and Smyrna because the roads to Constantinople are impassable."

Seba ran his fingers through his hair and blew out a loud breath of air. "I can't stand this waiting, but it seems like I have no choice. Stavros says that as soon as any ships from the north arrive with news of Constantinople's harbor, he'll make sure that Hector and Marco get the information to him immediately. Apparently, the henchmen, as you call them, spend a good bit of their time on the wharf, patrolling and protecting the Alkeidis exports."

Meleia said, "Ha! Those two thugs. I wouldn't trust any news they have—it's more likely coerced than true. They're no better than the pirates who raid the ships and ride off with the ill-gotten booty. In fact, I wouldn't be surprised if they helped the pirates raid ships of Stavros's competitors. That sounds like one way Stavros would ensure dominance over his competition."

Seba was undeterred by Meleia's cynicism. "Stavros said they work to *protect* the cargo from pirates, not steal it. It seems like a reasonable action for someone who trades in such luxurious merchandise." Seba jutted out his chin. "Stavros is offering me a kindness by allowing me to learn the silk trade from one of the best shops in the city while I'm forced to wait for news about my father." He held up his bandaged wrist. "It's the most I could hope for, given the circumstances."

Meleia sighed. "Stavros doesn't have any kindness inside him. He's always scheming and plotting—mostly ways to gain more wealth and crush his competitors. He's like a poisonous spider, spinning his web and drawing you in until you're close enough for him to sink his fangs into you."

Seba shuddered at the mention of fangs. Although he didn't mind spiders, he had an unnatural fear of snakes—the result of a face-to-face encounter with a deadly Ottoman viper as a child. Meleia's mention of fangs took him back to the day he accidentally stumbled into the Ottoman viper's lair, his face inches away from the snake's fangs. Somehow, he had escaped that Ottoman viper, and now, years, later, he was going to help his father escape a different kind of Ottoman viper: the sultan.

Meleia continued, "Has Stavros even mentioned your father?"

"Not exactly. He said that he's expecting a few ships from Bursa to arrive in the next several weeks. That's the closest trading port to Constantinople, and he said that is our best hope for news of my father and the Ottoman merchant fleet."

"What about Nasir? He seems like he has more contacts in the maritime trade than Stavros. And he's Captain Paşa's nephew, admiral of the Ottoman navy. They're the ones who protect the merchant ships from raiders and pirates. I had never met him before, but I could tell immediately that he is an honest man with principles. Can't you talk to him?"

Seba puffed out his cheeks. "I would if I saw him. Stavros has me so busy doing errands for him around the workshop that I haven't had time to look for Nasir. I don't believe he's been in the factory this week, and I don't know how often he inspects the tapestries or records the collection of tariffs. It's so confusing, because some of the tariffs are paid by the ship's owners, but others are paid at the workshop. I think it depends on the customer and the type of transaction. I'll admit, I don't understand it all, and every time I try to talk to any of my coworkers, it seems like Hector or Marco appears out of nowhere, eavesdropping on our conversations."

Seba traced his finger around the top of the coffee cup and didn't look up as he said, "Also, I got the feeling that Stavros doesn't want me to talk to Nasir. Did you notice when we were in the warehouse that Stavros was grumbling? I think it was because Nasir was getting all the attention."

Meleia nodded emphatically. "I remember. Stavros doesn't want you to speak with Nasir because he wants to keep you under his thumb for as long as possible, until he crushes your spirit and all that's left is an empty shell of your former self."

Seba took a swig from the tiny stoneware cup. The contrast of the warm, comforting coffee and Meleia's harsh words was disquieting. "Thank you for your optimism."

"Seba, I worry about you, and I'm trying to protect you. Look what Stavros did to my father, and to that poor boy who was butchered like an Easter lamb."

Seba picked up his coffee cup and thwacked it on the bar. "I've told you a thousand times, I'm not a child and I don't need any protection. Growing up on Chios, my mother tried to run my life, and it felt like being smothered. I didn't come to Smyrna for more of the same."

For once, Meleia was not interested in an argument. In

fact, she looked at him inquisitively, as if she was trying to figure him out. Then she held up a finger, then ran into the kitchen. She returned with three plates of food. "I understand, Seba. I don't like being told what to do either. How about we agree that I won't tell you what to do with your life if you take these plates to the table by the front door?"

Seba laughed and said, "Agreed." He hopped off the stool and carried the plates steaming with thin slices of doner chicken blanketed in roasted tomatoes, green peppers, eggplant, and a generous portion of tangy sheep's-milk yogurt. They were served alongside warm stacks of pita, the steam escaping from the fluffy pillows of bread. Seba had helped his old friend Sotirios with his coffee shop when he was a boy, but never any meals as mouthwatering as these. Sotirios generally did not serve food, other than cookies and cakes to accompany his coffee, or the occasional pot of *avgolemono*.

When he returned to the bar, Meleia said, "You're a fine hand, and even though your coffee-making skills are deplorable, you can be helpful sometimes. Are you planning to stay in Smyrna after you find your father?"

Seba blushed, thinking that Meleia was flirting with him. "I don't think I can go back to Chios." He frowned, remembering the argument he had with his Uncle Phillip before he left Sessera. Seba had called him a traitor and a puppet for the Ottoman empire. *You don't say that to the leader of the mastic council and get away with it.* Seba had longed to leave the island to search for his father, and his argument with Sessera's highest-ranking official, his uncle, propelled him into action. Now he knew he was no longer welcome in the village where he had been raised.

Meleia stared at him, and he wanted to tell her more, but

instead he said, "Smyrna is an exciting place. When I find my father, maybe my whole family will move here. I could bring my mother and grandfather from Chios, and we could be together again."

Meleia smiled, but her eyes were sad. "Family is a blessing."

"How is your father?"

"He has some good days, but mostly he lives in the past—the time when Stavros offered to help him and then plunged a knife into his back. When I show him how successful the Aigokeros is now, he looks through me, willfully ignoring how blessed we are. It feels like he is stuck in a loop, preparing to do battle with his demons, not recognizing that the demons left the fight years ago."

"I'm sorry. Both of our fathers suffered tragedies that they didn't deserve. Sometimes I wonder if my father will be the same person I remember. For all I know, they are keeping him locked up and forcing him to work as a slave to build ships day and night. What if I don't recognize him anymore? I was only nine years old when they ripped him away from our family."

Meleia put her hand on Seba's, sending warmth all the way up to his shoulder. "That's exactly how I feel. I know my father is in there somewhere, but I can't get to him."

"You know who reminds me of my father?"

Meleia shook her head. Her hand was on his, and he felt the heat spread to the tips of his toes.

"Nasir. He knows more than everyone else in the room, but he never makes anyone else feel as if they are less than him. That's the opposite of many people I've met in Smyrna, most of whom go out of their way to tell you what merchants they work for, why their business is the best, how much more they know about the east or west than the next person, and when their next great opportunity is coming. Nasir has that rare quality of remaining humble in all circumstances, not needing to prove his worth to anyone else. That's exactly how my father was, and it's why I have to find him."

Meleia nodded and moved her hand away from Seba's. "I understand. It feels like my father was taken away from me as well. The man who lives in our house and walks these streets like a ghost is not the man who raised me. That man is gone."

With a rare timbre of indulgence in her voice, Meleia said, "I wish you could have seen what my father was like before Stavros ruined his life. When something like that happens, it's hard not to feel resentment. I want to make sure that it never happens to anyone else again, especially you."

"I'm not your father. You can't expect the same thing to happen to me."

"My father was a successful businessman when Stavros destroyed him. You're a mastiha farmer who never lived in a city until a few weeks ago."

Seba banged his fist on the bar, splashing coffee on the wooden surface and surprising himself almost as much as Meleia. "I don't know why I ever asked you to help me—all you do is make me feel weak and inferior!" He stormed out the door of the taverna, leaving his half-finished coffee cup on the bar.

Meleia ran after him and reached him in the street, where he was walking quickly toward Buğra's loft. She put her hand on his shoulder, but he refused to turn around.

"Seba, don't go. You're right. People have misjudged me and underestimated me my whole life, so I shouldn't do it to you."

Seba was facing away from her, but he had stopped walking and he crossed his arms in front of his chest.

"I hate it when people treat me like I can't do things, especially because I am a woman. Do you notice how everyone addresses me as 'my dear,'? It's so demeaning. They assume that I am weak. It makes me feel so angry that I could fight an army of Ottoman soldiers with my own two hands. I don't like it when people judge me as less than I am, and I understand that you wouldn't appreciate it, either. As you can see, the subject of my father is difficult for me, and as much as I try to control my temper, this is the one area in my life where I haven't figured it out yet. Please accept my apology."

Seba turned around and offered a truce.

"Why don't we make an agreement not to discuss our fathers during French lessons? If you can restrain yourself, then so can I."

They shook hands, rather formally, and Meleia surprised him with a hug.

Then she said with a wink, "*Peut-être.*" Perhaps.

11 TAPESTRY

With every day he spent in the workshop, Seba studied the operation of the textile factory like a Greek scholar learning the mysteries of the world. In fact, he felt like an explorer in a new land. On the island of Chios, his life consisted of toiling in the skinos groves all day and then being locked up by the Ottoman guards at night inside the thick stone walls of his village. Sessera was one of the medieval enclaves built by the Genoese rulers of the fourteenth century to keep the famed Tears of Chios safe from marauders, pirates, and thieves. The Ottomans liked to say that they were keeping the villagers safe, but really it was the sparkling little nuggets of mastiha that necessitated the excessive security precautions. Seba knew that the precious Tears of Chios were harvested from the trees so they could be sent to royals and aristocrats from the Far East to the New World, but how the precious mastiha actually got there was, for the most part, a mystery. He was now getting a glimpse into the inner workings of the maritime merchant trade—from the spice farmer to the porter who offloaded the cargo at its destination, and everything in between. The fact that these wooden vessels, built by the hands of shipwrights like his father, could battle the currents, storms, and squalls to bring these treasures to people who had never even seen a skinos tree was almost too much for his mind to comprehend.

The secluded farming culture in which Seba was raised did not prepare him for life in a booming city, where all manner of languages, customs, foods, sounds, luxuries, and activities were on display. He felt akin to Odysseus, entering the land of the lotus-eaters, where the inhabitants were so different and their dependence on the drug of the lotus flower was so deep-rooted, that everything and everyone else no longer mattered. In the case of Smyrna, it was not a lotus flower that carried the enchantment, but rather the allure of untold riches made manifest through the exchange of foreign goods. Everyone in the city was obsessed with the best-quality silks and velvets, and the most exotic fruits and spices. Not to mention the opium, tea, gemstones and minerals like jade and lapis lazuli, and the prestige of participating in the trading network that connected all four corners of the globe.

And now Seba was working for one of the titans of Smyrna, a man with expertly styled hair, fashionable silk kaftans, and manicured hands, which looked like they had never touched a loom, weft, warp, or vat of indigo dye. His eyes were as black as Brother Tim's and Eleni's, but without the sparkle of mischief. His air of confidence permeated his whole being like an impenetrable citadel.

Seba only had a few moments every day to assess Stavros's grooming techniques, however, because Stavros kept him busy. There was no opportunity for slacking when your employer never slept. Seba had originally thought, after his meeting with Nasir, that he would be engaging with customers and boarding ships to assess their speed and seaworthiness. Stavros had said that he intended the Alkeidis Tapestry Workshop's goods to be sent to only the best manors, estates, and castles in Europe, and the way to accomplish that was by ensuring that the Alkeidis silks arrived at their destinations while the competitors were floundering at sea. Instead of spending time on the ships (and looking for information about his father), however, Seba found himself lugging huge wool tapestries from the weaving room to the warehouse, carrying spools of cotton and wool from the spinning room to the workers at their looms, and dragging indigo-dyed fabrics from the sludge-filled stinking vats of fermented indigo plants to the drying room. The fact that it was almost mid-summer in Smyrna made all of these tasks sweaty, difficult, and exhausting. *If this is what I have to do to find my father, I will.*

Stavros required Seba to report to his office each morning, where Stavros made a point to stand and greet him. Stavros was a fraction of an inch taller than Seba, and as they shook hands, it was clear that Stavros both noted the difference and used it as a measurement of worth, leaving Seba with the impression that he had already lost a point in the comparison. At least he didn't try to rip Seba's arm off, as he had attempted with Meleia on the day of their first meeting. Subtle though all of these mannerisms were, Seba felt the intent behind the gestures. Every interaction with Stavros was an assessment and test of power.

One day, when Seba arrived after sunrise, Stavros squeezed his hand so hard that Seba involuntarily flinched. Stavros said, "Nervous, are you? You told me you were loyal. You don't have anything to hide, do you?"

"Well, anyone in the presence of the great Stavros Alkeidis would be a fool not to feel a little nervous." Seba was proud of himself for that response—he had been observing and assimilating the technique of disarmament from Stavros since his first day in the workshop. If flattery mixed with self-confidence was all it took to be a successful businessman, then Seba could play that game with the best of them.

Eleni happened to have walked by the office at that moment, and hearing Seba's false compliment, she rolled her eyes comically so that Seba could see them, but Stavros could not. Seba stifled a laugh as Stavros appeared to revel in Seba's praise.

"I couldn't agree more, Sebastian. I recognize your talents more and more each day that we work together, and I see that you are an autodidact. I'm also pleased to see that you are no longer using the sling, although your wrist is bandaged. Is it healing well?"

Seba squeezed his left hand into a fist and released it. "Yes, it's much better, thanks to Dr. Robin."

Stavros looked surprised. "You were treated by Dr. Robin rather than one of our local Greek doctors? I'm surprised. What were you doing on Frank Street?"

"Meleia suggested it. She said that Dr. Robin's family was originally from France, but they had been in Smyrna for so many generations that they were considered part of the Greek community here."

Stavros looked skeptical. "I see. I used to have faith in Dr. Robin, but once her cousin Maria Gracia married that scoundrel Turnbull, I began to wonder where her loyalties lie."

Seba said, "She set the bone in my wrist, and it seems to be healing properly, so I have no cause to complain."

Stavros twisted the ring—the one with the gold strands—as Seba had seen him do when they first met. "And have you seen the good doctor since then?"

"No, that's the only time I've been on Frank Street."

Stavros seemed pleased with Seba's response. "Good. I'd advise you to stay away from Dr. Robin, at least until her cousin's troublesome husband, Turnbull, is chased out of Smyrna. That man is not to be trusted, and the sooner he's gone from our beautiful city, the better."

Seba said, "That's what Meleia said. She kicked him out of her taverna and threw a bottle of wine at his head in the process."

Stavros laughed heartily. "I would like to have seen that, Sebastian. I'd do the same or worse if he ever stepped foot in my shop—which I hope, for his sake, he never does. Speaking of my little workshop, what do you think of it?" Stavros swept his arms in an arc, a grand gesture meant to convey the message that although he used the words "little workshop," he knew it was anything but. Seba marveled at Stavros's ability to use self-effacing words while simultaneously conveying the raw power of his presence. It was masterful, and Seba remembered what Meleia said about observing one's enemies. Stavros didn't quite feel like an enemy to Seba, though. Powerful and self-absorbed, yes, but not an enemy, at least not yet.

"Well, sir, I've never seen anything so magnificent, and Timotheos always told me that you were the best businessman in Smyrna."

"Younger brothers will say such things, you know." Stavros looked thoughtful. "We have supplied several gold- and silver-embroidered silk fabrics to Nea Moni since I took over this business from my father. Have you ever seen any of the gorgeous tapestries in the sanctuary there?"

"Yes, as a matter of fact, I have." Seba pointed to a tapestry hanging on the wall behind Stavros's desk. Seba had been so intent on maintaining eye contact with Stavros every morning since his hire that he had failed to notice the tapestry before today.

"However, I've never seen one as intricately or delicately woven as the one on the wall behind you."

It had a subtle sheen that changed colors with the varying light in the room. Seba had learned from Eleni that this was a clear indicator of silk fabric and was one of the many reasons why the lustrous fibers were so expensive and adored by royalty. Stavros's indigo tapestry was approximately eight feet across and five feet high, bigger than any tapestry Seba had ever seen hanging in the sanctuary of Nea Moni. Of course, it was indigo because that color was the most difficult to produce, and it saturated the fabric with a hue so deep and magical that it resembled a twilight sky. It was no surprise that this was the predominant color for Stavros's prized possession.

At first glance, it was clear that the indigo silk was a huge spiderweb, its silver filaments extending in a spiral from the center to every corner of the tapestry. The primary feature, which struck fear into Seba's heart, was a sparkling brown spider, outlined in glowing white silk with an abdomen almost three times the length of the head. The spider's back displayed a complex yet unmistakable shining white, gold, and silver cross. It was stunning. Seba found himself drawn into the spider's web, yet slightly unnerved by it. He wasn't quite sure why, because it was an absolute marvel of color and composition. The shining argentine orb spanned out to the edges of the tapestry, with animals, plants, and flowers spilling out in all directions from the silvery strands.

The spider's eight legs were thick and striped, with

prickly hairs jutting out from each of them like the spines of a mace. Next to the spider's elongated face were two shorter legs, with the same barbed protrusions. Seba found himself counting the legs. There were eight long ones, in addition to the two short ones by the face. He had never gotten close enough to a spider to know whether the two shorter legs were an accurate depiction, and he didn't intend to. He was happy that the spider's fangs were not visible beneath its eight gleaming black eyes.

The tapestry's border was an intricate pattern of gold vines and leaves connecting tiny vermilion-centered flowers with bright white petals. Seba observed that the flowers' centers were not only embroidered red, but they also had cherubic faces with closed eyes, tiny indications of a nose, and a serene mouth, in the repose of prayer. It looked like a host of angels surrounded the spider in its all-consuming web.

"Ah, you noticed my modest piece of art? You must have seen much more elaborate decorations at my brother's monastery. They have quite a collection, I hear, and they've purchased many of Eleni's splendid designs over the years."

"Did Eleni design this one?"

"No, this is something that came from my own imagination. I commissioned our most prized weavers to create this to my precise specifications."

"Is that a cross on the spider's back?" Seba was trying to understand the meaning of Stavros's prized possession.

"Yes, the cross-backed orb weaver is native to Anatolia. Have you not seen them on the island of Chios?"

Seba shook his head. "No, I've never seen anything like it before."

Stavros nodded. "I quite like that this creature carries

the cross on its back, much like our Lord Jesus Christ, and weaves the most beautiful tapestries in the animal kingdom, much like I strive to do with my humble workshop."

Seba said nothing, mostly because he was trying to understand the imagery. The centerpiece was one of God's creatures, a weaver no less, surrounded by a multitude of animals, fish, and birds, all ringed by sweet cupid-mouthed cherubs. It might be a bit unsettling at first glance, but now, as Seba considered it, the tapestry could be Stavros's depiction of appreciation for his work and his place in God's creation. *He does call the workers his little silkworms, after all.*

"Ah, a man of few words, are you? In fact, my brother mentioned that in his letter to me. Of course, I haven't spoken to him in many years, and I've learned that it's best to make decisions based on my own experience. It has served me well—after my brother left us and my father died, we struggled to continue the business."

"It must have been difficult for you." Seba was thinking of the days immediately following his father's capture.

Stavros waved his arm, dismissing the emotions. "There's no place for sentiment here. That's all in the past now. I am ready to expand again, and our creations are in high demand. I think we are now in a position to move to a more exclusive clientele and sell our goods at an even higher price than before. That is why your appearance intrigued me so much, Sebastian. You arrived at precisely the right time—it was puzzling, actually." Stavros spun the ring on his finger, the one with the gold filaments that now reminded Seba of a spider's web.

Seba, feeling surprisingly confident, said, "I remember my father saying this: *'There is an appointed time for everything. And there is a time for every matter under heaven.'* I think it's from the book of Ecclesiastes. Maybe it was God's timing that brought us together when we needed each other."

Stavros raised his eyebrows. "A Bible scholar, too, Sebastian? I wonder what other hidden talents lie under that dark mop of hair on your head."

Seba grinned. "I would be happy to help you expand your business, or whatever else you need. Your offer to help me find my father is what I've dreamed about ever since the day the Ottomans took him away. I'm sure we'll be getting news from Constantinople any day now." Seba felt a rush of emotion, and hoped he wasn't sharing too much. He continued, "You know I'm capable—I've been transporting fabrics, threads, spools, and dyes around the workshop every day that I've been here, and my wrist is getting stronger. I've already learned a great deal about silk, wool, and cotton. Now that I know more about the manufacturing process, I'm ready to spend more time on the wharf, and I'm sure I can be more helpful to you there. I can even let you know when your contacts from Constantinople, or Bursa, arrive, so we can find out about my father."

Stavros raised his eyebrows and Seba added, "I can also use what I learned from my father to help you get your goods on the fastest ships to the richest customers."

Stavros eyed the center of his tapestry. "I hope that's exactly what you'll be able to do."

12 THE WAVE

As the next several days dragged on, Seba began to wonder if he was being duped by Stavros, as Meleia had warned. Seba noticed new ships arriving in the port every few days, and it was inconceivable to him that none of them came from Bursa, or hadn't brought some news of Constantinople's flood. He had asked Stavros for more assignments at the wharf, and Stavros appeared to agree, but then he continued assigning him to the warehouse. Seba needed to take control of his own destiny and search the waterfront for information about his father—that is, if he could somehow get away from the workshop, if even for a few hours.

It was as if God heard Seba's desperate plea, because that very day, the hottest that Seba had experienced since arriving in Smyrna, Eleni sent him on an errand to the harbor to deliver a çatma that the weavers had worked on all night to finish for a well-paying French customer. Eleni wrapped the çatma in burlap and said sternly, "I'm trusting you with this, Seba. Don't disappoint me; it is one of our most valuable pieces. Please take it to the *Endeavor*, which is moored at one of the southernmost berths. Ask for Captain Bisset, and make sure it is delivered directly into the hands of Monsieur Ducasse."

Seba was elated. He would deliver the çatma, but then he would use the rest of the day to ask every sailor he could find about his father.

The docks were bustling with activity, and Seba felt the salt air on his face along with the midday heat. The sun beamed directly overhead, and the water shone bright blue, with sparkles of gold and white dancing along the surface. South of the shipping docks, the fishmongers unloaded their catches onto wooden carts, with barbouni, mullet, sea bream, and turbot piled so high that it took several of them to get the wheels moving over the cobbled streets that led to the markets. Each fishmonger had a helper, probably a young relative, whose job it was to keep the pelicans and cats away from the carts as they lumbered up the road toward the hills. The incline from the harbor toward the mountains was not steep in this area, but the grade was such that the fishmongers were huffing and puffing the further they traveled from the wharf, stopping only to wipe their sweaty brows and hands with cotton cloths they wore under their caps.

The activity around the pier reminded Seba of a colony of ants, moving in lines to and from the ships and up the hills toward the Caravan Bridge. Just like the little insects carrying leaves and crumbs ten times their size, some of the laborers carried crates on their backs so big that Seba thought they looked like versions of Atlas holding up the world.

After he found Captain Bisset and delivered the çatma

to Monsieur Ducasse, he asked if anyone knew about the earthquake and tsunami that had deluged Constantinople. Many of the sailors knew about it, but Seba's French was not good enough to have a meaningful conversation with the crew on the *Endeavor*. He needed to find a Greek crew so he could get some answers.

He paced up and down the dock, walking past the ships and listening to the languages being spoken. Unfortunately, none of the ships that were moored close to the *Endeavor* had any Greek crews. As he tried to stop people and ask them about his father with no results, he became more discouraged. No one knew anything about Kostas Krizomatis, the famous shipwright of Chios. Seba began to wonder if his father was alive. What if the Ottomans had beaten him so badly that he never survived the voyage to Constantinople? Seba shook his head; he refused to believe it. If the sultan wanted Papa so badly that he was willing to tear apart Seba's family to get him, the sultan wouldn't have let his guards kill him. Seba had to keep searching until he found someone with answers.

"What are you doing here?"

Seba wheeled around at the sound of Paolo's voice. The sweltering June heat had matted Paolo's hair to the top of his head, and his shirt was rumpled and dirty. His face was florid and covered in sweat, as if he had been running.

Seba said, "I had to deliver a silk çatma for Eleni, and now I'm trying to find someone with information about my father. I'm not having any luck, though. What are you doing here?"

Paolo bent over and put his hands on his thighs. "I just quit my job."

"What? Why?"

Paolo smacked both hands on his knees, which threw up

149

a little puff of dirt. "I can't work for those barge owners another day. Today was the final straw—Peter accidentally dropped an amphora of olive oil into the sea while we were loading cargo, and the owner took off his belt and whipped him right there in front of all of us. It was awful! It's not like Peter did it on purpose—he was exhausted and tried to carry too much by himself. The owner said the mistake cost him 350 silver *thaler*, and he was going to make Peter pay it back to him if it took him twenty years. They treat us like dogs, and I'm not going to be subjected to that kind of abuse, especially for the small pay they give us."

Seba's eyes were wide. "I didn't know it was so bad. Haven't you worked in that job for a long time?"

Paolo grimaced. "Yes, I have, Seba. Too long. There are so many other opportunities in Smyrna." He pointed around the wharf. "Look at this place! Merchants are scrambling for any kind of advantage they can find, and everyone needs workers. It's not a coincidence that we found each other here, today, Seba. I've been thinking about the Alkeidis factory. They hired you on the spot; do you think they need additional workers?"

Seba cocked his head. "I'm not sure. Stavros keeps talking about expanding, but I haven't seen any new workers lately." He made a sweaty fist and felt the perspiration trickle down the back of his wrist. The sun burned his head, and he wished he had remembered to cover it before he left the workshop. "I feel like you— Stavros is not helping me find my father, so I've got to take control of my own destiny if I want to make any progress."

Paolo's face brightened. "If you get me a job at the silk workshop, then I could help you change your circumstances. Maybe if both of us were reminding Stavros of his promise to help you, he'd have no choice but to do it."

"I appreciate the offer, Paolo, but I haven't been there that long, and I don't know how long I'm going to stay, especially with Stavros stringing me along like a stray dog."

Paolo grinned. "Then I could take your job if you hop on one of these ships bound for Constantinople."

A raspy whisper of a voice behind them said, "No ships are bound for Constantinople, and they won't be for a long time."

Both boys turned quickly to see an ancient-looking old sailor, wrinkled and weathered, his skin looking like cow's leather that had been tanned too long and then stomped on by the cow's brothers and sisters. The decrepit mariner was hunched over, his clothes hanging off him like laundry hanging on a line. His eyes were slits, the folds of his eyelids gathered up like fabric, and his gray beard was so wiry that Seba thought it would draw blood if he touched it. He had a clay pipe hanging loosely from the corner of his mouth, and when he coughed, it sounded like the wheezing of a broken accordion.

Paolo was about to tell the man to shut up and leave them alone, but Seba said, "What do you mean?"

The mariner perked up, as if glad to have an audience. "The earthquake, son. The harbor in Constantinople is gone. No ships getting in or out. It wouldn't matter if there were any ships, because there is no cargo. The warehouses along the wharf were washed away, like seashells in a storm." He took a deep breath, and it was such a slow, wet, and rasping sound that Seba wondered if any air was getting to the sailor's lungs. Then he started to cough again, and Seba realized that it might be a laugh. "All those Silk Road goods, they're at the bottom of the Sea of Marmara." He continued the croaking, coughing laugh so long that Seba thought he was going to be sick.

Paolo said impatiently, "Yes, yes, old man, we heard about the earthquake, and we've all seen floods, but I don't understand why this one was so bad."

The old sailor eyed him skeptically. "Too young to know the ways of the world, you are. I've traveled on ships since before I could walk. Trust me, you don't ever want to see this kind of water. If you didn't believe in Poseidon, you would after you saw a gargantuan wave like that. If you lived, that is. Water can be calm and serene, like the Meles River under the Caravan Bridge up there." The sailor pointed a bony finger toward the eastern mountains, where the Caravan Bridge welcomed Silk Road travelers to Smyrna. "But after an earthquake, the water becomes as hardened as a mountain when it rises up from the seabed toward land. The ships anchored in Constantinople ended up three miles inland. I wouldn't be surprised if Poseidon himself picked them all up and threw them on the ground, miles away. No one could survive that kind of force."

Seba put his face in his hands. "It couldn't have been that bad."

"You look like your jib's too tight, son. What's wrong?"

"My father," Seba choked out, as he slumped over, his hands on his knees.

Paolo grabbed the sailor's shoulders. "Look what you did to my friend, you crusty old codger! We don't want to hear your lies. Everyone can't be dead—I'm sure some people survived." He gestured toward Seba with his head as he shook the man back and forth. "Tell him his father's alive, you senile old muck-spout!"

The old man cried, "Help! These villains are attacking me."

Nasir walked down the gangplank of the ship nearest Seba and Paolo, moving quickly despite the use of his cane.

"What's this? Do you need assistance, sir?"

Paolo immediately let go of the old man, who crumpled to the ground in a heap. Paolo froze when he saw Nasir.

Nasir looked at Paolo and Seba, and his face relaxed upon recognizing the latter. "Oh, Sebastian, it's you. I heard someone crying for help. What's going on?"

Seba could barely speak. "I'm looking for my father—he was in Constantinople—and this man says everyone in Constantinople who worked in the harbor was drowned. He said no one survived. I've come so far; I can't believe it's true."

Paolo, now confident that Nasir did not recognize him, said, "This man was telling tales, like the fish stories old curs tell in the tavernas. But his story was about my friend's father, not a fish." He pointed at Seba, whose face was drained of color despite the heat. "Look what he's done. I was telling him to be careful with his words because they can be hurtful."

The old man said, "Humph," but didn't seek to defend himself to Nasir. He seemed more interested in the drama that was playing out—something that would make for a juicy tale to tell later on.

Seba looked at Nasir and whispered, "Is it true?"

Nasir sighed. "Yes, the harbor was decimated, but we don't know who was lost." He rubbed his chin thoughtfully. "You know who was near there, but not actually moored in the port? That Englishman, Dr. Turnbull. My recollection is that he said he was testing out some new ship designs to speed his merchant ships. You might want to ask him if he knows anything about your father."

Seba gawked at Nasir. "Wasn't your uncle trying to arrest Dr. Turnbull? At the Aigokeros it seemed like the Englishman was not welcome in Smyrna. I thought I might get in trouble if I spoke to him. Isn't it dangerous to consort with the enemy of the Ottoman government?"

Nasir looked at Seba thoughtfully. "Yes, Dr. Turnbull has been raising my uncle's hackles for pulling into ports all over Turkey and trying to solicit volunteers for his East Florida venture. However, his situation is a bit different in Smyrna because his wife's family is here. In fact, I believe that one or more of his children were born here—legitimate citizens of Smyrna. His wife is the cousin of Dr. Robin, the woman who treated me when I was so regrettably incapacitated at the Aigokeros. Dr. Turnbull has somewhat of a complicated relationship with Smyrna, one that has confounded my uncle, to be honest."

Nasir continued, "Dr. Turnbull spent many years in this city, so he puts my uncle in a difficult position. I asked my uncle to give him some time to visit with his family, including Dr. Robin, before he ejects Dr. Turnbull from his wife's place of birth. Dr. Turnbull was very lucky that his ship was not lost in Constantinople. He's one of the few merchants who might have some idea of what happened there, but he'll only be here a short time, so if you want information, you'll have to act quickly."

Paolo said belligerently, "You're no better than this old dog. Seba doesn't need another wild-goose chase, he needs some answers. You work for the navy; are you telling me there is no one else in the whole of Smyrna with information about Constantinople?"

Nasir considered Paolo carefully, and Seba's heart rate increased as he worried whether Nasir would recognize him.

Nasir inhaled slowly and said, "I've told you everything I know, young man. It is not my nature to withhold information or cause pain to anyone. It is clear to me that

Sebastian is worried for his father, and if I had any means to assuage that pain, I would do so in a heartbeat. As would you, I presume. I can see that Seba is fortunate to have such a good friend in you."

Seba replied, "Nasir, are you sure it's not too dangerous for me to speak with Dr. Turnbull? Stavros Alkeidis told me to have nothing to do with the Englishman. In addition, I don't hold the same place in society that you do, and I can't find my father if I'm thrown in jail."

Nasir said, "I understand your concern, young man, but if you want answers, sometimes you have to travel to places that you might fear to tread."

13 NIGHTMARES

Seba slept fitfully that night, and his dreams were as vibrant as the tapestry behind Stavros's desk. In one dream, he was a sailor in the crow's nest of a sailing ship in Constantinople and the first to spot a large wall of water, higher than the mountains of Chios, moving toward the ship and the harbor. He could see his father on the wharf at Constantinople, chained to a group of men who were banging away, constructing the hull of the sultan's newest sailing ship. Seba was screaming at his father and the other men to run away, trying to warn them of the tsunami that was moving directly toward them. Paolo was on the ship with him, and he yelled for Paolo to shoot a gun in the air, anything to get his father's attention. The water was drawing closer to the shore, rising several feet in height with every second that passed. Paolo looked up and grabbed the gun, shooting it in the air as Seba continued to shriek at his father and the chain gang, who were oblivious to the sounds. His father looked up as Paolo's gun went off, but an Ottoman guard took out a whip and flogged his father across the back. Seba yelled, "No, Papa, no!" The water rose higher as it approached the harbor, and Seba felt as if his chest would explode from his ribs. He woke up covered in sweat, his throat raw and his head pounding. His screams were so loud that the donkeys and horses below rustled and brayed their unease.

It was only a dream. My father is alive. Everything's fine.

Seba knew he wouldn't be able to get back to sleep, so he got dressed and ate some dried apples, cheese, and pita that Buğra had left for him the evening before, and then he walked to the workshop. He knew a few of the weavers would be there; they often worked all night if they were in the middle of a particularly difficult pattern, but Seba did not expect Linus, the busybody of the workshop, to be there at this hour. Linus was one of Eleni's and Stavros's most senior employees, acting as an overseer of sorts. Linus had his hands in every part of the Alkeidis Tapestry Workshop, and never ceased to tell anyone who would listen. Seba often avoided him, primarily because he couldn't bear Linus's nonstop barrage of words. Once Linus had cornered Seba, and by the time Seba extricated himself from the conversation, he had to miss dinner at the Aigokeros to make up the work he hadn't completed. Seba couldn't believe that Linus accomplished anything, because he was always busy bloviating about one topic or another. Today it was food, which Seba found comical, because Linus was the skinniest person that Seba had met in Smyrna.

"Hello, Seba! You're here early. Have you eaten breakfast?" Linus, dressed in a white cotton shirt over dark amethyst-colored trousers, was holding a small leatherbound book in his hands, something that Seba had never seen Linus without. Seba wondered what kinds of things Linus wrote in that book, and if it was information for Eleni and Stavros, or something that was for Linus's own use. As usual, Linus didn't wait for Seba's response to his question. "My favorite breakfast is *çilbir*—have you ever eaten it?"

Seba was stunned by the pace of Linus's chatter, but he did love food, so he shook his head no. The workday hadn't officially begun, and if Linus had to talk Seba to death, maybe talking about food wouldn't be so bad. Also, Seba thought that maybe he'd get a glimpse of what Linus wrote in that mysterious leather journal.

Linus continued, "I made some this morning. It's the absolute best way to make eggs—lightly poached and served over a heaping dollop of yogurt. Of course, the yogurt must be mixed with finely minced garlic, salt, and pepper for proper çilbir, then drizzled with gently heated olive oil and Aleppo pepper flakes. If you overheat the olive oil, you'll ruin it, Seba! I like to top mine with mint and fennel. And you can't forget the pita sprinkled with black cumin seeds for sopping up all the delicious goodness! Fresh baked pita is the best, isn't it, Seba?"

Linus patted his nonexistent stomach and didn't wait for a response. "I probably shouldn't have eaten so much, but you know, it's good to have energy for the workday, isn't it? Especially in the dyeing room. Mixing the indigo dye is hard work, and hot. Not as bad as the silk room, of course."

Seba wasn't sure if Linus had taken a breath yet, and he was surprised when Linus stopped and looked concerned.

Linus said accusingly, "You're awfully quiet this morning, Seba. Did you stay out drinking at the Aigokeros too late last night? I heard Meleia has been celebrating even bigger crowds since the re-opening of her taverna. Speaking of celebrating, are you excited for the Festival of Saint John?

159

It's my favorite time of year! All the fruits are ripening, and the weather is fine. My sister will be making several cakes. What's your favorite cake, Seba? I'll ask her to make it for you. Mine is *galaktoboureko*—I could eat a whole one right now thinking about it; the taste of the cheese is divine. What does Eleni have you working on? I saw you talking to some of those French merchants in her office yesterday. Were they from Marseilles? I'd love to travel on a ship to Marseilles one day. The French are so sophisticated and exotic, aren't they?"

Seba didn't know whether Linus intended him to answer the torrent of questions that spewed from his thin lips, but Linus never paused long enough for anyone to respond, so the point was moot.

"Speaking of exotic, have you told Stavros and Eleni that you were learning English in addition to French?"

Seba's brow creased, wondering how Linus could possibly know that. "No, I did not tell Eleni about my English lessons, and I'd appreciate it if you would keep it to yourself."

"Why? There's nothing wrong with learning English."

As Linus said the word "English," Stavros exited his office and stepped into the hallway. Seba hadn't expected Stavros to be at the workshop so early.

"Who's learning English?" Stavros frowned, and his voice was low and gravelly.

Linus, looking as happy as a dog with two tails, could not contain his enthusiasm. "Seba's learning English from Meleia at the Aigokeros. He's getting really good. Seba, say something for us in English."

If looks could kill, Linus would be on the ground with both of those tails between his legs. *Linus, no.*

Seba said quietly, "Meleia taught me a few words, that's

all."

Stavros's eyes flashed, although his voice was calm. "I thought we agreed that she would teach you French. Didn't I make it clear to you that France is where we are focusing our business? Eleni mentioned that you are communicating competently with our longtime brokers from Marseilles, and I've noticed your progress as well. You have an aptitude for languages, if I'm any judge."

All the muscles in Seba's body tensed as Stavros continued, "Two languages aren't enough for you? Why would you need to speak English? You're not in bed with that scoundrel Turnbull, are you? I thought I explained myself clearly on the subject of loyalty."

Seba could feel his shoulders tightening, and he willed himself to stand tall. "No, sir. I was doing well in French, and I wanted to test myself. I was trying out a few words. It's nothing."

Linus clapped Seba on the shoulder, as if they were best friends. "Oh, come now, Seba, that's not what I've heard — by all accounts, your English is very good already! Everyone's talking about it."

Stavros crossed his arms in front of his chest. "Is there something you're not telling me, Sebastian?"

"No, sir, I really don't know the language at all. It was a silly game with Meleia to mimic a few sounds. Linus is mistaken." In his head, Seba desperately pleaded for Linus to stop talking.

Miraculously, the heavens cooperated, and it worked this time.

"Well, Seba, as you know, I speak fluent French, which is required by my position here as owner of the workshop. It is the language we use to conduct business with the merchants who order our textiles for royalty and the wealthy families of Europe. That language has become the lifeblood of this business. Anyone learning French would have an advantage in the textile business, but I'm not so sure about English. Especially since there is a certain Englishman in Smyrna making quite a bad impression on the Ottoman government in recent days. I've told Hector and Marco to keep a watchful eye, and if that criminal comes within five hundred feet of this workshop, they know what to do. The English are nothing but trouble."

"Yes, sir." *That's exactly what Meleia said.*

"Now stop dawdling and get back to work, both of you." Stavros turned and walked back to his office. Linus's gossip must have been what brought Stavros out into the hallway. Seba thought about the spider in the center of the tapestry and the thin shining filaments of the web that stretched everywhere. He wondered if Linus was some kind of secret informant for Stavros. *He couldn't be, could he? He seems too oblivious, but maybe that's part of his act.* Seba vowed to avoid Linus from now on, at all costs.

Linus said innocently, "I think Stavros was really impressed, Seba. He commented that you had an aptitude for languages, and I think he's right. You don't have to thank me for bringing it to his attention, I'd do it for anyone in our workshop."

Seba ground his teeth and fought back the urge to punch Linus right in his pointy nose.

"I'll see you around, Seba. And if you want my sister's recipe for çilbir, let me know. *Adieu!* Or, if you prefer, *Cheerio!*" Linus waved his hand with a flourish, and he was off to the dyeing room.

Several nights later, Seba had another nightmare, but this time it was not the sea that caused him to toss and turn. In this dream, he was a brown spotted moth living on the right side of Stavros's tapestry. He had a sudden urge to travel across the indigo silk, and he left the comfort of his home to venture to the opposite side. He had an inner knowing that something awaited him on the tapestry's far edge, but as hard as he tried, he couldn't remember what it was. He understood only that something significant and valuable was calling to him, and he had to follow the little silver filaments of the web to reach his destination. The problem was that every time he managed to find a filament leading to the other side, it turned and meandered around toward the center of the tapestry. There was a prize that awaited him if he refused to give up, but no matter how hard he strove to make forward progress, the filaments led him in circles.

A fuzzy, striped honeybee warned him to keep clear of the shining silver web and to stay along the edges of the tapestry, where the cherubic little angels floated above the labyrinth. Seba tried to reach the topmost border, but every time he turned toward the tiny flowers with bright white petals and angel-faced centers, the silver web led him back toward the center, toward the cross-backed orb weaver.

Next, he passed a bright green grasshopper that warned him that the closer he got to the center, the stickier the strands of the web. The grasshopper was sitting at the far corner of the web, shouting for Seba to stay to the outer edges. The warnings came too late. Seba struggled against the sticky strands, and as he looked down, he saw that he was between the two short legs of the spider, unable to escape from the web. The tangle of filaments increasingly tightened around him the more he strained against them. He kicked, shrieked, and called for help, but the web continued to close in. He awoke in a pool of sweat, with the cotton sheet tangled around his legs and one arm. The horses and donkeys again brayed their displeasure with Seba's unsettling nightmares. The loft above Buğra's stable was dark, but he could hear the owls calling to each other, signaling that the sky would soon lighten.

Again, he knew he wouldn't be able to go back to sleep, and he thought that seeing Meleia would chase the darkness away, so he got dressed and climbed down the ladder to the stable. He walked to the Aigokeros in the early morning hours, the sound of the nightjars clucking from the scrubby bushes in the hills. He found Meleia behind her taverna, putting chickens on the spit. In several hours, they would be ready for the midday meal. He told her about his conversation with Linus the day before.

"Of course, I have a great recipe for çilbir, Seba! I was born and raised in Smyrna, wasn't I?" Meleia squinted at Seba and jutted out her chin.

Seba grinned. "And I bet you have a special way of making it, like the coffee, don't you?"

She smiled and nodded knowingly. "You're right, I do."

"Are you going to share your secret with me? I won't tell anyone. I probably wouldn't remember it anyway—the ingredients that Linus described were new to me. In fact, I don't even know what Aleppo peppers are."

Meleia's face lit up. "Oh, Seba, they're wonderful, crimson-colored peppers with a hint of heat and a fruity, tangy taste on the tongue. They ripen in August, and you'll see every street in Smyrna festooned with garlands of them drying in the sun in late summer. It's too early for them now, but I have dried pepper flakes from last season that I've stored in my ceramic çini jars over the winter. They are the key to a good çilbir. In fact, I think I will make it for Klydonas tomorrow. Thanks for the idea!"

After talking to Meleia, the memory of Seba's nightmare

faded quickly. She was too busy to talk any longer, however, so Seba wished her a good day and they planned to see each other at Klydonas.

The Greek citizens of Smyrna had celebrated Klydonas, the annual feast day of Saint John the Baptist, every Midsummer's Day since the fourth century AD in honor of the birth of Saint John. Seba knew that although the other saints of the Bible were celebrated on the dates of their deaths, Saint John the Baptist was celebrated on the date of his birth. The Gospel of Luke stated that John the Baptist was born six months earlier than Jesus. And since Jesus's birth was celebrated on Midwinter's Day, the Greek Orthodox church logically determined that six months before that was Midsummer's Day, the right time to celebrate the prophet who was famous for eating locusts and honey.

It also was a time when the sun, a symbol of fire, movement, creativity, and life, was at its strongest. Seba had always been captivated by fire, ever since he was a small boy sitting on his father's lap in front of the hearth, watching the logs crackle and spark. His father said the sun was a great ball of fire, and sometimes when it was setting upon a long summer day, Seba thought he could see the orb pulsing and sending out waves of heat and light upon the earth. Once, when Seba was only five or six years old, he sat on his father's lap while his grandfather told him the story of Hephaestus, god of forge and fire.

Now Seba, I have told you of the births of Athena, Ares, Aphrodite, Hermes, Dionysus, and the twins Apollo and Artemis. They are the offspring of Zeus and his sister wife, Hera. But the birth of their son Hephaestus was altogether different. You see, when Hephaestus was born, Hera did not think he was as beautiful as the child of a goddess should be. No, she found him so ugly that

165

she cast him off Mount Olympus, and he fell for more than a day. The landing did not kill him, but it did render him lame. If not for the kindness of the sea goddesses, Thetis and Eurynome, Hephaestus might not have survived. They nurtured and cared for him, surrounded by Oceanus, and encouraged his inventions and beautiful creations, formed from the fires of undersea volcanoes. He thrived under their care and returned to Olympus a master craftsman, triumphant with the passion for creation that he cultivated under the protection and tutelage of the sea goddesses.

However, when he returned to Mount Olympus, his siblings could not see past his deformities. They thought him inferior, solely because he required the assistance of two gold canes to traverse the royal pathways of Mount Olympus. They had no appreciation for the artistry and ingenuity of Hephaestus's creations or the fact that he created those gorgeous machines that enabled him to walk. He fashioned his golden canes from the fires of his volcanic forge, along with many other ornaments and magical trinkets of his brilliant imagination, yet they dismissed him as subordinate to their greatness. It was not until they needed tools, weapons, shields, and other magical apparatuses that they came to understand his value. They begged Hephaestus to shower them with his extraordinary creations, and he had every right to refuse his siblings, who had derisively taunted him his whole life.

He did not do it, Seba! Hephaestus is a shining example of what we all should be. He forgave his siblings and got to work at his volcanic forge. He made Apollo's sword and shield, Hermes's helmet and winged sandals, Athena's spear and shield, Aphrodite's belt, Artemis's arrows, and Ares's chariot. He also made the shield of Achilles, Heracles's breastplate, and the adamantine blade that Perseus used to behead the gorgon Medusa. In addition to weapons and armor, Hephaestus created the exquisite palaces of each of the Olympians, golden attendants to assist him with his creations, the crown of Pandora, and the *necklace of Harmonia.*

Hephaestus is the god of fire and the forge, and he is the smith and armorer of the gods. He is the patron god of both smiths and weavers, with great healing powers because of his kind, peace-loving nature. All of these creations came from fire, which is why I became a blacksmith, working the forge like the patron of all master craftsmen, Hephaestus. With fire, my grandson, you can make and create anything, including, like Hephaestus, a life of beauty and art from the inspiration of the mind.

Ever since he had heard that story from his grandfather, Seba had associated fire with creativity and potential. And every time he thought of his father, his heart burned as if there were a fire inside him—one that would continue to grow until he accomplished his goal. He *would* find his father. That's why this time of year gave him hope—he felt like he could do anything. The Festival of Saint John was named for one of the Bible's most fiery characters, and it was celebrated at the time of year when the sun's fire burned the brightest. Probably the most popular part of the Festival of Saint John, however, was the Klydonas tradition of fire jumping.

On the eve of Saint John's Day, in accordance with tradition, unmarried women of Smyrna gathered in one of the homes of the Greek quarter, and one of them would fetch water from the neighborhood's well. This woman was said to bring the *siopyló neró*, or silent water, back to the home. The water, of course, was always silent, but in this case, it was doubly silent because the woman fetching the water was forbidden to speak to anyone on her return from the neighborhood's well.

Once the silent water carrier entered the house, she carefully poured her haul into a clay pot. Each unmarried woman from the quarter then placed a personal trinket inside the pot. Then the pot was covered with a heavy stone disc, around which a long red sash was tied. That evening, the girls prayed to Saint John to bring them blessings in the coming year. The pot was then carried out into the center of the Greek quarter, and fresh flowers and greenery were placed around it and left overnight. A girl from Seba's village, Xenia, who had chased after him for years, once told him that she had dreamed about marrying him on the eve of Saint John's Day. He was mortified and thought she must be mistaken, but after investigation, he learned that girls who place trinkets in the pot will dream and see their future husband.

Seba was beginning to understand the mix of cultures in Smyrna. He had not expected that Greek Christians would be permitted to practice their religion in the Ottoman city, but he was pleasantly surprised when he was disavowed of that incorrect assumption. As he walked through Enymeria Market on the day before the festival, he encountered Buğra, who was Seba's resident expert on all things Ottoman, and who was happy to educate him.

"Sultan Mustafa III is generally lenient when it comes to religious freedoms across the empire. If I'm correct, your Ottoman overseers on Chios were more concerned with your treatment of the mastiha than they were with your exercise of Christianity."

Seba nodded thoughtfully. "You're right. Most of the punishments came from people stealing mastiha, not from any Christian activities. And we went to church every day during the Christmas and Epiphany celebrations. I guess I never thought about it."

Buğra said, "The same applies here in Smyrna—even more so perhaps—because the European merchants provide immense amounts of wealth through trade with the empire, and they are predominantly Christian."

"What do you mean?" Seba knew that Buğra had a unique perspective, because Buğra and his father worked in the Ottoman clerk's office. They understood the day-to-day affairs of residents of all of the Smyrnean neighborhoods, each a unique and important part of the whole.

"Haven't you noticed that here in the Greek quarter, it's almost like you are living as Greeks did prior to the ascension of the Ottoman empire?"

"Yes, that surprised me very much when I arrived."

"Well, it's the same for the other neighborhoods. I'm guessing you may not have ventured into the Jewish, Armenian, and Levantine areas, but they enjoy the same freedoms as the Greek Christians to express their cultural and religious beliefs."

Seba said, "It's hard to comprehend, because I was raised to understand that the Ottomans were our oppressors. That fact was confirmed the day they kidnapped my father and whisked him away to Constantinople."

"I'm sorry that happened to you, Seba. That is not our experience with the Ottoman government in Smyrna. We work together cooperatively, for the good of all the citizens of our great city. The sultan understands that managing his citizens is like holding grains of sand in his hands: the more he tightens his grip, the more sand disappears through his fingers."

"I wish that also applied to mastiha and building ships. Maybe then my family would be together."

"Cheer up, Seba. You'll find your father. You were brave enough to cross the Strait of Chios without a boat, and act befitting of the heroes of ancient Greece."

"Thank you, Buğra. Every time I talk to you, I feel better."

"We'll all feel better when we've celebrated the day of John, Son of Zechariah, one of Allah's greatest prophets."

"Wait, don't tell me that Muslims celebrate Saint John's Day, too?"

Buğra laughed. "Seba, it amazes me how you like to create division between the Christians and Muslims. As I said, I am born of both worlds, and I see the similarities much more than the differences. John the Baptist is known as Yahya, a prophet of Islam. His birth was a miracle, as he was the son of two elderly parents: Elizabeth and the prophet Zechariah. You may recall that Zechariah was the uncle and protector of Mary, mother of Jesus. Yahya lived a simple and ascetic life, grateful for all he was given. He baptized people during his lifetime to cleanse them in spirituality, bringing them closer to Allah, or God."

Seba smiled. "I can see that Meleia is not my only teacher in this city. She might be tutoring me in foreign languages, but you're teaching me about life. I appreciate it, my friend, and I feel lucky to have met you."

"Let's see how much luck you have staying sober at the festival tomorrow." Buğra lifted an imaginary mug to his mouth and pretended to drink it.

14 FESTIVAL OF SAINT JOHN

June 24, the day of the Klydonas festival, dawned just as fiery as the saint for which it was named. Shimmering waves of heat rose up from the cobbled stones of the Greek quarter even though the midsummer sun had scarcely crested the eastern mountains surrounding Smyrna.

Each family had donated something to the feast day, and Enymeria Market was bustling with the happy sounds of neighborhood partygoers preparing for the celebration that would begin later that afternoon. All of the roads leading into the bazaar had been blocked off from the usual traffic of donkeys, ponies, and camels, and tables of food were installed around the perimeter of the market square. Meleia had been slow-roasting lamb kebabs for over twenty-four hours, and they were expertly spiced with lemon, oregano, paprika, thyme, and black pepper. The Grey Heron had donated its summer specialty, as well: finger-sized dolmas filled with savory ground meats, vegetables, and brown rice, covered in a thick avgolemono sauce of lemon, olives, and egg.

Anything and everything that could be cooked over a fire had been duly seared, from guinea fowl and lamb to sea bream and prawns pulled out of the harbor before sunrise. The city's great brick ovens had been used to bake *pastitsio*, *spanikopita*, and layers of tomato-simmered *moussaka*. The bakeries supplied their favorite cakes, from honey-dripped, fruited yeast cakes to delicate galaktoboureko filled with a creamy, lighter-than-air cheese.

When it was time for the celebration to begin in earnest, Seba, Paolo, and Buğra searched for the best location to view the festivities. They found a bench on the northern side of the market square, not far from the many tables of food. Two younger boys had tried to stake out the same location, but given the fact that this bench was particularly close to the huge stone jars of wine and ale, Paolo explained to them rather convincingly that it was in their best interest to find another spot.

"The younger generation becomes bolder with every passing year," Paolo said, clapping his hands together several times, as if he had just taken out the garbage.

Buğra chuckled. "You didn't have to threaten them with bodily harm. It is the Klydonas festival, after all."

"Yes, and just like Saint John, these youngsters need to understand their place in the world."

Seba said, "Well, you just made it very clear that their place is nowhere near these jars of wine."

Paolo held up his mug in agreement, flexing his bicep at the same time. *"Apolytos."* Absolutely. Seba laughed so hard that the avgolemono sauce on the dolmas he had just eaten threatened to come out his nose.

As the afternoon progressed, Paolo and Buğra regaled Seba with stories of their childhoods in Smyrna, and Seba reflected on the contrast of growing up in a large metropolitan area versus his sheltered youth in the remote Chian village of Sessera.

They gorged themselves for several hours, filled their mugs liberally from the stone amphorae, played games with the children, listened to what Paolo said were the same stories the older generation had told at every Klydonas festival since he could remember, and watched the cats and dogs chase each other around the square. Seba noted that like in Sessera, the citizens worked very hard, but during the festival days, they put even more energy into celebrating. As the sun waned in the western sky, the neighborhood's best musicians took the stage, and an air of eager anticipation fell over the square.

Seba looked around to see almost everyone in the square remove some kind of musical instrument from their pockets or a nearby basket. The instruments ranged from the rudimentary, such as a pair of wooden sticks, to the elaborate, such as large round-holed *flogheras* and various sizes of long-necked lutes.

Buğra reached into the pocket of his trousers and offered Seba a harmonica. "Seba, you look like you could play one of these."

Seba took the harmonica and blew into it, searching his memory for a tune that his grandfather, Papouli, had taught him. "Thanks, Buğra. I used to play this back home on Chios. I hope I remember."

Fortunately, the wine and barley ale had lubricated his memory. The musicians were playing a traditional Greek dance, and Seba recognized it, so he began playing, at first tentatively, but then with confidence as the memory of the tune returned to him. By the end of the song, Seba's face was glowing and his cheeks were red from puffing in and out.

Seba took a break and walked to the stone jar that was filled with water. He knew that he would be asleep before long if he tried to maintain Paolo's wine-guzzling pace.

As he looked around, he spotted Meleia, who was dressed even more brightly than usual, and whose curls were not pinned up in a knot on her head. Seba had never seen her with her hair down, and he didn't believe it was possible, but she was more beautiful than ever. Meleia danced with everyone, her face flushed as she threw her head back and laughed when the owner of the Grey Heron spun her around like a top. As Seba gulped several cups of water, the band launched into a tripatos, and Seba felt a twinge of nostalgia, remembering the many festivals that he had shared with his family on Chios. His grandfather was a great dancer, often singing and stepping the tripatos. He put his cup down and both hands dropped to his sides. *I miss my family.* He knew that Mama and Papouli were probably singing and dancing in Sessera, and sharing dolmas with avgolemono. Before Seba could fall deeper into melancholy, he felt Paolo's hands on his back, shoving him toward Meleia.

Meleia grabbed Seba's hands and whirled with him in the open air, dancing the three steps all around Enymeria Square. Seba could have danced with her until sunrise. At some point, she leaned in toward his ear and said, "You didn't tell me you were such a good dancer," as they stepped and turned through the tripatos.

Seba replied, "Especially when I have a good partner," and he gave a little kick of his heels like his Papouli always did when he was entertaining a crowd.

Meleia laughed heartily and they continued to strut and step along with the other dancers until they were so out of breath that they fell onto the benches by the side of the street, faces red and beaming with joy. Meleia had cured him of his melancholy.

The atmosphere changed to one of unbridled excitement as the sun sank lower over the western stalls of the market. It was then that three piles of sand, spaced a few yards apart in a straight line in the center of the street, became the focus of everyone's attention. The children ran back to their homes and returned with armfuls of dried flowers, wreaths, and stems, which they placed reverently on the piles of sand. In a matter of minutes, the stacks of twigs and flowers became precariously positioned towers that, by the time twilight beckoned, were almost as tall as Seba. People were laughing, talking, and drinking everything from tea to raki. Paolo, the self-appointed keeper of the *aqua vitae*, made sure the stone amphorae remained full of wine and ale. Children were running around everywhere, full of sugar and zeal. As the deepening twilight made it more difficult for Seba to see his hand in front of his face, the local priest lit the fires.

The three towers flamed up immediately, the sun-baked wreaths and dried flowers serving as ideal fuel to ignite the fire. In a flash, the fires were raging, taller than a man standing on another's shoulders, but people continued to throw more wreaths on the blazes, causing them to crackle and snap with fierce energy. The priest then gave a short speech, thanking God for the beauty and bounty of the earth, thanking John the Baptist for paving the way for the teachings of Jesus to be heard and understood by everyone in the land, and thanking the citizens of Smyrna for joining in the feast of Saint John.

"And now we ask our children to show their bravery. Who will show the strength of their ancient Greek heritage by jumping the fire? Who will show that they walk with Jesus and will not be burned by the flames? Who will have the courage to face their fears and emerge victorious, warding off evil, pestilence, and disease in the coming year?"

The children all yelled loudly, some of them throwing their hands in the air, but when the priest gestured at the first red-hot fire, the children looked at the flames, as high as a man's head, and swiftly retreated behind their mothers' skirts.

Seba could see the fear in their faces. He had jumped the fire in the village square in Sessera every year since he could remember. He had been as scared as these children the first time, but Brother Tim had encouraged him with enthusiasm and confidence, and after he had jumped the fire, he felt like the most powerful boy on earth! Now, as a young man, he knew that he could give these frightened children the same gift that Brother Tim had given him. They needed the fiery confidence and creativity of Hephaestus to run through their veins, and Seba knew what to do to inspire it.

He jumped on a bench and called out to the children, "We are Greek, aren't we?"

The children responded cautiously from behind their mothers' skirts. "Yes."

"Our brother Jesus walks by our side, doesn't He?"

"Yes!" The response was a bit louder this time.

"We have no reason to fear the fire when the courage of our ancestors, our heroes, and the blood of Jesus course through our veins!"

"Yes!"

"Will you follow me in jumping the fire?"

Seba jumped off the bench and ran to the first flaming mound.

"Yes!" A few of the braver children were now approaching the fires.

"Join hands and follow me!" Seba reached for the hand of an older boy who had been encouraged by Seba's words. That boy held on tight to Seba and took his sister's hand. As he looked over his shoulder, Seba saw a chain of children forming behind him. Seba led the parade of children to the first blazing fire and he nodded to the boy and his sister. *You can do it.*

Seba crouched down, showing the boy and his sister how to ready their legs like two springs that when released, would launch them over the fire. He ran and jumped, lifting the boy and his sister over the first flaming mound, and everyone cheered! As they catapulted over the second and third fires, Seba turned and saw that the chain of children was unbroken. He watched as each child triumphed over the final flaming tower, and the children who had gone before them laughed and hugged each other, raising the youngest ones above their heads in celebration. Their parents clapped and shouted, and as the chain continued to leapfrog over the fires, some of the children who had conquered their fears ran into the crowd, taking the shy ones' hands and helping them to jump the fires. Some of the older boys and girls lifted the babies out of their mothers' arms and carried them through the fires, to make sure that they would be protected in the coming year and that they could proclaim that they had the courage to jump the fire the first year after they were born.

After every child and infant had jumped the fire as many times as they wanted, the flames slowly dwindled until they were three crimson heaps smoldering in the dark. At that point, the women carried the silent water pot from its place of prominence and poured it over the fires to put them out.

They all held up their cups, and Meleia handed Seba a mug of raki. "Congratulations! Those children needed a bit of inspiration, and you gave it to them. I'm proud of you."

Seba took the mug from Meleia and tipped the entire contents of it into his upturned mouth. It burned his throat and made his eyes water, but he didn't care, because he was a man who had seen the fear in those children's eyes and encouraged them to overcome it. Seba felt like Hephaestus triumphing over his detractors. Hephaestus created his own reality, rising above his siblings' cruel contempt, and Seba felt as if the fire jumping gave him the courage to make his own reality, too. *I'm going to find my father.*

As the bright glow of a full moon shone through the square, the assembly of musicians played the traditional folk dances. Whereas the late afternoon dancing had been a free-for-all, these dances were more formal, and involved the partygoers following the steps together. The revelers linked arms, sang, danced, clapped, snapped, tapped, and enjoyed the time-honored traditions that had been passed down to them for centuries. The June evening air from the Gulf of Smyrna had cooled the heat of the day, but Seba remained warm in the glow of the merriment. Buğra's face was red with exertion from the dancing, and Paolo was sweating as he managed to lock arms with every girl in the neighborhood. Seba laughed as Paolo threw his hands in the air and kicked his boots in time to the music.

Seba said to Meleia, "Thank you. It's a beautiful night, isn't it?"

She was standing with her hands on her hips in a bright red skirt with a white blouse and a dark blue sash. Her face was flushed pink from all of the dancing, and she smiled sweetly at Seba. Seba had a full stomach, he had enjoyed a wonderful celebration of the feast of Saint John the Baptist with his new friends in the city of Smyrna, and the girl of his dreams had just congratulated him. The moonlight peeking between the buildings in the square reflected in Meleia's eyes, and she looked like Aphrodite. Not that he would ever mention that again.

"Yes, it is," Meleia replied contentedly.

"Now that I've proven myself as a good dancer and expert fire jumper, would you like to share another dance with me?"

Seba expected a sassy reply, but instead, she placed her hands on his shoulders and said, "How could I refuse those gray-green eyes?"

Meleia was not the first person to mention Seba's eyes. Xenia, the girl from his village who had been trying to marry Seba since they were eight years old, had said his eyes were the color of the raging sea in winter. Seba had considered Xenia a pest and a busybody like Linus, but the last time they had spoken, she admitted that she loved Seba, and she wanted them to be together. Seba had not been interested in getting married to Xenia; she didn't seem to understand that he did not want a life of slavery on Chios.

Meleia was different, however, because she was more worldly, and she had a fire inside her that Seba found enticing. If Meleia said she couldn't refuse Seba's eyes, that was fine with him. Seba took Meleia's hand and jumped into the circle alongside Paolo, Buğra, and the crowd of dancers. They danced and sang to the traditional midsummer melodies, fingers locked together as they and the others moved through the streets in a circle.

To Seba's surprise, one of the women playing the *kithara* began calling for Meleia to join them on the stage. Another musician held out a *tambouras*, gesturing for Meleia to take it from her.

He looked at Meleia. She had never mentioned being a musician. *Could she be any more perfect?*

Aloud, Seba asked, "Do you play the tambouras?"

Meleia was waving her arms across her chest, signifying to the woman playing the kithara that she did not want to join them. The other musician had been walking toward Meleia with the tambouras in her hand but stopped at the sight of Meleia's frowning face.

"I did when I was a child. They want me to sing. But I haven't sung in years, and I don't intend to do it now."

"I'll bet your voice is beautiful, like you."

Meleia looked flattered, and Seba was pleasantly surprised that he hadn't been chastised for complimenting her. However, he was shocked when Meleia released his hand, looked around, and said, "Fine, I'll sing a song. But only one."

She took the tambouras, strummed it a few times to ensure it was in tune, and began:

*Το γιασεμί στην πόρτα σου
γιασεμί μου
ήρθα να το κλαδέψω ωχ
γιαβρί μου
και νόμισε η μάνα σου
γιασεμί μου
πως ήρθα να σε κλέψω ωχ
γιαβρί μου

Το γιασεμί στην πόρτα σου
γιασεμί μου
μοσκοβολά τις στράτες ωχ
γιαβρί μου
κι η μυρωδιά του η πολλή
γιασεμί μου
σκλαβώνει τους διαβάτες ωχ

γιαβρί μου

*This jasmine outside your door
My jasmine
I came to prune it
 Oh, my love
And your mother thought that
My jasmine
I came to steal you
Oh, my love

This jasmine outside your door
My jasmine
Smells divine
And its abundance
My jasmine
Enslaves all who pass
Oh, my love

Seba had heard that song six short months ago, at the celebration of Saint Vasilios in his village of Sessera. He knew it was a love song because his grandfather's future wife had sung it to him with such adoration in her eyes that he understood what it meant to be in love.

The fact that Meleia chose to sing this song made Seba feel warm inside, like everything and everyone in the world were exactly as they should be. He had not come to Smyrna to find love, but it seemed to be finding him. Seba noticed that several snow-white butterflies appeared in the square, flitting and floating toward Meleia's hands as she strummed the accompaniment to her angelic voice. In fact, the little white butterflies looked like tiny angels with wings that were undulating along with the vibrations of the song.

Seba wished that he could capture this moment: the beauty of Meleia's voice, the tambouras in her hand, her radiant face, and the little white butterflies that couldn't help but join her in this intimate sharing of her soul through music.

When the song was over, everyone clapped enthusiastically, and Seba motioned for Meleia to join him. Embarrassed by all the attention, she waved off the praise and walked over to Seba, who was staring at her dreamily.

Meleia snapped her fingers in front of Seba's face. "Was it so bad that I put you to sleep?"

"No, it was beautiful. Especially with those white butterflies dancing all around you."

Meleia groaned. "Don't start on that business about Aphrodite again. You remember what happened the last time you made that mistake."

"Can't we enjoy this evening?"

"Not if you're always imagining me as Aphrodite!"

"Why not? Don't you feel the same about me? You held my hand when we were practicing French the other day, we danced together, you said you couldn't refuse my eyes, and then you sang that love song—"

"Will you stop mentioning that stupid love song? I knew I shouldn't have sung it. I only sang it because my father sang it to my mother every night when I was a child. He played the tambouras beautifully, and his voice was warm and heavenly, like being swaddled by an angel. I thought maybe if he heard his own daughter singing that song, it might shock him into reality." She hung her head as she pointed to her father, who was on a nearby bench, leaning his back against a post, oblivious to the world. "Obviously, it didn't work."

"I'm sorry. I didn't know."

"That's because you think everything is about you.

Sometimes, I wonder if you really see me for who I am."

Meleia's words were making Seba dizzy. Or maybe it was the raki. He remembered similar words that the girl, Xenia, from Sessera, had said to him, and he tottered over to a bench under a pomegranate tree, whose bright red flowers were beginning to fruit. As he looked up, he saw Meleia hurrying away toward the musicians.

A hand tapped him on the shoulder, and as Seba turned, an old man was offering him a half-empty bottle of wine. The man said, "When a man is exhausted, wine will build his strength."

Seba looked past the bottle and realized that he had stumbled onto the bench occupied by Meleia's besotted father. However, the words that came from his mouth were from Homer's renowned epic poem, the *Iliad*. He hadn't expected Meleia's father to quote the great Greek poet. Meleia made it seem as if he wasn't even lucid.

Taking the bottle and raising it to his lips, Seba said, "I could use some strength right now. It seems like everything I say and do turns into a disaster."

"I know how that feels." The despair in the man's voice struck Seba like a wave.

"Did you quote from Homer's *Iliad*?"

"Yes. He was born in Smyrna, like me. On the banks of the Meles river, by the Caravan Bridge. That's why they called him *Melesigenes*, son of Meles."

Seba now understood Meleia's concerns about her father. *His brain must have been curdled by too much drink.* Seba said gently, "I think you're mistaken, sir. Homer was born on Chios. That's what my grandfather taught me."

Meleia's father laughed, and Seba could see that the few teeth he had were a dark yellow color. The breath that burst past his gap-toothed smile was so foul that Seba had to turn away. Seba pursed his lips and waited for the man to respond before he inhaled again.

"The Chians will try to get ahead any way they can. Homer narrated a few poems on the *Daskelopetra* over there, but he was born here in Smyrna, like me." Meleia's father held out his hand, and Seba returned the wine bottle to him, which he tilted into his open mouth and guzzled until the remaining liquid in the bottle was gone.

Seba was perplexed. Meleia's father wasn't even slurring his words. He sounded like he was Homer's contemporary. And the quote about turning to wine when he was exhausted felt significant, even poignant. It explained exactly how Seba was feeling at the moment.

"Is there anything I can do for you, sir?"

Meleia's father didn't seem to hear Seba. With his eyes closed, he said in a low murmur,

"Even in our sleep, pain which cannot forget
falls drop by drop upon the heart
until, in our own despair, against our will,
comes wisdom through the awful grace of God."

Seba tapped his shoulder, but Meleia's father didn't respond. He had drifted into unconsciousness, where it appeared that even there, he could not escape his pain.

The words of Aeschylus were so full of truth and sorrow that Seba ran through the alley and retched in a barrel filled with food scraps for the animals. He knelt there with his hands around the top of the barrel for a long time. How did he go from being on top of the world, the fire jumper leading the children with courage and heart, to the idiot boy of Sessera who couldn't do or say anything right?

He felt a hand on the back of his neck.

"Did you drink too much raki? I probably shouldn't have given you that last one." The concern in Meleia's voice sounded genuine.

"No, leave me alone." Seba didn't want to talk to Meleia right now.

She said kindly, "You're drunk and I get upset when I think about what happened to my father. Don't worry about it. We'll both feel better in the morning." She rubbed her hand in a circle on Seba's back.

"And by the way, those 'white butterflies' you mentioned are silk moths. You're working in the silk capital of the Ottoman empire; you should at least be able to recognize them."

Seba groaned. *She thinks I'm an imbecile.*

Meleia asked, "Do you want me to ask Buğra to take you home?"

"No, I'm fine. I'm really sorry."

"I know." Meleia gave an exasperated sigh. "Good night, Seba."

15 FISHING

The next day, Seba, Buğra, and Paolo were fishing on the south side of the harbor, hoping the fresh salt air would cure their hangovers. It was so early that the sun had not yet ascended beyond the eastern mountains of Smyrna, and the breeze coming from the Aegean Sea felt good on their faces. Seba's stomach was queasy, but being near the water and breathing in the fresh salt air was a reliable cure. The three of them had done well that morning, each having caught a decent-sized barbouni that would satisfy their appetites for the evening meal. Sometimes they dropped their catches off at the Aigokeros, and Meleia cooked them for dinner when the workday was over. They hoped that today would be one of those days.

Paolo dipped his line in the water and asked, "Where did you disappear to last night, Seba? One moment you were dancing with Meleia, and the next you were gone."

Seba didn't want to talk about it. "Nowhere."

"You drank too much raki, didn't you? I told Buğra that

you weren't accustomed to the level of celebrations we have here in Smyrna. Have you ever had a hangover before?"

Seba was indignant. "No, it wasn't that, it's that I always seem to say the wrong thing to Meleia, and I can't figure out why."

"What did you say to her? I told you if she was unhappy, she might spit in our food." Paolo held up the creel containing the fish they had caught so far that morning. "Or what if she burns our dinner on purpose?"

"It was nothing."

Buğra blinked his eyes several times but remained silent. Seba was grateful; it was one of the many reasons that Buğra was such a good friend.

Paolo said, "By the way, did you ever ask Stavros for a job for me? I need wages in order to satisfy my stomach. I'm not that good of a fisherman."

Seba replied, "He isn't happy with me right now, because the workshop's resident busybody told him that Meleia was teaching me a few English words, and Stavros gets angry any time someone mentions England or anything English. I'm not in a position to ask him anything at the moment."

Paolo's face fell, and he stared at his basket of fish, mournfully imagining life as a fisherman.

He looked so pitiful that Seba said, "I could ask Eleni. She's much easier to talk to, although I'm not sure if she has the authority to hire anyone. It seems like Stavros has the final word on those kinds of things."

Paolo put his arm on Seba's shoulder. "I'd appreciate anything you can do to help. If my sisters were here, they'd be so proud to know that I landed a job at a Smyrnean silk factory."

True to his word, Seba brought Paolo to work with him that day. He knew that Paolo made a good first impression with his size and muscularity, not nearly as big as Hector and Marco, but similar in build.

They walked together into Eleni's office and Seba closed the door behind them. Paolo whistled as he looked around at all the books, and his eyes focused on the clepsydra.

"Eleni, this is my friend, Paolo. As you can see, he is strong, and he is a hard worker. He has not been treated fairly by the barge owners, and I told him that you, in particular, cared for your workers as if they were your family. We were hoping that you might find a position for him here."

Eleni's gaze drifted from Paolo to Seba and back again. Despite being ambushed, she appeared pleased at the interruption.

"A pleasure to make your acquaintance, Paolo. Your timing is impeccable. Stavros and I were talking about our employees last evening, although I wish he would stop calling them his little silkworms—it's demeaning. Stavros wants to hire a replacement for the employee who used to maintain the ledger book. He and his brother no longer work here, and Stavros can't function unless he knows exactly who visited the factory, including their arrival and exit times. In fact, Stavros was planning to send Linus down to the harbor this evening to solicit a clerk."

Paolo clapped his hands and said, "To work personally with the great Stavros Alkeidis? My grandmother would be so proud. She worked for your father many years ago."

Seba's jaw dropped and his head whipped around to face Paolo. "She did? You never mentioned her."

Paolo was ebullient. "Yes, when Mr. Alkeidis operated the tailoring and mending shop, he became so busy that he needed a few additional seamstresses to complete his orders. My grandmother said it was her honor to work for him, and he was very kind and fair as an employer."

Eleni smiled. "He was a very kind and fair father as well. If you have no qualms about keeping a ledger, then I believe we can welcome you to our happy textile family. I'm sure Stavros won't mind that I've hired you—he'll appreciate your size as you greet the visitors—the same way he loves Hector and Marco lurking around the shop, keeping everyone in line."

Paolo was nearly bouncing out of his boots with excitement. "When should I start? I can't believe that I'm going to work for the illustrious Stavros Alkeidis. Thank you so much!"

Eleni crinkled her nose. "On second thought, I don't know if I can stomach another of my brother's worshipers working for us. One Linus at the Alkeidis factory is enough for me."

Seba laughed, but Paolo turned serious. "I meant no offense. I promise I'll keep my worshiping to myself."

Now it was Eleni's turn to chuckle at Paolo's earnestness. "Seba, why don't you show Paolo around the workshop before you begin your tasks for the day? And Paolo, meet me back here in my office later this afternoon so I can explain the ledger to you."

Seba couldn't tell whether he or Paolo was more pleased that day, and they walked the halls together, Paolo's head on a swivel as he absorbed as much as he could of his new workplace. The most entertaining part of the day for Seba, however, was when he introduced Paolo to Linus.

"Linus, this is my friend, Paolo. He's going to be keeping

the visitor ledger for Stavros."

"Oh, Seba, you've brought one of your friends to work with us at the shop? Any friend of yours is sure to be one of mine. This is wonderful! And you've saved me a trip to the wharf, because Eleni mentioned something about me going to the docks to find a clerk."

Paolo extended a hand, but Linus had already engulfed Paolo in an embrace as if they were long-lost relatives. "My name is Linus, and I've worked here for many years. In fact, you could consider me one of Stavros's closest confidants — after his sister Eleni, of course. I know all of the employees by name, their families, and how long they've worked here, so if there is ever anything you need to know about the Alkeidis Tapestry Workshop, please do not hesitate to look for me. I'm often in the dyeing room, but I also help Eleni with anything she needs to make the workshop run most efficiently. She says I'm her most dependable employee. No offense, Seba."

Seba fought to choke back the peals of laughter that were trying to escape, and he croaked, "None taken."

Linus continued talking and hugging Paolo, at the same time patting him on the back. Paolo was trying to extricate himself without appearing rude. Linus was so small and skinny, and Paolo so big and muscular, that Seba knew Paolo could have escaped in the fraction of a second if he wanted to. Seeing Paolo squirm uncomfortably was so comical that Seba couldn't wait to get to the Aigokeros that evening and tell Buğra all about it.

Paolo managed to pull away, saying, "Thank you, Linus. I will be sure to call on you when I have a question." Then Paolo looked pleadingly at Seba, which made him laugh out loud.

A frown passed over Linus's face. "What's so funny,

Seba?"

"I'm so happy that we all will be working together— I can't contain my joy."

Linus's countenance brightened, and he patted Seba warmly on the shoulder. "I know how you feel! I love it when someone new comes to work at the shop. We'd rather see them coming than leaving." He put his arm conspiratorially around Paolo's shoulder. "We had a bad time several weeks ago. One of the employees was caught stealing. Of course, his brother said he didn't do it, but you know that twins will defend each other no matter the circumstances. We lost two employees that day, so it's good to have our ranks growing again. I'll have to show you the indigo dyeing room. You'll need a handkerchief to wear over your nose, though. I'm used to it, of course, but it's quite a bad smell. Oh, never mind me, I don't want to put you off this work on your first day. I think we're going to be great friends, Paolo. . . ."

Linus was talking as Seba walked away, chuckling to himself.

#

Paolo's enthusiasm for the workshop was contagious. He always arrived early, greeted all of the workers with a hearty "good morning," and asked every worker if he could be of assistance to them. He quickly became a favorite of the women working the looms, and didn't even complain about the awful smell coming from the indigo dyeing room. *Working on the barges must be much harder than I thought, if Paolo is this thrilled to be here.*

One of the jobs Paolo was given was to make sure that Stavros received a list, at the end of the day, of every broker, trader, and customer who had any business in the shop. It wasn't a difficult job, because everyone who walked through the workshop's doors to conduct business had to sign a ledger that included their name, whom they met with, and whom they represented. Paolo's job was to keep the ledger and bring the list of visitors to Stavros at the end of each day. Previously, Stavros had retrieved the list himself, but Seba could tell that Stavros enjoyed the idea of having Paolo as his personal errand boy, and Paolo enjoyed what he considered to be a place of prominence working for the great Stavros Alkeidis.

That was until several days later, when someone failed to sign the ledger.

"You are lying to me!" Seba heard Stavros's voice booming from inside his office at the end of the day. Paolo had passed him with the day's page from the ledger in his hand, so Seba knew that Paolo was in Stavros's office and that Stavros was probably directing his accusations at his friend.

Seba couldn't tell what Paolo was saying in response, but Stavros was screaming at the top of his lungs, his gravelly voice reverberating through the hallways.

"I will not tolerate anyone hiding anything from me in my own workshop! Nothing escapes my attention, and no one will take one step in this factory without my knowledge or approval!"

Seba heard more indistinguishable mumbling, which must have been Paolo trying to defend himself.

"I trusted you to work for me, and this is how you repay me? I saw Monsieur Ducasse in the shop, and his name is not on the list! I demand to know what game you're playing at."

Seba ran back to the front door where the ledger was

kept and searched feverishly for Monsieur Ducasse's name. After frantically thumbing through the remaining pages, Seba saw what had happened. Monsieur Ducasse had run out of space and had flipped several pages ahead in the ledger, which Paolo must not have seen because there were several blank pages between them. Seba pulled the page with Monsieur Ducasse's name on it and ran to Stavros's office, knocking loudly on the door.

"What is it?" Stavros boomed.

"Uh, there was a page that was stuck in the ledger, and I heard you mention Monsieur Ducasse. Can I come in?"

The door swung open with a great force, and Seba saw Paolo standing next to Stavros's desk, face red and looking stunned. Seba held the paper up to Stavros, whose expression was contorted with rage.

Stavros snatched the paper out of Seba's hand and stomped over to his desk. He pulled the magnifying glass from his desk and examined the paper. When he spoke again, his voice was its typical low tenor. "Paolo, why didn't you see this page?"

Seba started to answer, but Stavros held up a hand and glared at him.

Paolo said, "I looked at the page behind today's ledger sheet, but it was blank, so I thought it was the complete list. I'm sorry, I didn't know."

Stavros twisted the gold ring around his finger. "Trust and excellence are two of the most important attributes that I require of my silkworms. I thought I could depend on you, Paolo, but now I don't know."

Seba blurted out, "Paolo is one of the most loyal people I know. He wasn't used to looking for the additional pages, and Monsieur Ducasse doesn't have the best eyesight, so he probably didn't notice he was signing the wrong page. Eleni had me deliver a çatma to him on the *Endeavor* a few days ago, because he's one of our more difficult customers. Don't worry, I'll make sure Paolo doesn't make any mistakes."

Stavros glared at Seba. "Fine. If you're going to guarantee that Paolo does his job competently, then I'll hold you both responsible for any future mistakes."

Seba swallowed hard. He didn't need any more responsibilities that would keep him from searching the docks for his father, but he couldn't let Stavros treat Paolo like a criminal for making a simple error in delivering the day's visitor ledger.

"Get out, both of you, and I don't want to see your faces until tomorrow morning."

Paolo jumped out of the chair and practically ran past Seba out of Stavros's office and out the back door. Seba followed behind. As they walked to the Aigokeros, they didn't speak to each other.

#

Eleni must have heard what happened to the boys (probably from Linus, Seba thought), because she sent word to them at the Aigokeros that evening to meet her in the workshop's kitchen the next morning for a special treat. In what appeared to be a gesture of apology for her brother's temper, she invited them to learn another aspect of the business. Although Seba would have preferred to spend the morning on the waterfront asking questions about his father's whereabouts, Eleni had been so generous and gracious that he could not refuse her request.

Paolo was sulking over what he called Stavros's overreaction, and Eleni seemed to understand his frustration. Walking to the workshop's kitchen, Eleni asked,

"Have you ever heard the advice of Hippocrates regarding bad moods?"

Paolo and Seba replied that they hadn't.

"He says, 'If you are in a bad mood go for a walk. If you continue in a bad mood, go for another walk,' but I've improved upon it in this way: If you are in a bad mood, drink a glass of tea. If you continue in a bad mood, drink another glass of tea."

Seba could tell from Paolo's expression that he did not think tea was going to solve his dilemma with Stavros, but he brightened when Eleni continued, "Although that advice is more of a personal nature, I find tea to be an integral part of the Alkeidis business model. Tea happens to play a great role in our ability to attract and retain the best customers. Our hospitality is what sets the Alkeidis Tapestry Workshop apart from our competitors, and today I'm going to show you the right way to offer hospitality."

"You mean we're going to learn how to serve tea to the guests?" A smile began to appear on Paolo's face. "I thought that you and Linus were the only ones who were allowed to serve the guests."

"Yes, Paolo, that's exactly what I mean. Linus and I have been very busy, and we have many more customers these days, especially from France. It would be helpful to us if you and Seba could assist us in this part of our business."

Paolo asked, "Does this mean that I'm not in trouble anymore?"

Eleni sighed. "You made a mistake, Paolo, and sometimes my brother reacts a bit too strongly when people make mistakes. You're not in trouble. And if you and Seba learn how to offer hospitality to our guests and make them feel welcome, you will be providing a valuable service to your employer."

Seba said, "I've heard some of the merchants mention that you make the best tea in Smyrna."

Eleni smiled and said, "I'm glad, Seba. The success of a business is not based solely on monetary transactions. There is much more involved, including making our customers feel so comfortable, so at home here, that they could not imagine doing business with any other textile workshop. They would feel like they were abandoning their family."

Eleni walked over to a cabinet that held several glass jars full of what appeared to be earthy bricks, dark green and brown. Lifting one of the lids from a glass jar, Eleni said, "The best Turkish tea must have the best leaves, which is why my prized bricks of *pu-erh* tea create the best-tasting brew in the city. I purchased these bricks from a Silk Road trader who said if I wanted to buy the tea prior to its arrival at the port for weighing, I'd have to climb atop the camel myself and pull it from the leather pouch hanging from the camel's hump. So, I did exactly that! To think that this little brick came all the way from the city of Yunnan in China. It's an extraordinary time we live in, isn't it?"

Seba and Paolo agreed heartily.

"Do you know the best way to test whether tea leaves are of the highest quality?"

Seba and Paolo shook their heads in unison.

"Well, the simplest way, as I was taught by my mother, is to test a leaf by floating it in a cup of cold water. If it changes color slowly, it is a good leaf. The goal is to have absolutely no trace of bitterness in the tea, which means the water cannot be overboiled or too hot when it touches the leaves."

She retrieved a dark brick of tea from the glass jar and broke a piece off the corner of the brick. She then returned the brick to the jar and replaced the lid. She worked the little clump of tea between her fingers until all the leaves separated. She put them in a small ceramic dish and set them aside.

Seba was thinking of the difference between Turkish coffee, which, according to Meleia, had to be boiled twice, and Turkish tea, which Eleni cautioned should not be overboiled or too hot. *These women know more about hospitality than I'll ever know.*

"In addition, the leaves and water should not be stirred together violently. They should dance naturally, not like a whirling dervish, but like delicate leaves floating from the branches of the beech trees in autumn."

As she spoke, she removed the *caydanlik*, which was a double-stacked teapot, from its place on a table next to a cast-iron stove. The caydanlik's bottom was a copper pot, decorated with thick horizontal magenta stripes, inside which bright daisies were painted blue, yellow, and green. It had a handle and a spout but no lid. The top teapot was slightly smaller but with exactly the same shape, spout, handle, and decoration, and the addition of a magenta-striped copper lid.

Eleni poured water into the bottom pot and put it over the stove, which was heated by fire. She brought the little ceramic dish of tea leaves from the cabinet, lifted the lid from the smaller pot, and delicately sprinkled the leaves from the dish into the smaller pot. She then placed the smaller pot over the larger pot on the stove.

As the water was heating, she took a slim-waisted glass in her hand, saying, "You see that this little tulip glass, the *ince belli bardak*, has no handles. That means that the guest will be holding the hot glass with two fingers, presumably at the top, where it is slightly wider. As such, we will leave space at the top of the glass when we pour the tea, so the guests will be able to drink the tea without burning their fingers."

The water began to boil, and Eleni poured the water from the bottom pot into the smaller pot that contained the tea leaves. She steeped it for a short time and then placed a sieve over the glasses and poured tea from the top pot. When it became a rich caramel color, she added water to the glasses from the bottom pot, which diluted the color slightly. Eleni then poured again from the top pot, blending the tea and water until it was a bright translucent amber.

As they sipped the tea from the tulip-shaped glasses, Seba said solemnly, "This is delicious. Thank you for sharing this tea ritual with us, Eleni. I've already learned so much from you these last few weeks, and I am grateful for your generosity and everything you've taught us about the silk business."

Eleni looked up from her glass. "It appears that you are about to add a caveat, Sebastian."

"I don't want to seem ungrateful, but you know I'm looking for my father. Stavros promised to speak to his contacts, but whenever I ask him about it, he brushes me away with a wave of his hand, saying that the *meltemi* winds are very difficult this year, keeping the ships away. I don't have access to those same contacts, and it's very frustrating to have come all this way, to be stuck again."

Eleni nodded, and she set her glass of tea on the table.

Seba continued, "I observe ships coming in from the north every week, and I'm wondering why Stavros has no news." Seba felt braver saying this in front of Paolo. If Eleni reprimanded him for being ungrateful, at least he knew Paolo would take his side.

"I see." Eleni's mouth was drawn in a thin line. It was that same worried look she had worn on the day she and

Seba had met—the day the boy's twin brother came to plead his case.

"I'm not asking you to say anything to him. I'm wondering, well, if you could give me the names of a few merchants or captains that I can speak to. I came a long way through extremely difficult circumstances to find my father and try to put my family back together again, and I feel like I'm not getting anywhere."

Paolo leaned forward and said to Eleni conspiratorially, "It's all he has talked about ever since we met. In fact, he's built this man up so much that I feel like if I get to meet him, I won't know how to act. The renowned shipbuilder Kostas Krizomatis is a legend in this city, and he never even lived here."

Eleni took a sip of her tea. "I understand. My father loomed large in my life, and I'm sure it was the same for my siblings. I can relate to the feeling of wanting life to be as it once was."

Paolo crossed his arms in front of him approvingly, as if his words had moved Eleni to agreement.

Seba wasn't so sure, however, and his fears were confirmed when Eleni said, "I'm afraid, however, that life does not move backward. The lives we lived in the past are that—passed. Our job in the present is to move forward doing the best job we know how, without attachment to what the future holds. That is my advice for you."

Eleni's words struck Seba like a bucket of ice-cold seawater. It was as if she was telling him that he was not going to find what he was looking for. The magical atmosphere of the tea-drinking ceremony was abruptly broken, and Seba felt the black tea now gurgling in his stomach. He wanted to run from the room and never smell the loamy scent of tea leaves again.

Paolo put his arm around Seba's shoulders. "I think we should get back to work."

Eleni stood and gathered up the glasses and caydanlik. "You two really remind me of my brothers. Timotheos always said that my conveyance of the truth was accurate, but not as gentle as he would like. I'm sorry, Seba. I've had my hopes with regard to my family's reconciliation dashed so many times that it is hard for me to envision it anymore. Don't let my experience with my brothers dampen your enthusiasm. If you are meant to find your father, I'm sure you will. And if I think of any individuals who might be able to help you, I'll make sure to give you their names."

That didn't make Seba feel any better, although he appreciated Eleni's kindness. *I don't care what she says or what happened in her family; I will find my father.*

16 BROKEN GLASS

The next few days were difficult for Seba because he felt like every time he passed Eleni in the shop, she looked at him with a combination of sadness and pity. *I wish I hadn't confided in her about my father. I can't stand the way she looks at me, like I'm an orphaned puppy.*

Paolo tried to cheer him up in the warehouse as they worked together to match invoices to the finished tapestries for Eleni. "She doesn't know what she's talking about. She's caught between a brother who chose the church and another who is one of the richest men in Smyrna. There are bound to be disagreements and arguments with those two powerful forces at play. She doesn't know anything about your circumstances or your relationship with your father. Plus, she probably feels bad because she knows what an ass Stavros is, and yet she has to work with him every day."

"I hope you're right."

"Of course I'm right, Seba." After being unfairly accused by Stavros, Paolo had redoubled his efforts to prove that he was the best employee the Alkeidis silk factory had ever seen. He worked even longer hours than Seba, and his way of managing Stavros's outbursts was to make sure that he anticipated anything that Stavros wanted. Seba also knew that Paolo appreciated how Seba had defended him in front of Stavros, despite how terrified they both had been.

Seba said, "I'm grateful that you're trying to help me and make me feel better, but the truth is that it doesn't really make me feel any better."

"Really? Jesus and me dancing the tripatos for you doesn't lift your spirits? I don't think your friend the monk would be happy to hear that." Paolo did a little dance step, as he had on the first day they met.

Seba exhaled loudly as he reached for a saffron-colored silk çatma brocaded with silver threads. "I worked so hard to get here, but now I am stuck again, in a different location. I had a friend named Thaddeus in my village on Chios, and he said that because we cultivated the mastiha for the Ottoman empire, we were like donkeys, yoked to a cart and imprisoned by our masters, doomed to drudgery when we really wanted to frolic out in the fields. I somehow managed to escape that form of slavery, only to exchange it for another. I thought I'd be further along in my search for my father by now. He always told me we are descended from the great shipbuilders of ancient Greece, and I feel that call to find him and reclaim my legacy. So why am I slaving away in a textile workshop? I expected Stavros to help me before now."

"I know what you mean. When we first met, I didn't think you would be in Smyrna very long. After that incident with the ledger, I think I understand Stavros a bit better, and he seems to appreciate my strength. He's told me to learn everything I can from Hector and Marco, almost as if he's grooming me to work with them. I don't know if I want to, though, because they seem to fuel his awful temper. He does respond well to flattery, however, like the barge owners I used to work for. Do you want me to talk to him for you?"

"No!"

Paolo jumped back, surprised by the force and volume of Seba's voice.

"I don't need you to fight any battles for me, and I can talk to Stavros myself."

Paolo pinned an invoice on a cyan-colored silk velvet with a design of gilded carnations and tulips. "You let Meleia talk to Stavros for you, but you won't let me?"

Seba grumbled, "I did not let Meleia talk to Stavros for me. She and I were arguing about approaching Stavros, so we did it together. I'm the one who did most of the talking."

"Look what good that did. And now you and Meleia seem to have had a lovers' tiff, although it might be because you drank too much at Klydonas. If you don't want me to talk to Stavros, do you want me to talk to Meleia for you?"

"No!"

Paolo pursed his lips skeptically and crossed his arms over his chest.

Seba said, "Look, Paolo, as I've mentioned to you many times, I appreciate all the help you have given me, and I appreciate that you want to fix things for me. However, it makes me feel inferior, and I don't like that you treat me like a child. There are some things that I need to do for myself — as a man, as the son of Kostas Krizomatis, and as someone who is trying to make a life for myself. You can't live my life for me, and I don't try to live yours for you. Could we agree to treat each other as equals?"

Paolo tilted his head, unconvinced.

"Please? Jesus treated everyone as his equal, and you are his special friend, after all."

Finally, Paolo laughed and held out his hand. "Understood. And so it is, my friend."

They shook, and Seba actually felt much better. It was amazing the change that he felt throughout his body when he stood his ground and told the truth, even when it was uncomfortable and difficult. Feeling inspired, he said, "In fact, I'm going to do something for myself right now. I'm going to confront Stavros and tell him that I will not wait forever for him to help me find my father. He promised he would do it, and I will hold him to that promise."

"Now that's the Sebastian Krizomatis who swam the Strait of Chios! Godspeed and good luck." Paolo made the sign of the cross and then waved Seba out of the warehouse and back to the shop.

Seba threw his shoulders back and tried to channel the confidence of Heracles as he walked into the workshop.

#

Fresh from his talk with Paolo, Seba strode toward Stavros's office feeling strong and confident. He would get his answers, and he might even get them from Eleni *and* Stavros.

Eleni was like Brother Tim—she would be true to her word, and would share a few names of ship captains or officers as soon as she could; Seba knew it. Contemplating Eleni's promise, Seba reached the back door of the workshop and caught a movement from the corner of his eye. He thought he saw a streak of red flash around the corner. *Who would be running away from the workshop in such a hurry?* Even Linus wasn't that fast. Seba considered

206

running after the person, but decided it could have been a trick of the light, especially because he had been lost in thought at the time. He couldn't allow any further distractions from his mission to elicit Stavros's assistance, whether Stavros liked it or not. Seba's chest was puffed out, and his shoulders were pulled back as he strode purposefully toward Stavros's office.

Seba's confidence immediately deflated at the sound of Stavros's angry voice, which was blasting out of Eleni's office. Stavros's rages were becoming more frequent, like the one Seba had witnessed with Paolo a few days earlier. Paolo was right; Stavros's temper was awful.

From inside Eleni's office, Stavros howled, "Don't tell me that you actually met with that poacher! You're plotting against me, aren't you?"

"Stavros, it isn't like that, and you know I would never plot against you. This is our family business."

"I know what I saw—that scoundrel Turnbull walked out the back door. Don't deny it!"

"I'm not denying that he was here, I'm saying that no one is plotting against you. He asked about my designs and inquired whether we were willing to trade with the Levant Company in the New World. I told him we were focusing on France at that moment, but that we might consider other options in the future."

"You expect me to believe that nonsense? He was trying to steal you away from me, wasn't he? He's luring our silkworms away to start a new silk business in East Florida, and he's enticing you to abandon me! That will ruin our business!"

"No! You're letting your imagination get the better of you. Calm down, brother."

"I will not calm down! If it was business, then why did

he run out the back door like a common criminal? Where are Hector and Marco?"

Seba heard something slam on the desk, like a book or a fist. Stavros's voice was at a fever pitch. "How dare you do this to me, your own flesh and blood—it's like Timotheos—he abandoned us before our father died, and now it's happening to me again. You will not get away with it!"

"Brother, your paranoia is clouding your judgment. As it did with Michalis. He didn't deserve to lose his hand, and you jumped to false conclusions. You didn't even give him a chance to—"

"How dare you tell me how to run my business, you traitor!"

"Traitor? I'm the only reason we have a business! I have to go behind you and clean up all your messes because you can't control your temper!"

"*My* messes? You coddle these employees—my silkworms—like they are babies, when we have a substantial business to run. You're probably inciting them to stab me in the back—that's why you met with that English pilferer!"

Seba heard a crash, as if books were falling on the floor, and Eleni screamed, "Stop!"

"I always knew you were against me! You always favored Timotheos! You were waiting for your chance to demolish my life's work!"

Another crash, but this time it was the sound of breaking glass, and Eleni shrieked, "Don't!"

Stavros whipped open the door to Eleni's office and stormed past Seba, not even noticing he was there. Seba rushed into Eleni's office, where the clepsydra was shattered into thousands of pieces of colored glass all over the floor.

Eleni was curled up on the ground, her bloody hands holding the siphon that had been connecting the glass cylinders of the clepsydra. Seba put his hand on her back, and when she looked up, he was horrified to see shards of glass in her face and neck as she sobbed uncontrollably.

"We've got to get you some help."

"No!" She was holding her bloody hands across her face. "No one can know."

"Your face and neck are bleeding, and there's glass everywhere." He looked at her hands and arms, which had tiny flecks of glass in them, from which blood was trickling in little rivulets down between her fingers and onto the floor.

"Go to the kitchen and get some boiling water and towels. Do not speak to anyone."

Seba did as instructed and returned with a stack of cotton towels and a bowl of boiling water. He dipped the towels into the water and helped to clean Eleni's wounds, carefully picking the tiny slivers of glass from her skin.

Eleni's voice was hoarse from screaming at her brother. "Seba, what did you hear?"

"I heard that your brother is uncontrollably violent and that you are in danger."

"You can't tell anyone about this. I haven't seen Stavros this angry since the day Timotheos left for the monastery. Soon after, my father passed away and Stavros felt betrayed by both of them. His paranoia grew and he began acting as if everyone and everything was against him. His obsession with loyalty has magnified so much that I barely recognize him."

Seba said nothing but continued to pick tiny bits of glass from Eleni's face and neck.

"It was very difficult after my father died. Stavros and I

worked tirelessly, and I could see that the more money and power he gained, the less he felt betrayed. I think he views this business as his only means of security, and he protects it like a citadel. I thought that he felt safe when he became one of the most prominent businessmen in Smyrna. But that changed when Dr. Turnbull arrived. Stavros feels threatened by Dr. Turnbull, and Stavros's paranoia has resurfaced. It doesn't help that he spends so much time with Hector and Marco. They're violent, and I'm sure they have ties to the pirates that are the bane of every merchant's existence here. He's not the brother I remember from my childhood anymore."

As Seba swept up the glass and placed it in the garbage bin, he realized that everything Meleia had told him about Stavros rang true. What he had done to Meleia's father, and to the twin brothers who did nothing but their best work for him, and now even his own sister, the only one who understood him.

When the books had been placed back on the shelves, the glass had been cleaned from the furniture, floors, and Eleni's skin, and the blood had been mopped up, Eleni said, "Go out back and burn these cloths, and tell no one of what happened. If Stavros finds out that you know, I cannot predict what he might do."

"But what about your face? The workers are going to see it."

"I'll say there was an accident in my kitchen. If anyone asks you, tell them you don't know anything about it. Especially Linus."

#

At the Aigokeros that evening, Seba couldn't eat, and he

210

hated keeping this horrible secret from Paolo and Buğra. He remembered the scar on Eleni's temple the first day he had met her. *Has Stavros attacked her in the past? Is this a remnant of the earlier time that Stavros felt betrayed?* Seba didn't know what to think. He felt like he was being given strands of information and asked to weave them into the truth. The problem was that he didn't have enough threads. Paolo and Buğra were talking about Dr. Turnbull, as it seemed every citizen in all quarters had been doing for the last few weeks. Seba had been so busy scouring the docks to find sailors with information that he had all but forgotten about Turnbull until he learned that the flash of red he had seen scurrying away from the workshop was the Englishman. Now he considered the doctor with renewed interest.

Buğra said, "Before Meleia threw him out, Turnbull said that Smyrna was the last city he was visiting because he had already gathered volunteers from Italy and the Peloponnese and taken them to the island of Menorca while he searched for additional volunteers. He said Smyrna was his last chance to find some strong candidates to work on his new plantation in the garden of Eden on the other side of the world."

Paolo was dipping pieces of flatbread into Meleia's famous curried goat stew, which was hot and spicy. Meleia had placed a small crock with some yogurt in it on the table, which Paolo generously spooned onto his flatbread. He was alternating bites of curry with a fermented peach cider, and looked as if he had recovered well from being castigated by Stavros. "I haven't decided yet what I might do."

Buğra smiled. "You just got the job working for Stavros. Would you really leave such a good opportunity to go to the New World?"

Paolo spoke slowly, between bites of curried stew and

pita. "I think East Florida sounds exotic, the opportunity of a lifetime. On the other hand, the Alkeidis factory is expanding its business contacts with France. Then there's Stavros's temper to contend with. It's a difficult decision."

Seba was dumbfounded. "Are you seriously considering Turnbull's offer?"

Paolo bent down over his curry. "You wouldn't say anything to Stavros, would you?"

Seba shook his head in the negative. "Absolutely not. Especially after what we've been through. You were there—I told him I would watch over you. I'm certainly not going to say anything if you decide to leave. He might take it out on me anyway, because you and I are friends." If Stavros found out that Paolo was thinking of leaving the workshop, Seba could imagine how Stavros would take the news, especially after what he had witnessed in Eleni's office. Seba twitched his head back and forth, trying to dismiss the vision.

Paolo poured a long draught of peach cider into his upturned mouth. "Well, I haven't decided yet, so there's nothing to say."

Buğra was staunchly on the side of the government. "My father says that it is dishonest and cowardly to solicit the citizens of another country for some venture on the other side of the globe. He wants to know why the English don't solicit their own citizens if it's such a great venture. He says anyone who goes with Dr. Turnbull is exchanging freedom in the most successful port city in the Ottoman empire for slavery in a foreign land. The Ottoman government is concerned that its citizens are being swindled. And once they are gone, there will be no way to rescue them from their foolish decision."

Paolo replied, "Why shouldn't people be able to make

their own choices? If it turns out to be a bad decision, at least they've made it for themselves, and the government hasn't made it for them. And what about the adventure? We could be pioneers, like the first Greek mariners who sailed to Egypt! Can you imagine? Don't you want to see things you've never seen before, and do things you've never done before? And it doesn't appear that this Turnbull character has a temper like Stavros. He seems fairly benign to me."

Seba imagined Paolo telling Stavros that he was quitting, and try as he might, he couldn't shake the vision. "Paolo, you begged me to get you that job with Stavros. What if he punishes me because I brought you to him in the first place? He'll accuse us both of betrayal!"

"Well, as I said, I haven't decided yet. Remember what Eleni told us? She said not to worry about the future before it gets here. Besides, if you get some news from the ships coming in from Bursa, you might be gone before me anyway."

Paolo tapped his toes under the table, that little tripatos dance he did whenever he was feeling full of himself.

Paolo set his fork down and put his hands on Seba's and Buğra's shoulders, stretching his arms across the table. "My friends, if I decide to join the East Florida adventure, I would love it if you would join me. Can you imagine the fun we'd have in a new land, experiencing paradise together, growing old in a community that we built with our very own hands? Buğra, you've never left this city before, and Seba lived in a small village until he recently arrived in Smyrna. I have worked the barges between Smyrna and Çeşme, and I've met sailors from around the world. All I ask is that you give it the same consideration that I am. I don't want to be trapped in a life that isn't my own. If there is more for me out there, I want the

213

opportunity to find it myself."

The thought of freedom encouraged Seba's appetite to return, and he joined Paolo and Buğra in downing several more mugs of peach cider. Meleia even gave them heaping servings of her famous galaktoboureko for dessert. The cheese was mild and delicate, with the slightest tang of lemon, and the pastry surrounding it was so flaky that Seba thought it might float off his plate like a feather on a tuft of air. He could have picked up the whole pastry in one hand and shoved it down his throat, which is exactly what Paolo did, but Seba chose instead to savor each tiny bite. Buğra and Paolo tried to convince Seba to stay for another round, but he needed to be alone with his thoughts.

Walking back to Buğra's house, Seba noticed the nightingales singing, and the hum of the city's inhabitants winding down their day was oddly comforting. He passed through the main thoroughfare of Enymeria Market, where vendors had closed their stalls to customers and were usually enjoying tea and chatting about the day's sales. This evening, however, the subject was one that Seba could not avoid.

"Did you see his buttons? Pure gold, I tell you."

"They say East Florida is full of gold. That's why the Spanish went there centuries ago."

"This Turnbull fellow seems to think that's not all the Spanish found."

"What do you mean?"

"I heard a story of a magic fountain discovered by one of the Spanish explorers. Anyone who drinks from the fountain will never age."

"I could use some of that. My feet are killing me. I've been standing since before sunrise."

"They're killing me, too. Why don't you go and wash

them?"

"My sister says the Englishman is married to the French physician's cousin."

"Which physician? Dr. Robin? I like her—she gave me a salve for a rash of red bumps I had on my legs. The scourge went away by the next morning. It was a miracle."

"I saw him eat fifty oysters in one sitting."

"The Englishman? Yes, he's quite fat, isn't he?"

"And jolly—he can tell a tale almost as well as my Greek grandfather, and that is a compliment I do not give lightly."

"Yes! That story about the man and his elephant in Constantinople? I almost wet myself, I laughed so hard."

"Can you imagine an elephant sticking its trunk—"

"George, that's enough! I've heard that story three times this week, and I don't need to hear it again."

"He's got a thousand lively tales like that one—he had us all falling off our chairs at the Golden Bull last night."

Seba realized that everywhere he turned, the infamous Dr. Turnbull was there. Meleia hated the sight of him, Stavros went insane at the thought of him, and Buğra thought he was a swindler, trying to lure Smyrna's citizens away from their homeland. What was it about the English? An English ship captain had tried to save Seba's father when the Ottomans kidnapped him, but the captain had no authority under Sultan Mustafa III. Now Seba thought back to Nasir's words, telling Seba to ask Turnbull about his father. As he walked toward his loft above Buğra's stable, he wondered if a path that included Turnbull was somewhere he feared to tread.

17 SILKWORM

Seba never made it back to the loft, however, because Stavros accosted him on the street. He was coming from the direction of the Turkish quarter, which was unusual, because Seba knew he did not live there.

"Sebastian, come with me." It wasn't a request; it was a directive.

"Where are we going?"

"I want to show you something in the silk room."

"But you never let anyone but the silk room workers in there—what do you have to show me?"

"You'll find out when we get there. I have some new information that I want to share with you."

Seba's heart skipped a beat. Stavros was finally going to give him information about his father!

They walked in silence toward the factory and entered through the back door. As they neared the silk room, Seba could hear the low murmurs of people talking inside. He knocked on the door, and the voices abruptly went silent.

Stavros said, "Nasir, what a surprise. I didn't expect you here this evening. Inspecting our silkworms, I see?"

Nasir looked from Stavros to Seba and said, "Yes, everything appears to be in order. As you know, my uncle wants to ensure that the quality of the empire's silk is the best in the world. I was just leaving."

Stavros said, "Don't forget our conversation of this morning. You have heard my concerns, and if I don't get satisfaction, I'll reach out to Governor Paşa myself." Stavros waved his arm in the direction of the factory's exit doors. "Nasir, please use the back door. Hector or Marco will unlock it and escort you from the workshop. Intruders have been spotted on the premises in recent days, and unfortunately, we've had to institute additional security precautions."

Stavros walked into the silk room, and as Seba was about to follow him inside, Nasir touched his shoulder and whispered, "Be careful."

Seba hesitated outside the door. "Be careful of what?"

"Take care of your—"

"Sebastian, are you following? I thought you were right behind me." Stavros called reproachfully from inside the silk room.

With that, Nasir turned and strode quickly toward the exit. Seba's head was thrumming as he followed Stavros to the silk room. He had always wanted to see what was in that room, but it seemed an odd choice for the place where Stavros would tell him about his father.

The silk room was dark, with an enormous stone furnace in one corner that reminded Seba of the blacksmith's forges he had seen in his home village of Sessera. The fire was throwing out waves of heat, and there was a stack of wood as tall as Seba that ran along the wall next to the furnace.

There was a large grate over the furnace's fire, upon which sat three large copper cauldrons. Aside from the fire, the only light in the room came from a dozen thick pillar candles set out around the perimeter and on a large wooden table in the middle of the room. The table held several tools—large metal tongs, wooden spools that were three feet tall and almost a foot thick, wooden rods and pegs of various sizes, and a pair of scissors that were as long as Seba's forearm.

The rest of the room was occupied by ten wooden barrels, each bearing an identical copper cauldron full of steaming water. Beside each barrel was a wooden box on four legs, and inside each box was a wheel with six spokes, connected to the box by a dowel that ran through the wheel's hub. Outside each box, connected to the dowel, was a hand crank that spun the wheel. Each barrel had one silk filament that was raised up from the water, threaded through hooks mounted on several wooden pegs that were attached to the wooden box closest to the barrel, and fed onto the wheel. It looked very similar to the spinning wheel that Seba's grandfather had fixed for Mrs. Lampros the previous winter.

There was a woman at each barrel, cranking the handles to spin the silk from the barrels of steaming water onto the wheels. Seba was shocked that he had never seen these women at the workshop before. It was as if they were ghosts, flitting in and out of the factory without being seen. Most surprising of all, however, was that Linus was tending the fire, keeping the pots over the flames full of boiling water. *The biggest blabbermouth in the factory works in the silk room?*

Stavros called out, "My little silkworms, you've had a long day, and because I am a magnanimous employer, I am giving you permission to go home early. Sebastian and I will finish up your work here. The two of us have a bit of business to discuss, and as it relates to our silk production, we need to speak in this room. As you may know, Eleni had a bit of an accident in the kitchen the other day, but she managed to bake some delicious *revani*, which she left for all of us, so help yourselves before you leave. I'll see you in the morning."

Seba bristled to hear Stavros speak so heartlessly about his sister, and he felt his fingers curl into a fist. He took a deep breath to calm himself. As the workers cleaned up to leave, Linus walked by Seba and said, "What a wonderful surprise! Have you ever tasted Eleni's revani? I am not exaggerating when I say it is heavenly. Orange-infused semolina cake, dripping in sugar syrup and covered with crushed pistachios—yum! I'll save you a piece."

Seba stared, incredulous, as Linus picked up his small leather journal from the table and walked out the door with the other workers.

When everyone was gone, Stavros said, "Sebastian, this is something that is to be between us. I don't want you to mention it to anyone, not even Eleni. She worries about me, and I would not like to give her any additional reasons for concern."

Seba fought the urge to gag at Stavros's hubris. It was clear that Stavros thought his attack on his sister was a secret, but Seba knew better, and it made him sick to think that Stavros could speak that way about his own flesh and blood.

Seba managed to hide his disgust. "Is that why you wanted to meet here?"

Stavros smiled, and the flickering candlelight gave him an evil, ominous look. Seba told himself it was an illusion caused by the shadows, but fear was creeping up his body like a mist rising from the ground.

"You've done well for me in your short time here, Sebastian. Almost too well. You understand that it was quite an unusual turn of events that brought you to me. And the fact that you were sent by my dear brother Timotheos made our encounter all the more intriguing, especially because Eleni and I have not seen or heard from him in many years."

Stavros continued, "You must admit that your story was quite extraordinary. That, in addition to the fact that you were not offering yourself to work for me—you were asking for something in return—raised my curiosity."

"I wasn't try—"

Stavros held up his hand. "Sebastian, let me finish."

Seba stood erect, feeling more uncomfortable with every passing tick of the clock.

"I have asked myself why my brother, who has not communicated with me for ages, now sends me a young man asking for a favor. A favor that relates to this boy's vendetta against the Ottoman empire, possibly even against Sultan Mustafa III himself, and to something that happened to his father when the boy was nine years old. The same Ottoman empire that regulates all of the production and sale of the goods that move in and out of this workshop. To be frank, I wondered whether my brother had sent someone to spy on me."

"I'm not a spy!"

Stavros pushed his raised hand out toward Seba. "You would not be here without my charity, I believe the least you could do is respect my time and allow me to finish."

"I apologize."

"That's better." Stavros walked over to one of the

steaming barrels. "Do you know how my business began, Sebastian?"

"No."

"My father was a tailor when I was young, mending clothes for the Greek merchants who inhabited this beautiful city. We didn't have much, but my father was talented, and he had a dream of creating exquisite, grand fabrics to share with the world. He loved color, and he experimented with ways to dye the yarn to create hues that had not been seen before, as well as combinations of colors that were stunning and evoked emotion, much like this tapestry that I commissioned. My father gained a reputation for not only mending clothes with perfect stitches that were so pristine that anyone would have thought them brand new, but also for creating textiles that breathed new life into the world of weaving. In addition, he was efficient, making a spool of cotton last longer than the sun in midsummer, and wasting nothing in the production process. In time, he slowly expanded into creating silk fabrics for the elite in Smyrna, and he opened a small workshop on this very ground."

Seba leaned forward, despite the flutter in his stomach.

"As my brother and I got older, we helped my father in the workshop, and when my sisters came along, they added their input, helping my father to create more and more beautiful designs; soon the European merchants were requesting çatmas, tapestries, and even garments for special occasions.

"My mother cared for all of us, keeping us grounded and reminding us of our roots, so that we would not become lost in the world, jumping at the next trend or overextending ourselves. We stayed true to my father's vision and worked long hours, making gorgeous shimmering art that was as

222

beautiful to touch as it was to observe. It was the happiest time in my life."

Seba nodded his head in agreement. "My mother took pains to remind me of my roots as well."

Stavros absently moved his hand over the steam that rose from the barrel closest to him as he continued, "When Timotheos and I got older, we realized that the shop was my father's dream, not ours. My father had plenty of employees, and he encouraged Timotheos and me to follow our own dreams. Timotheos was interested in academic pursuits, particularly the teachings of the church, and my heart was set on opening a restaurant. I had always loved food and often helped my mother with baking since the time I could walk. I began to apprentice to one of the bakers here in Smyrna, and I couldn't have been more pleased with my prospects for the future.

"It soon fell apart. My father's health began to falter, and so did his workshop. My father came to me and Timotheos, telling us that the future of our family depended on the two of us, as the boys in the family. My mother and my sisters would not be able to survive unless we kept the business alive. Timotheos and I protested, saying that we could support our mother and our sisters with our own dreams, but he would not hear of it.

"We begged and pleaded with him to let us strike out on our own, and we promised to support our family. We tried to convince him to sell the business, but he refused, and he said if we did not continue his legacy, we would be disgracing the Alkeidis name. We had no choice—we could not deprive our father of his dying wish. I left my apprenticeship to the baker and took over my father's business."

Stavros's eyes flashed. "It was then that my brother

broke my father's heart. He said that the call of the church was too great, and the legacy of God was more important than the legacy of one family. He said we are all God's family; Jesus was not beholden to Mary and Joseph, and he could not be beholden to us. He told my father he was going to study at Nea Moni. He abandoned my father, and all of us, in our time of need.

"His cowardly act and his betrayal of our family was the final straw that killed my father. Timotheos left on a ship bound for Chios on a Tuesday morning, and by Wednesday evening, my father was dead." Stavros spat, the spittle landing on the floor beside a barrel of boiling water. "What's worse is that it was all done in the name of God, so of course, we couldn't say anything about his choice, lest we be considered ungrateful—or worse, un-Christian.

"I was the only one left who could save my father's legacy, and it was my loyalty that did exactly that. That Wednesday, on my father's deathbed, I vowed that I would make Alkeidis the most successful textile workshop in all of the Ottoman empire, far surpassing my father's original dream and showing what could be accomplished in the name of loyalty and legacy."

Seba's mind traveled back to the tapestry in Stavros's office, and he fought the overwhelming urge to turn and run from the silk room as fast as his boots would carry him. He willed his feet to remain planted.

"I hope you will not do to me what my brother did, Sebastian. His disloyalty killed my father." He pointed to the corner of the room. "See that woven basket covered with a cloth? Please bring it over to the fire."

Seba brought the basket over to one of the copper cauldrons and removed the cloth. There were little white shapes in the basket like hundreds of tiny birds' eggs. Seba realized that these were the silkworms' cocoons.

He said, "There are so many cocoons, this must make miles of silk."

Stavros shook his head scornfully. "Not quite, Sebastian. It takes three thousand cocoons to make one yard of woven silk fabric."

"What? That's impossible. There aren't that many silkworms in the world."

"Don't be obtuse, Sebastian. Now please gently pour the contents of the basket into this copper cauldron. Linus left us with a roaring fire, and the water is boiling well."

Seba's head was spinning as he tried to imagine how many millions of silkworms had donated their cocoons for the thousands of tapestries he had seen in the weeks he had been employed at the workshop. Every little skein of silk surrounding each weaver's loom must have been given by several thousand cocoons. The sheer volume of numbers boggled Seba's mind.

Seba held the rattan basket by its handles and carefully tilted it over the boiling cauldron. He watched as the cocoons dropped to the bottom of the pot and then rose so they were floating on top of the bubbling water.

After the basket was empty, Seba asked, "Why are we putting the cocoons in boiling water? Are we softening the silk?"

Stavros laughed. "No, Seba, we have to boil them to kill the silkworms."

Seba dropped the basket, which made a smacking sound against the floor and rolled past his feet. "What?"

Stavros's eerie smile reappeared. "You've worked for me for all these weeks and never took the time to learn the process? I'm a bit disappointed in you, Sebastian."

Seba frowned. "I don't understand. I thought the

cocoons were harvested after the silkworms were finished with them, after they had emerged as butterflies."

Stavros picked up the basket, placed the cloth inside, and laid it on the table with the tools. He retrieved a long wooden paddle from the table and stepped toward the boiling copper pot.

"That's a precious thought, but a bit naive, I'm afraid. I was similarly immature in my younger days, but that quickly changed after Timotheos betrayed our family and killed our father." Stavros put the paddle in the boiling water and swirled it around the bobbing cocoons.

"You see, when the silk moths are ready to emerge, the silk strands harden, which is nature's way of making it easier for the moths to eat through them and escape their confinement. However, the hardened strands are not the best quality for silk production, so we must extract the silk before it hardens. In addition, it is much easier to unwind one strand from a whole cocoon than to gather many pieces of half-eaten strands. We choose just the right time, when the silk is at its softest and in one whole long strand, which is before the moths emerge. It is a fact of life, like my being forced to leave my chosen profession to secure my family's well-being. These silkworms sacrifice themselves so we can produce the most beautiful textile artwork in the world."

"You're boiling them alive? Right now?"

"You just did, Sebastian." Stavros continued to slowly stir the boiling water with the wooden paddle. He looked as calm as if he were stirring avgolemono over a fire.

"And please, there is no need to be so dramatic. We are preparing the cocoons to be spun onto spools to be taken to the dyeing room."

Seba remembered the night of the Festival of Saint John and those ethereal little white silk moths floating around

Meleia's hands as she played the tambouras. The thousands of silkworms in this room would never be given that chance.

Seba felt the bile rising up in his throat, and his eyes were stinging with rage that was bubbling inside. He ran out the back door of the silk room and into the alley behind the workshop. He vomited between two large scrubby trees, his mind racing. *He's boiling those beautiful creatures alive. Those beautiful silk moths that want to be free to dance and spread their wings.*

As Seba said those words to himself, he retched again. He was transported back to the day that his father's freedom was abruptly taken from him. Those old feelings of grief and rage surged back into his body, and he was nine years old again, trying to understand why these things were happening to him.

Stavros called from the silk room, "You'll need to develop a firmer constitution, Sebastian. A few dead worms are nothing to be sick over. And we have work to do. In fact, I have a special project for you."

As Seba returned to the silk room, he noticed that Stavros continued to swirl the wooden paddle in the boiling water. "Unless, of course, you intend to breach our agreement, and no longer need my assistance with your search for your father."

Seba wiped his chin with the back of his hand and stood up, facing Stavros. "I *am* pursuing the path to my father. His life was taken away before he reached his full potential, like these innocent silkworms. I refuse to believe that is the end for him, and I will do whatever it takes to find him."

"I'm glad to hear that, because I require something from you before I bring you to your father."

"What? You know where he is? Why didn't you tell me?"

"All in due time. I had to make sure of your loyalty, and

after this display with the silkworms, I'm not convinced. I need you to do one thing for me, and then we will see about your father."

"Is he in Smyrna? If he's here, I have to leave right now. I'll search this whole city until I find him. How could you not tell me he was here?"

"Not so fast, Sebastian." Stavros put the wooden paddle on the table and reached into the pocket of his silk trousers. Staring at Stavros's silk pants, Seba wondered how many silkworms were boiled alive to create them.

"I don't think you should be going anywhere in the city right now, except where I tell you."

"Why not?"

Stavros pulled out a velvet pouch and dangled it in front of him, admiring it. On his finger was a ring with the sultan's tughra on it—the one that Seba had found on the ship the day his father was taken away. Seba felt an explosion inside his chest as the realization hit him.

"Where did you get those?" Seba's voice was barely a whisper.

Stavros pulled the cord, opening the pouch. Seba could smell the contents before his sight confirmed it. Stavros picked a tiny jewel-like pebble of mastiha from the pouch and slowly put it on his tongue, then crunched through the pebble's exterior, releasing the resin of mastic gum into his mouth.

"I told you, my web extends throughout the entirety of Smyrna. Nothing escapes my silvery strands."

"But that pouch was in my room, in my lodgings, hidden away. I didn't even tell anyone I had it."

"No one escapes my reach, Sebastian. And Hector loves to visit the animals in the stables of Smyrna. He says he finds their braying to be soothing to his nerves."

"You have no right to take that ring and pouch of mastiha. That's stealing!"

"My thoughts exactly. I wonder what would happen should I notify the Ottoman authorities that I discovered a mastiha thief in my workshop. And one who was mysteriously found to have a ring bearing the sultan's seal, although he claims to have been a Greek Christian in the self-governing area of the mastichochoria. Why would a fifteen-year-old young man have a ring that is restricted to the Ottoman government's ruling class? Possibly because he is a spy, sent to plant this in my shop and call the authorities to shut down my business? I knew my brother was against me, but I didn't think he would sink to this level."

"That's not what happened! I found —"

"Save your lies for someone else, Sebastian. You've got work to do, and I've noticed that you continue to favor your left wrist. The Ottomans could take care of that problem for you—they'd be happy to remove your left hand, and then your wrist would be the least of your problems."

"No! I came here in good faith, upon your brother's recommendation. He said you would help me. Why would you do this to me?"

"You're too young to understand the ways of the world. You put your trust in the wrong person, the same one I did many years ago. And now I can't even trust my own sister." He held up the pouch. "It appears that I can't trust you either."

"I didn't steal that mastiha, if that's what you mean. It was given to me by my Uncle Phillip, after I learned how to embroider the skinos trees."

"Maybe that's true, but I can't be sure. What I am sure of is that if you want to avoid immediate arrest by the Ottoman government, you will do something for me. Then I'll find out where your loyalties truly lie."

Seba's shoulders slumped. He knew that he had no choice. He would never find his father if he was in jail, and he might not survive the amputation of his left hand if Stavros followed through on his threat of bodily harm.

"What is it?" Again, Seba barely found his voice. The conversation, the flickering candlelight, the dead silkworms, the bile stinging his throat—it was all like a horrible nightmare. But this time, he did not awake from the nightmare in his loft, tangled up in a sheet. This time, his nightmare was his reality.

Stavros reached into his other pocket and pulled out a blade, approximately five inches long, beveled on the top and flat on the bottom, with a slight curve. Seba recognized this as a carpentry knife that he had seem many years ago at his father's shipyard. It was used to shave planks of wood into a smooth surface. Seba remembered the fresh-smelling curls of pine shavings that dotted his father's shipyard on Chios. He wondered if Stavros was testing him again to see what he knew about ships.

"This is a carpenter's knife. It's extremely sharp. I suppose you may have seen one of these, if your father was the superior shipbuilder you claim he was."

"He was! I mean, he is!"

Stavros raised his hand. "No need to be so sensitive, Sebastian. As you may have guessed, I am careful with my words, as I am with everything that affects my business. Now, what I want you to do is steal onto the ship that scoundrel Turnbull has at anchor in the Smyrna harbor, and use this tool to remove all of the Ottoman seals from every pallet, box, barrel, and container in the hold of that ship."

"Why?"

"Forgive me if I don't find it necessary to share my reasons with you. Turnbull is a menace, and he needs to be stopped. You are going to help me stop him."

"By removing the sultan's tughra? What will that do?"

"When the Ottoman tariff collectors are alerted to the fact that the cargo on Dr. Turnbull's ship is missing the tariff seals, he'll be punished severely. We'll never see his face in Smyrna again—that is, if they let him live."

"Won't the tax collectors be able to tell that the wood was shaved?"

"Not if you do a good job."

"I'm not a carpenter—what if I fail?"

Stavros held up the pouch of mastiha with one hand, the sultan's gold ring on the tip of his first finger. "I think we've gone over that already. Make sure you don't fail."

"How am I supposed to get on the ship? Every merchant ship in Smyrna's harbor is guarded, in case any pirates attack."

"You've shown yourself to be quite resourceful thus far, and my holier-than-thou brother seems to think highly of you, so I'm sure you'll figure something out." Stavros took another nugget, one of the Tears of Chios, from the pouch, and popped it into his mouth.

"And what if I get caught?"

Stavros twirled the strings of the pouch between his fingers. "Really, Sebastian, I thought that you were smarter than that. I've already told you that it is in your best interest to make sure that doesn't happen."

"You're saying that if I shave these tughras from all of the wooden crates, you'll take me to my father?"

"If you prove yourself to be true to your word. Which, by the way, you have not done thus far."

"And if I don't do it, or I get caught, you're going to turn me into the authorities as a mastiha thief?"

Stavros sneered, "You are so dramatic that maybe you should consider a career in the theater. Either that or a town crier, since you seem to revel in repeating yourself."

"And when am I supposed to do this?"

"Why, as soon as possible, of course. You never know when the Ottoman tax collectors will be given a tip to board Turnbull's ship and inspect the cargo. Captain Paşa has been very slow in ejecting Dr. Turnbull from the city. I'm simply hastening the Englishman's exit."

Seba had been holding his breath, which he now exhaled slowly. He reached for the carpenter's knife. "Fine. I'll be back soon, and when I am, I want you to take me to my father immediately."

Stavros taunted, "If you're successful, I might even consider returning this pouch to you. Get going."

18 TURNBULL'S SHIP

Seba was shaking as he advanced quickly to the harbor. Stavros said that Turnbull's ship was called the *New Fortuna*. By asking around, Seba learned that the captain of the *New Fortuna* was a Greek man, Alexander Alexiano, so Seba believed that was a good sign for his ability to gain access. Hopefully some of the crew was Greek, or at least spoke Greek. It seemed plausible, given that Dr. Turnbull's wife was Greek. Seba's English was rudimentary at best, and he was afraid that speaking French would upset anyone on the ship who was English. He had learned from Meleia that France and England had been at war with each other for at least six hundred years.

Seba hid behind several crates of potatoes heaped in a pell-mell stack beside one of the waterfront's warehouses. He needed a safe place to wait until the sky darkened completely, because he couldn't risk being seen by anyone. Looking out over the Gulf of Smyrna, he saw Mars, the red planet, appear clear and bright in the western sky. Seba preferred the Greek name, Ares, the god of fire and action. He took it as a sign that it was time to move, so he crawled slowly from behind the crates and quietly approached the *New Fortuna*. There were a few sailors standing on the dock where the *New Fortuna*'s gangplank ended, but it was near the time when they would return to the ship's galley to find a cup of tea or, more likely, a bottle of raki. The moon was a waning crescent, with enough light reflecting off the water to allow Seba to pick his way toward the ship. As the sailors walked back up the gangplank, sharing a pipe between the two of them, Seba stood tall and followed behind them silently, staying far enough back that they didn't hear him but close enough that someone patrolling the docks would see three sailors returning to a ship for a night of cards or dice.

He made it! Seba was so excited that for a moment, he gazed around for someone to celebrate with. Then he realized how foolish that was, hastily crouching down lest he be seen by any crew members on the night watch. He heard a few men talking to each other from the ship's bow, and he froze. Seba observed that they were engaged in a spirited debate about the existence of mermaids, and it became clear that they were too distracted to notice anything but their own opinions.

Seba spotted a ladder poking out of the ship's hold, which was a few feet away in the center of the main deck. He hastily looked around in the scant moonlight, scouring the ship for any other sailors who might be watching for intruders. He could taste the bitter stomach juices that had plastered his throat earlier outside the silk room. He put both hands on the deck to steady himself. *Pull yourself together, or you're going to end up a one-handed convict wasting away in an Ottoman prison.*

Seba crawled on his hands and knees toward the hatch leading into the hold and looked around before scrambling down the ladder. When he reached the bottom, and his feet hit the floorboards of the hold, he looked around before stepping away from the ladder. It was pitch black and deadly silent. The only light in the space was the pale moonlight, making a tiny square at the bottom of the ladder. His heart sank and his body buzzed with fear. He couldn't scrape the tughras from the crates if he couldn't see them.

Then Seba remembered a conversation with his father at the shipyard many years ago. His father said there were pegs built into the support posts of every ship's hold for the purpose of hanging lanterns. According to his father, the lanterns would be suspended from metal rings attached to the pegs, and there would be a little metal box nearby, filled with twisted bits of paper, called spills, that were used to light the lanterns. He felt around in the dark until his hands landed on a post. He ran his hand up the post, and was elated when his fingers alighted on a lantern. His father had been correct—there was a metal box nailed to the post that contained several paper spills. Now he had to find a way to light the spill, but the hold was steeped in blackness, with no flame in sight. *Why can't this be easy?*

Seba removed the spill and climbed back up the ladder. He ducked as he saw two sailors checking the stern lines before exiting the ship. They were laughing and speaking Greek, and Seba guessed that they were on their way to a delicious meal at the Aigokeros. He wished he could say the same for himself. However, hearing his native language made him feel better. If he was caught on this ship, he could act like he was visiting a friend or relative, or acting on official business for a Greek merchant.

From his position on the ladder peeking up from the

hold, Seba spied a huge lantern mounted at the ship's stern. It was fastened to post that jutted up from the back of the ship's balustrade, and Seba knew that it was used to mark the boundary of the ship, in order to prevent nearby ships from anchoring too closely. He scrambled over to the stern until he was just below the large lantern. As he was about to poke the paper spill into the flame above the lantern's wick, he heard a shout from the starboard side of the ship and dropped the spill. It was one of the ship's officers, mistaking him for a member of the crew, and yelling at him in Greek.

"You there! Have you filled the stern lantern with oil? No going ashore until all of your duties are complete!"

Seba resisted the urge to bend over and look for the spill, and instead stood erect and nodded, giving a hand gesture of assent as well. He had seen the crews at the shipyard do the same whenever they were given orders by their commanders, and he hoped he was doing it correctly. However, the officer seemed irritated. "Cat got your tongue? You answer your commanding officer when he asks you a question."

Seba cleared his throat and made his voice as deep and different sounding as he could muster. "*Nai. Malista Kyrie!*" Yes. Yes, sir!

The officer nodded in approval. "That's more like it. Go about your business, and get snappy!"

Again, Seba responded in his deepest voice. "*Malista Kyrie!*" Yes, sir!

The man, who must have been the second mate or some other midlevel officer on the ship, turned and quickly walked toward the officers' quarters.

Seba knew he didn't have much time, and these encounters showed that there was more activity on the ship

236

than he had expected. He felt around on the deck until his fingers brushed across the paper spill. He rapidly jabbed the spill into the lantern, and as soon as it flared, he ran toward the ladder, cupping the flame with his other hand while he awkwardly descended the ladder into the hold, using his elbows for balance. He leaped toward the closest lantern and touched the spill, which had almost burned out, to the wick. It sparked to life and illuminated the hold.

There were boxes, crates, pallets, casks, and barrels, all decorated with the sultan's tughra. Dr. Turnbull had obviously paid the taxes on these goods, or his brokers had done so on his behalf, but all of that was about to be wiped out.

Seba swiped the knife across the side of a barrel and realized that not only was the blade extremely sharp, the sultan's seal was not deep. On some crates and casks it had been stamped, and others, which were the heavier boxes, it had been branded. However, even the branded tughras came off in two swipes of the sharp blade. Seba moved quickly from one box to the next, picking up the small, shaved curls from the ground and shoving them in his pockets to make sure that there was no evidence of what he had done.

He attacked the stamped and branded seals with the knife, swiftly and carefully shaving each one before moving to the next. When the last tughra had been removed, Seba viewed his work, commenting to himself that not even the person who packed these boxes would know that they had been tampered with. He blew out the lantern and put the knife back in his pocket, wondering how he had ever gotten into this predicament.

Everything was deadly quiet on the ship as Seba climbed the ladder out of the hold. He could hear the distant voices of the local citizens talking and laughing in the tavernas. As he slunk by the officer's quarters on his way back to the gangplank, he saw Dr. Turnbull's silhouette inside the room's window. The Englishman was talking to someone, but both men's voices were so quiet that Seba thought they must be discussing something secretive.

Deciding that his situation couldn't get any worse, and hoping that he might learn something that could save him from Stavros's evil web, he lingered outside the window. He didn't trust Turnbull, but at this point, he had no other options. *The enemy of my enemy is my friend.* Was it Meleia who had said that? Or something about being close to one's enemies? His brain was a jumble, his heart was beating out of his chest, and he could scarcely remember his own name.

"The poor boy has been in Smyrna for the last few months, looking for his father. It's awful." Seba thought he recognized the voice speaking to Turnbull as belonging to Nasir, but it was so low that he couldn't be sure.

Then Seba heard a third voice. "I can understand the boy's despair. I don't even know if my son is alive."

Seba heard Nasir draw a long breath, as if he were pulling on a pipe. "Family is important. My uncle has been like a father to me ever since I lost both of my parents in that horrible fire that ravaged Smyrna three years ago."

Seba could not see Nasir or the third man, but Turnbull, who was closest to the window, was popping strawberries into his mouth as he spoke. "Ah, yes, the fire of seventeen sixty-three. My wife's cousin, Dr. Robin, told us all about it. She said it was an awful tragedy. Fortunately, my family was in England at the time, but several of Maria Gracia's cousins perished in the blaze. We've had quite our share of disasters in this part of the world, haven't we, Nasir?"

Nasir agreed, and Dr. Turnbull continued, "By all

accounts from the sailors I've spoken with, the wall of water was more than fifty feet high when it reached Constantinople's port. It picked up the ships closest to the wharf and deposited them three miles inland. I've heard these ships are strewn about the city like children's toys. The sailors from East Asia call it a tsunami, which I believe means 'harbor wave' in Japanese. And this atrocity was compounded by the complete devastation of those buildings from the shaking of the earth that came before the great wave."

The third voice said, "I'm glad my family was not with me in Constantinople."

Turnbull said, "Yes, we were lucky. I can't imagine the ruination and carnage. If anything happened to my Maria Gracia, I would be shattered."

Nasir's voice pitched up. "I agree, and yet I feel terrible for this boy. I told him I would help him. He said his father was an engineer in Constantinople, brought there by order of the sultan himself. One of the old sea dogs had told the boy that every person within three miles of the harbor was drowned. The old mariner said there were no survivors, and I could see the pain in this boy's eyes. I advised him to talk to you, Andrew, but I don't think he trusts my judgment. Something about an altercation between you and Miss Kokokis at the Aigokeros has put him off. Do you know anything about a Greek engineer from Chios who was in the harbor that day?"

Turnbull swallowed a large strawberry that he had been chewing, and said, "Why don't you tell him, Kostas?"

The third voice said, "As a matter of fact, there was such a Greek engineer, but he was *not* on the dock when the tsunami hit. In a stroke of good luck, one of the Danish captains who had designed the hull of the *New Fortuna* happened to be in port. The Greek engineer and his crew were working on an Ottoman ship docked at the wharf, and Captain Alexiano invited them to see the Dane's design in action, by sailing around the Sea of Marmara for a few hours. Captain Alexiano said the Danish captain could accompany them and demonstrate the design, as well as answer any questions the crew posed about the construction. The sultan's overseer, realizing that this information might benefit his own fleet and raise his status in the sultan's eyes, permitted the Greek engineer to accompany Captain Alexiano and the Danish captain for the demonstration."

Nasir said, "Was his name Kostas Krizomatis?"

Seba couldn't believe his ears. He whispered to himself, "Papa?" Seba wondered if his hearing had deceived him. His heart was thumping so loudly, and he wanted to find his father so desperately, that he wasn't sure what he heard. He inched his head upward from his hiding place until his chin was even with the windowsill.

Nasir was sitting in a red velvet high-backed chair, pulling on a long-stemmed pipe that was almost the length of his forearm. Wisps of tobacco smoke drifted up and swirled above his head. In the dim light, Seba observed that the bruises on Nasir's face had all but disappeared, and the skin around his eyes was no longer swollen. Dr. Turnbull was seated at an immense mahogany dining table, a delicate blue and white bowl of strawberries and a similarly-decorated pitcher of cream in front of him. Several large pillar candles were situated in the center of the table, casting light on Turnbull and creating shadows across the rest of what appeared to be his dining quarters. There was a banquette on the wall next to Nasir, and a third man was seated there, his feet resting on a stool that was covered with an indigo embroidered çatma. Several lanterns were mounted on the wall behind the banquette, and Seba thought he could make out the design of white dolphins and yellow seahorses over a field of indigo on the footstool. A thick wool hand-knotted carpet stretched across the wooden floor, bearing an intricate Ottoman pattern of tulips and palm trees in colors of gold and vermilion. The man seated at the banquette was thin, with a bushy beard and wild, unkempt hair. His collarbones were prominent, and his face was drawn, making his features look sharp and angular. He looked like he hadn't eaten for many months. Seba squinted, searching the man's features for something recognizable.

When Seba stood up to look closer, the knife fell out of his pocket and clattered onto the deck. All three men's heads pivoted toward the window, where Seba quickly crouched back down and groped along the deckboards until his fingers felt the cold metal of the knife. He curled his fingers around the knife's handle and jammed it back in his pocket as a shadow passed over his head.

It was Dr. Turnbull, hands red with strawberry juice, his large round pate protruding out from the window like the head of a hog on a spit. "Look now, what's this? An intruder?"

Seba reached up and grabbed Turnbull's hands in his own until their faces were only inches apart. "No, please, sir, don't raise an alarm. I'm Sebastian Krizomatis, and I think my father is in there with you."

Nasir called, "Turnbull, are you alright? What's going on over there?"

Turnbull winked at Seba and jerked his head toward the door. He held his finger to his lips, directing Seba to come to the door and remain silent.

"It has recently come to my attention that we have a special delivery for our friend here. Please remain seated, and give me a moment, Nasir. I promise you will enjoy this." Turnbull walked to the door and motioned for Seba to follow him inside. Turnbull was so fat that he completely obscured the other men's view of Seba, who stood behind him at the threshhold.

When Seba was fully inside the room, Turnbull stepped aside with a flourish and put his hand behind Seba's back, thrusting Seba into the center of the room. "Surprise!"

Seba's hands hung at his sides, and he stood there, slack-jawed and unable to move. The man seated on the banquette looked somewhat like his father, but he couldn't be sure. He was so gaunt and bony, and so much older than he remembered his father being, that Seba thought he must be mistaken. The thin man jumped up from the chair he was sitting in and hobbled to Seba, knocking the footstool over in the process. He was limping badly, and Seba watched as he winced in pain when his right foot touched the ground.

"Seba? Is it really you?"

As the thin man came near, and Seba heard his voice, he realized it truly was his father. Seba dropped to his knees—his legs could no longer support his body, and he felt as if everything inside his skin had liquified into jelly. Emotions welled up in him and bubbled over like water from a deep spring.

Nasir stood and positioned himself behind Seba, ready to catch him should he topple to the ground. Seba heard his father say, "Praise be to God, the Saints, the Angels, and the Holy Spirit! My prayers have been answered."

Seba looked up and felt the arms of his father encircle him; he was transported to his childhood, remembering the warm refuge of his father's embrace. Tears streamed down his cheeks as he wrapped his arms around the best man that he had ever known.

Seba had no idea how much time had passed or whether he was experiencing a dream. In his mind, he had died and gone to heaven. He would have endured thousands of nightmares like those in the loft, if they led to this moment. At some point, which could have been minutes or hours later, Seba heard Dr. Turnbull say, "I haven't been so touched since the day my little Jenny was born, right here in this very city. It warms my heart, I tell you."

Nasir laughed, and Kostas laughed along with him, drawing back from his only son and looking into the gray-green eyes that were just like his own.

"Sebastian, I have dreamed of this meeting every night for the last six years. That's more than two thousand one hundred and ninety nights. I never gave up hope that I would see you again. Without the presence and comfort of the Virgin Mary, I don't think I could have survived that lonely time."

Seba was sobbing so loudly that he could barely hear his father's voice. He tried to choke back the tears, but they had been bottled up for so long that they had multiplied a thousandfold. It would take time for them to find their way out.

"I've been searching for you ever since they took you away." Seba's voice was raw, and it cracked on the last syllable of "away."

Seba felt his father's hands stroking the top of his head. "Shhh, you don't have to say anything right now. I want to tell you that I couldn't be prouder of you than I am right now. Look at you, you're a grown man, with a sable-colored beard like mine. I'm so sorry that I wasn't there for you and your mother. I tried everything I could think of to escape."

He gestured with his arm, and as he did, Seba noticed thick bands of raised red welts above his elbow.

Seba looked down and saw that his father's leg was protruding from his hip at an unnatural angle.

"Papa, what did they do to you?"

"In due time, son, I'll tell you everything. Although it is a tale so dark that even Hades himself might cringe to hear it." He pulled Seba close to him. "But none of that matters now, because we've found each other, and everything will be fine.

"You know I would have done anything to return to you and your mother. Every time I devised a plan, something happened to thwart my escape. And every time I got caught, the punishment was more severe."

Seba looked at his father's wrists and remembered his nightmare. "Did they have you in irons? Were you chained to other workers on the dock?"

Kostas closed his eyes and took a deep breath. "Yes, it's true. But let's not speak of that now. My prayers were answered, even if it was by the frightful power of nature that caused so much death and destruction. I certainly did not pray for that, but here we are."

Seba said, "I'm sorry, I should have looked for you sooner. I let you down, Papa, and you suffered because of it. Please forgive me." Seba's tears were full of regret and shame, knowing that his father had suffered, and he had done nothing to help. He sobbed, "I'm sorry, I can't stop crying."

Seba felt his father pulling him to his feet. "Seba, please. You were only nine years old, and you couldn't have known what was happening. But also, never be embarrassed by your feelings. As your grandfather always says, 'We are Greek, for heaven's sake; we must show our emotions!'

Aside from the day you were born, this is the happiest day of my life."

Seba sniffed. "I missed you."

"I know, Seba. I missed you more than words can say. And I thank God that he brought these wonderful people into our lives who enabled our reunion." Kostas nodded to Dr. Turnbull and Nasir, who had seated themselves at the dining table and were sipping mulberry wine from long-stemmed wine glasses with a pattern of engraved butterflies and roses. Out of the corner of his eye, Seba could tell that Nasir was using his cloth serviette to dab at the corners of his eyes. Dr. Turnbull had taken out a pipe and was smoking it, looking as happy and content as a doctor who had saved a patient's life. Which, Seba thought, was exactly what he had done.

Dr. Turnbull said, "I guess I learned my lesson that on God's green earth, there is no such thing as coincidences." He drew on his pipe and chortled. "I had no idea that you were related, or that Kostas's son would be joining us for the evening meal. This is quite a treat, not only for the two of you, but also for Nasir and myself, who are honored to participate in your reunion."

"Do you think you can eat, Seba? You look thin. Dr. Turnbull's chef, Dmitri, rivals your mother's skill with food, and Dr. Turnbull has shown me the most cheerful hospitality ever since I stepped foot on this ship."

Seba was taken aback. "You look like you haven't eaten in six years, Papa."

His father smiled wanly. "You should have seen me the day I boarded this ship. When the guards took off my chains at the port of Constantinople, I nearly fell off the pier into the harbor. I was so weak I had to be helped up the ladder from the tender to the *New Fortuna*. In fact, one of Captain

Alexiano's crew nearly carried me up the ladder on his back. That was May twenty-second, I believe. And now it's already July. I've probably gained twenty pounds in the last two months."

Seba couldn't imagine his father twenty pounds lighter. He looked like he could blow away in a stiff wind across the Smyrnean mountains.

Dmitri brought out plates of grilled fish, dried figs, olives, that same crusty French bread that Seba had enjoyed in Dr. Robin's garden, and a dish in a casserole that Dr. Turnbull called "beef Bourguignon." According to Nasir, it was a French delicacy, and the chef was given a recipe from Dr. Turnbull's wife, Maria Gracia de Robin, who was Greek, but whose ancestors were French. It was a hearty stew with chunks of beef, mushrooms, garlic, little white pearl onions, carrots, thyme, beef stock, and red wine that Dr. Turnbull said came from somewhere called Burgundy. Seba didn't know what Burgundy was, but if it was a real place in the world, he thought he might like it very much. This particular meal danced happily on Seba's tastebuds, but he couldn't tell if that was because of Dmitri's extraordinary skill or because he was sitting across the table from his father.

They all talked and laughed as the crescent moon made its way toward the western horizon, Seba keeping all three men in stitches with his stories of the antics of Paolo and Buğra, and the embarrassing coffee incident at the Aigokeros.

Dr. Turnbull said "Ah, yes, the fiery disposition of Miss Kokokis is one I'll not soon forget. For you it was coffee, young man, and for me it was a sorely misused bottle of strawberry wine. A tragic end for one of my favorite fruits. I've always said that wine is made for drinking, not spilling, and definitely not for tossing at one's head!"

After they had shared stories for many hours, Nasir excused himself and said that he must be going home. Dr. Turnbull implored Nasir to stay the night on the ship in the guest's quarters, and Nasir finally relented, saying that the last time he stayed too long in one place after drinking, he ended up on Dr. Robin's surgery table.

Seba said, "I'm sorry that happened to you, Nasir. I'm glad Dr. Robin was able to treat your injuries so quickly."

Nasir's eyes were twinkling. "And I have you to thank for that. Even though you've never been given proper credit for saving my life."

Seba nearly choked on a strawberry. "What? You knew?"

Nasir said kindly, "What kind of port inspector would I be for my uncle if I couldn't find out who saved my own life?"

"How long have you known?"

"Since I was well enough to discuss the matter with Dr. Robin, of course."

Seba was nonplussed. "Why didn't you say anything?"

"It didn't seem pertinent, Sebastian. It was in the past, and I was thankful that you and your friend Paolo saved my life. I surmised that we would discuss it when you were ready, and it turns out that tonight is that time."

Kostas sat up a bit taller on the banquet. "My son saved your life?" He beamed at Seba, and his face looked like one of the saints from the sanctuary at Nea Moni, he was so proud. Kostas continued, "I'm not surprised at all. My heart is so light that I feel as if I might float away."

Dr. Turnbull said, "I'm turning in, gentlemen, but please, stay and catch up here in my dining quarters, or anywhere on deck. I'll let Captain Alexanio know that you are my honored guests this evening, and I'll have the crew make up a bed for Nasir. Make yourselves at home."

After Dr. Turnbull and Nasir retired to their beds, Seba told his father about swimming the Strait of Chios and how the dolphins had helped him in the final push to reach the shores of Turkey. He told his father of the wonderful friends he had met in the city, and the fact that the Muslims loved Mary as much as Seba's mother did.

"That's quite a statement, son. I've never known anyone more devoted to the Virgin Mary than your mother. And you say that the mother of your friend, Buğra, has a similar devotion? Well, I suppose I shouldn't be surprised. It reminds me of the words of Plotinus."

Before his father could complete the thought, however, Seba responded, "*It is in virtue of unity that beings are beings.*'"

His father laughed and patted Seba's arm. "How did you know I was going to say that?"

"I feel like it's something that God has been telling me ever since I stepped foot in the city of Smyrna. I've learned so much, and even though people here are from every corner of the world, there are many more similarities than differences."

Kostas nodded in agreement, but then his brow furrowed into a frown. "Speaking of your mother, what can you tell me? I've just realized that she must be in immense pain. I can't imagine how she is coping with the loss of her husband and her only son. She's all alone." Kostas's voice broke at the thought of his grief-stricken wife. "She must be devastated. We were each other's sun and moon, and she loves you more than life itself."

Seba felt his face grow warm as he imagined his mother puttering around their hearth in Sessera, baking bread and stirring soup without the men in her life to share it with. He hadn't realized until this moment what grief he must have caused her when he decided to swim the Strait of Chios and search for his father. It seemed like ages ago, though it had been only a few months. He knew his mother had a strong connection to the Virgin Mary, and he knew that she would have leaned on her for strength. A sob escaped Seba's throat as the guilt for what he had done welled up in him.

"I know, Papa. I don't think I understood her suffering until just now. I didn't realize what it would have felt like for her to lose both of us. The thought of finding you obscured everything else for me."

Kostas closed his eyes and nodded. That was something Seba had always appreciated about his father—Seba never felt judged by him, even when Seba judged himself.

"I guess I started to understand the feeling of loneliness when I came to Smyrna and I had no family here to support me. The donkeys and horses in Buğra's loft were the closest connection I had to home for a while. My friends have become my family in the short time I've been here, and I don't know what I would have done without them."

"Ah, yes, the scions of Smyrna. I can see you've learned much from them."

"Why do you call them that, Papa?"

"Well, from what you've told me, you and your friends, despite your different backgrounds, have struck out on your own and have made something new for yourselves in this city, which is exactly what a scion does."

"I've never heard that word, Papa."

Kostas laughed. "Don't tell your mother. Do you remember when Uncle Phillip took a cutting from a skinos tree and grafted it onto new stock? It was one of the primary techniques for propagating a stronger, more adaptable plant."

Seba nodded, remembering how Uncle Phillip used the *kentitiri* to cut the shoots from a well-producing tree and then band them to a young sapling that grew on a different part of the skinos terraces.

"Those cuttings are called scions, because they are taken from well-established stock, but when they are separated from the host, they unite with different varieties in order to make something new. The scions take the best of what's come before and create something better for the future. And the same goes for your friends."

"I don't understand."

"You, Paolo, Buğra, Meleia, Nasir, and even Dr. Turnbull have all branched out on your own, to make your own legacies. Your friends are descended from great stock, like we are descended from the ancient Greek heroes, yet you all have come together to make something new, not bound by what has come before. You are the Scions of Smyrna."

"I hope Mama feels that way. I have to tell her how sorry I am for leaving her alone."

"She will forgive you for trying to find me, even if she blames the adventure on your grandfather filling your head with stories of Heracles and Theseus." Kostas chuckled, and Seba thought it was the most magical sound he had ever heard.

"Yes, Papa, she will say it was all Papouli's fault." Seba sniffed happily, imagining his mother and his grandfather playfully arguing over the ancient Greek heroes, Mama imploring Papouli to focus on the heroes of the Bible instead. It was a memory that filled Seba with a warm feeling deep in his core that spread all the way to his fingers and toes.

Seba looked into his father's gray-green eyes, like his

own. "You should have seen the two of them dancing at my birthday celebration—you would have loved it."

Kostas laughed. "You're fifteen years old now, aren't you? You're a man, and I'm so proud of you."

Seba thought his ribs would burst open and his heart would escape, he was so filled with gratitude and happiness. "I knew I would find you."

Kostas's eyes misted, and he said, "There were days when I wondered if I would ever see my family again. That earthquake caused so much death and destruction, but I believe it brought us together. I'm sorry I missed so many birthdays."

Seba squeezed his father's hands. "It doesn't matter—all that matters is that we are together now."

Kostas smiled and said, "Speaking of celebrations, how is your grandfather? That man never missed a celebration, as I recall."

"He's as mischievous as ever, and he's getting married to Barbara Lampros."

"What? Now, that is something that I did not expect. I thought he enjoyed the bachelor life after your grandmother passed away."

"You should have seen when Mrs. Lampros sang to him—I thought he was going to melt into the floor. And you know she bakes the best *loukoumades* in Sessera. Papouli is going to be fat once he marries her!"

Father and son laughed, cried, and shared stories with each other as the moon sank low over the Gulf of Smyrna. They did their best to fit six years' worth of their lives into that evening.

"What are you going to do now, Papa? I don't think we can go back to live in Sessera."

"I agree, Seba. Dr. Turnbull has made a generous offer to

take me to East Florida, where I may build ships for him. Thinking that you were with your mother in Sessera, I asked him to sail to the shipyard on Chios, where I would entreat you both to join us. I know your mother's family has cultivated the skinos trees for generations—I hope that seeing me will entice her to leave with us on a new adventure. It will be a shock for her, and difficult for her to abandon what has been part of her ancestry for generations. As I recall, she does not welcome change, and it may take both of us to convince her to sail to the New World. That is, if you are coming with us."

"Of course, I'm coming with you! The only reason I came to Smyrna was to find you. Wherever you are going, I'll be there."

19 A PLAN

Dr. Turnbull had left instructions for Dmitri to continue bringing food to Seba and Kostas throughout the night, and Seba ate until he thought his trousers would split apart at the waist. As they reclined in the chairs that surrounded Dr. Turnbull's mahogany dining table, Seba pressed his father for information about his scars and his injured leg.

"Papa, was it horrible in Constantinople? Can you talk about it?"

Kostas sighed. "I guess it would be better for me to tell you now, because I won't be able to share these horrors with your mother. I think it would break her heart. It almost broke my spirit." He rubbed the area above his wrists, where the skin was a ghostly color and slightly misshapen, like the indentations on a donkey's back when it is saddled too tightly for too long.

"As I mentioned, when we first reached Constantinople, it was clear that I was not free, because there were guards everywhere, and my movements were monitored from sunup to sundown. They even posted a guard in our quarters at the harbor to make sure we wouldn't escape. You remember Samos, Ionnis, and Antonio, from the shipyard? They were with me, and we all slept in the same room—basically, a warehouse at the Constantinople harbor that had several cots on the floor. It wasn't even heated, and we weren't permitted to have a fire for cooking. Once I realized that Ahmed and his overseers were not going to agree to release us voluntarily, we thought that if we performed excellent work, we might be given certain privileges, and then we'd have more freedom to make our escape.

"How naive we were! And how hot-headed Antonio was—with good reason, of course. His wife was pregnant when we were kidnapped and taken away. As the months wore on, he made himself crazy, wondering if he had a little girl or little boy who would never know their father. The separation drove him insane, and he began to take risks that endangered us all. We tried to convince him to be patient, but we're Greek, for heaven's sake, and that is easier said than done.

"Antonio was always planning an escape, and it was all we could do to keep him subdued. After a time, he began to convince us that our plan to do excellent work to gain favor was a fool's errand. It was then that we actually supported several of his escape plans. Sometimes it was when we were taking a break for lunch, and other times in the middle of the night when we heard the guard snoring. Unfortunately, we were caught each time, and after the last one, in which Antonio, Ionnis, and I had made it onto a Dutch ship and were waiting for Samos to make it past the guard to join us, one of the Greek sailors whom we knew called out to Samos from the docks, and the guard woke up, caught him, and scoured all the ships moored in the harbor until they found us. We considered jumping overboard, but there was no way we could swim to freedom, and we couldn't bear to leave Samos to suffer alone in Constantinople. The punishment they would have inflicted on him for our escape would have killed him, I'm certain.

"After that time, we were chained together, with thick iron cuffs on our wrists and ankles. The shackles dug into our skin so deep that we bled every night for weeks until the callouses formed, and our flesh was on fire from the bruises that cut deep into our bones. After that, the few privileges we enjoyed were taken away. The guard carried a large whip, and if one of us made even a trivial mistake, we all suffered at least twenty lashes."

Kostas cringed, his shoulders hunching over as if imagining the whip cracking across his back. He continued, "We became skittish, jumping at any unexpected sound or happenstance. One time, we were installing a ship's wheel, and one of the spokes splintered, causing us to have to start its construction again from scratch. Ahmed's guard whipped us so violently that we all lost consciousness, even Antonio, who was the biggest and strongest among us. When I came to my senses after that beating, my hip was on fire. I think it had been dislocated—probably one of the guards had stomped or kicked me when I was passed out. But no matter how much I complained, the guards told me I was making up stories to try to escape. They refused my request for a physician."

Kostas pointed to his hip. "Look at it—I'm sure they could tell that it was severely displaced. They never allowed me to visit a doctor, and it never healed properly. It was awful. The only good days occurred if the crew on a ship we repaired took pity on us and smuggled fruit, bread, and cakes to us when no one was looking. Those days were rare. As a result of our ill treatment, our work suffered, and then we were punished even more severely for lack of production."

Kostas put his head in his hands. "I wouldn't wish that brutality on my worst enemy, Seba. Not in a million years." Seba leaned over and hugged his father. "You never deserved that, Papa. You're the best man I know, and I'm so sorry. I wish I would have come for you sooner."

Kostas broke away and hissed, "No! Seba, if you had come to Constantinople when we were enslaved there, you would have been treated the same way, and that would have been the circumstance that broke me. I thank God that you and your mother were safe all these years."

They were both quiet, and Seba thought he heard the morning birds calling. The sun would slowly rise over the mountains, sparkling on the water like precious gems. Then the large homes in the hills would become visible, and the wealthy boulevards surrounding Frank Street would spring to life. Although they couldn't yet see them, they could hear pelicans and seagulls soaring over the harbor, calling to each other as they fished in the last few moments of pre-dawn solitude. On the deck, Seba and his father could feel the dry breeze from the eastern mountains as it wafted toward the water, carrying with it the scents of citrus and ripening figs.

Kostas said brightly, "Let's talk of something happier. Tell me about this female scion of Smyrna. Based on what you and Dr. Turnbull mentioned, it appears that she is a woman much like your mother."

"Yes, she's taller than Mama, so I call her 'five and a half feet of fury' because her eyes spark like Mama's when she gets angry."

"Well, I can tell you must have a close relationship if you have experienced anger in addition to love." Kostas reached over and tickled Seba's beard. "Now that you're a man, it comes with the moniker."

Seba laughed. "Yes, Papa, ever since this hair on my chin began growing, I'm learning all about relationships. I can't wait for you to meet Meleia."

"Really? You believe I'll have a chance to meet her? It didn't seem as if she regards the doctor as well as I do, which means she's unlikely to visit this ship. And I'm not leaving this room until we reach Chios."

"I don't know, Papa. She's unlike anyone else I've ever met. She's infuriating, but I also want to be with her every minute of the day. She threw a bottle of wine at Dr. Turnbull when he visited her taverna in search of recruits, but maybe now if she knows that he saved your life, she'll reconsider. Paolo called Dr. Turnbull 'benign,' and I must agree. I think Meleia has misjudged him. Maybe I can convince her of this wonderful opportunity. I can't imagine being without her, because when she's not with me, I spend most of my time thinking about her."

Kostas tilted his head and cupped his chin in one hand. "It sounds like love to me."

Seba's face turned serious. "This night has been so wonderful that I almost forgot. I need to tell you something."

"Anything—we have all the time in the world now that we're together."

"That's just it. We *don't* have all the time in the world. I'm in trouble, and it's bad. Really bad. I don't want to put you in danger." As he said those words, Seba squeezed his eyes shut, pushing back the tears that tried to form behind his eyes. He couldn't lose his father after all they had suffered. He would not let Stavros near his father, no matter what happened.

Seba told him about the knife and scraping the tughras off the boxes of Turnbull's silk goods right below their feet in the hold.

Kostas was incredulous. "You say this is the older brother of our Timotheos, the priest?"

Seba nodded emphatically. "I know, I couldn't believe it either. They resemble each other physically, but they have nothing else in common. Stavros is horrible, the worst kind of slavedriver, and he calls his employees his 'little silkworms.' Papa, they boil the silkworms alive, before they get the chance to transform into beautiful white butterflies! It's all wrong."

Kostas pulled on his beard. "I agree, Seba. From what you've told me about Stavros Alkeidis, he sounds eerily similar to Ahmed, the sultan's cousin."

Seba agreed.

Kostas tapped his hands on his trousers emphatically. "In fact, I think we should act quickly. It seems like Stavros can't be trusted, and it also appears to me that he is playing both sides—acting as if he is working in conjunction with the Ottoman government but also consorting with pirates. I wonder if that's why he wanted you to scrape the sultan's seal from those crates—I'd wager that he's going to resell those goods as his own."

Seba's eyes grew wide as he absorbed what his father said. Now it all made sense—Hector and Marco, who looked and acted like pirates, Stavros's obsession with secrecy and loyalty, and his horrible temper. He was playing with the devil, appearing to all as if he were a legitimate businessman, but in reality, working with the pirates and profiting from the theft of his competitors' goods. *Why can't Stavros rely on Eleni's designs and run his business honorably? Does he think the only way he can succeed is by cheating? Is that why he's obsessed with loyalty? Because loyalty ensures that no one would reveal his cheating ways?*

Seba said, "We have to get out of here now, and go to Chios to get Mama before anyone finds out I'm here. Do you think it will work?"

"I hope so. For so many years, I thought that I would never see you or your mother again, and the pain was paralyzing."

"It was paralyzing for us, too, Papa. Mama was never the same after they took you away."

Immediately Seba wished he had not said that, because the sadness in his father's eyes was almost too much to bear. "I thought of you and your mother every day, and I never stopped thinking of a way to escape this slavery. I couldn't even think about the ships anymore. I hope this tragedy has not soured me altogether on the notion of shipbuilding."

Seba said, "I understand. That's why I came to find you."

"Yes, Seba, and I thank God with all my heart that you did. You say that you are in trouble, and so am I. No one knows that I survived the flood, and no one knows that I am on this ship—not that it is such a safe place, either, from what you've shared. All I know is that we have to get as far away from the Ottomans as possible, and it looks like Dr. Turnbull is our best chance for that. We need to entreat him to leave immediately, and when we get to Chios, we're going to sneak into Sessera and convince your mother to come with us, without getting caught."

Seba's eyes grew wide. He had escaped from Sessera less than two months ago, and he knew how difficult it was to get past the village's guards. *That's impossible.* Aloud, and despite his fear, he said, "I can do it, Papa."

259

Kostas believed that Dr. Turnbull would not leave until after sunrise, and therefore Seba had enough time to ask Meleia to join them before Stavros turned the officials onto Turnbull's ship. He left his knife with his father, who agreed to explain everything to Dr. Turnbull and Nasir, and to convey that it was Stavros's pirates who snuck aboard the ship to remove the tughras. Seba left a peeled stamp from one of the crates with his father as proof if someone questioned Dr. Turnbull before Seba could return. Seba hugged his father tightly, then opened the door to the main deck and gave his father a wave that was much more confident than he felt.

20 *NEW FORTUNA*

Seba ran down the gangplank, his mind racing with all the plans he and his father had discussed. He didn't even notice the sun as it peeked over the eastern mountains. Despite the July heat, Seba didn't stop running until he reached the Aigokeros, where Meleia was roasting the chickens and preparing the *adjuka* for the midday meal.

"*Kalimera*, Meleia!"

"Hello, Seba. You look like you've run a marathon. It seems a bit early in the morning for you to be out."

"I know, I've come from Dr. Turnbull's ship."

Meleia frowned. "I thought we had decided that you were going to stay away from him."

"Well, it's a good thing I didn't, because my father is with him. Dr. Turnbull saved my father from drowning in the tsunami at Constantinople!"

Meleia put down the chicken she was trussing for the spit. "Seba, that's wonderful! I didn't want you to get your hopes up of finding your father, because it seemed like such long odds that he would even be alive. I'm so happy for you!" She hugged him, and the joy he felt radiated outward from his heart.

She continued, "So that imbecile has done one thing right in his life, by saving your father. I'll grant him that, but nothing more." She was smiling so broadly that Seba knew she was teasing him.

"It was the best night of my life—we stayed up the whole evening on the ship, talking about the last six years. So much of our lives was exactly the same. I used to look up at the constellations from my roof at night and imagine that my father was viewing them, too. Orion, the Pleiades, and the Olympians, reminded me of the times we spent together when I was a boy, and gave me hope that we would find each other again. He said that he did the same. Even though we were apart, we were thinking of each other every day. And now we are together!"

A touch of sadness crossed Meleia's face, and Seba knew she was thinking of her own father. She said, "I'm glad for you, Seba. I remember what it was like when my father was himself, before the drinking. It felt safe, like nothing in the world could touch us. Celebrate that feeling; it doesn't always last."

"Well, this is going to last, because we are going to East Florida with Dr. Turnbull."

Meleia raised her eyebrow, an expression that Seba had come to love.

"And I want you to come with us. You can bring your father, and you can start a new taverna in East Florida. There will be so many workers that they will need a place to eat."

"Oh, the Englishman needs a cook on his little adventure, so now you're trying to enlist me as one of his workers?"

"No, no, no, it's more than that," Seba stammered. "The thought of leaving Smyrna without you is too much for me to bear. I want you to come with us."

"Why?"

"You know why. Are you going to make me say it?"

Meleia put her hands on her hips. "Yes."

"Because I'm in love with you."

Meleia's shoulders sagged. "Seba, I was afraid that's what you were going to say." She took a deep breath. "I know you have feelings for me, and I have feelings for you, too, but our relationship was always going to be temporary. I can't leave this city."

"I don't understand." Seba was gritting his teeth together, willing his eyes to stay dry. The last thing he wanted to do was cry in front of Meleia.

"You know all the work I put into this taverna. I can't leave it." Meleia's gold-flecked eyes were brimming with sadness. "And anyway, I'm too old for you."

Seba countered, "We're not that far apart in age. You're the same age as Paolo, and he's practically my best friend."

"It's not just that, Seba. My life is here, in this bustling city. I love this taverna, and I love the people of Smyrna. My family has been here for generations, and I feel like I belong to this city, like it belongs to me. I could never leave it! And my father is not well enough to leave, even if I wanted to."

"I think you're wrong about that. I spoke to him at Klydonas, and he quoted the *Iliad*. I think he's still in there. Maybe a change of location would bring him out."

Meleia stomped her foot and dropped the twine she was using to truss the chickens. Picking it up from the ground, she said, "Now you think you know my own father better than I do? Zeus was the most arrogant jackass in all of Greek mythology, but I think your ego is even bigger."

"But I thought—"

Meleia interrupted, "I know, I know. I really enjoy spending time with you, Seba, and you do have the most beautiful eyes I've ever seen. I'm afraid, however, that our timing is off. Maybe if we had met each other at another time, under different circumstances."

"Don't you see that we're meant for each other now? I see the way you look at me. Remember when we danced at Klydonas? We need to be together. I thought you felt the same way."

"I do, and I'm sorry, Seba. I am not Aphrodite, and I am not some manufactured goddess that fulfills your ideals. I'm a living, breathing, human being with my own hopes and dreams. You're going across the globe with your father and that damnable Englishman, and my dreams are here, in this city that I love. I'm not prepared to leave, even for you."

Seba felt like the room was spinning around him, and he clutched the kitchen washtub to steady himself. "Maybe I could convince my father to stay in Smyrna." He knew that was impossible, but he was grasping at anything that would make the pain of Meleia's words go away.

She put her hand on his shoulder. "You know that's not possible. Your whole life has revolved around finding your father. Now that you have reunited with him, you are not going to endanger his life."

"But what if—"

"No, Seba. Go with your father; you'll understand what I'm saying in due time. Let's remember the beautiful times we shared, and whenever you speak French, you'll think of me."

Seba turned on his heel and snapped, "I won't. I thought our relationship was special, but I guess I was wrong. I'm sorry I bothered you with all those French lessons, and I'm sorry I pestered you every night that I ate a meal in this taverna. It must have been a horrible imposition for you." *Don't cry in front of her, don't cry in front of her.*

Meleia called after him, "Seba, don't leave in this way. I'm not coming with you, but that doesn't mean we can't be friends."

He didn't respond, because in his mind, that's exactly what it meant.

#

Back on Turnbull's ship, Seba broke the news to his father, who remained in Dr. Turnbull's dining quarters, just as he had promised. It was good to see his father, who had suffered so much at the hands of the Ottomans, lounging on the velvet-covered couch, the oil lamps flickering, and the dining table overflowing with his favorite Greek delicacies. Even if Seba's heart had just been broken, at least he could be grateful that he was reunited with this father, especially with a large crock of avgolemono sitting on Dr. Turnbull's dining table. The unctuous chicken, barley, egg, and lemon soup was his favorite, something that both his mother and his father had made for him when he was a boy. Seba's mouth watered at the sight of it.

His father saw his gaze and limped over to the table to ladle the silky, comforting soup into a bowl for his son.

His eyes full of compassion as he handed the soup to Seba, Kostas said, "I'm so sorry, Seba. Heartbreak is one life experience that most of us suffer, but I had hoped that it might bypass you for at least a few more years. Did I ever tell you about the woman I courted before I married your mother?"

"No." Seba couldn't imagine his father with anyone else. Even though his parents were very different, they were a perfect match.

Seba looked at the soup in the bowl in front of him, and thought about all the days he couldn't eat it while his father was gone. And now Seba's heart was in pieces, but the fact that his father was there to share the grief with him made the soup feel like a comfort, as it had when he was a boy.

Kostas continued, "The girl who stole my heart when I was a young man was much like your Xenia, that girlfriend you had in Sessera." Seba balked at the description of Xenia as his girlfriend, but he did not want to contradict his father, so he continued to spoon the delicious egg and lemon soup into his mouth.

"Her name was Sophia, and she had long, brown hair always hanging in two tight braids down her back. She was the smartest girl I had ever met, and I adored her. I had every detail of our lives planned out—what church we would be married in, how many children we would bear, whether they would be boys or girls, where we would live, how many goats we would raise, and what musical instruments we would play in the winter evenings sitting by the hearth while the cold Chian winds blew outside our cozy home."

"That sounds wonderful." Seba was trying not to picture all of those scenes with him and Meleia.

"It was wonderful, but when I asked for her hand in marriage, she told me that I was too young for her, and she did not envision any of those experiences with me. She had her heart set on another boy in the village, and despite all the time we studied together in school and learned our Bible verses together, she told me that she only thought of me as a friend. I was devastated. My poor mother tried to console me for weeks—I wouldn't eat, I carried out my daily chores in a dull torpor, and I cried myself to sleep at night like a forlorn donkey. It was miserable."

"What did you do?" Seba again could see himself suffering in the exact same way as his father.

"Well, in time, I forgot about her, and it was your mother who helped me do that, with her fiery temper and passion for life. You'll find someone else, Seba. You have many years to find love, and I know that God has the right person waiting for you. They will appear when you are ready for them."

"But right now, it feels awful. What am I supposed to do?"

His father ladled the thick soup from the crock into a bowl for himself. He placed it on the table and put his hand on Seba's head. "Don't fight the pain—you must experience it and let all of the feelings flow through you, no matter how agonizing. I promise they will dissipate much more quickly if you can muster the energy to feel them fully."

"I don't want to do that."

Kostas wrapped his arms around Seba. "I know exactly how you feel. If you need to wallow in your misery, we will have plenty of time on the way to Chios, and then your mother may have some wise advice for you when we get to Sessera. Trust me—this too shall pass."

While embracing each other, they heard a crash, and Kostas jumped, releasing Seba and gaping at the door to Dr. Turnbull's dining quarters. Seba could see the whites of his father's eyes, like a frightened animal that had been cornered. Seba was more shocked by the sight of his father than the sounds coming from the deck. His father had never been afraid of anything, and now he was cowering behind the table, his eyes darting frantically around the room for a place to hide. *What have they done to you, Papa?*

Seba said with more confidence than he felt, "One of the crew must have dropped a crate; it's probably nothing."

Another crash, and the sound of angry voices on the deck.

"What if Ahmed found out I'm here? He's coming for me, Seba! You have to get away—I can't let them take us. We have to hide!"

Seba said, "You're scaring me, Papa. It's probably an argument between sailors. You know how they are. I'll go see what it is—you can stay here."

Kostas had pressed himself against a wall in the corner, but he reached a hand to grab Seba's arm. "Absolutely not. It might not be safe out there. Let's stay in here. Sometimes these ships are built with nooks and hiding places. Maybe we can find one." Kostas began haphazardly moving the carpets away from the floorboards and opening the cabinets.

Seba was chafing to get out and see what was happening, but he could feel his father's fragility, like wounded animal caught in a trap. Seba did not want to cause him any additional stress.

Someone rattled the door handle and shook the door violently.

Kostas whispered fiercely to Seba, "Come here, and get down!"

Seba turned to see his father kneeling on the floor, trying to squeeze himself into the base of Dr. Turnbull's immense liquor cabinet. Seba couldn't decide if the crashes outside or the sight of his frightened father were more unsettling.

They heard another crash and a cry of pain, but whoever had been at the door must have been pushed aside in the scuffle. Seba strained to distinguish any words from the shouting on deck, but the yelling and clanking and banging were so loud that he couldn't make out what they were saying or who was on board. It sounded very similar to the noise from the brawl at the Aigokeros, and Seba wondered if pirates were raiding the ship.

Kostas was almost wedged into the liquor cabinet. "Seba, you must find a place to hide. You can't let them find you. They'll take you away in chains, and I'll never see you again. I couldn't bear the sight of anyone beating my only son!"

The fighting went on for a long time, but no one ever breached Dr. Turnbull's dining room. Finally, Seba stood up, and said, "I'm going to see what's happening."

Before he could put his hands on the doorknob, his stomach lurched as he thought he recognized one of the voices that was shouting above the fray. *Why is Stavros on the ship?*

Seba pushed the door open wide enough for one eye to peek through the opening.

Dr. Turnbull's crew was fighting with a group of men that included Hector and Marco, as well as some others who looked like "thugs," as Meleia called them. Several men lay on the deck, bleeding and wounded, and many of the combatants were wielding knives. *I finally reunite with my father, only to be caught in a pirate raid? Please God, help me.*

Seba heard stomping on the gangplank and looked toward the port side of the ship. A bolt of terror shot through Seba's body—Stavros was wielding a knife that was twice the size of all the others, flailing it around indiscriminately like a whirling dervish carrying a blade. As Seba searched the deck for signs of Dr. Turnbull or Captain Alexiano, he saw Nasir emerge from the guest's quarters, holding a flintlock high in the air. Nasir fired it once, and immediately, the fighting stopped. Nasir bore an expression that was both dismayed and disappointed, as if he had expected Stavros to be here but hoped against hope that he was wrong.

Nasir said, "My friend, what are you doing on this ship? And why are you holding such a large knife?"

Stavros's eyes grew wide, and the hand holding the knife shook wildly. "That scoundrel Turnbull is stealing my silks and my silkworms. And he's transporting goods without paying the tariffs! If your uncle won't protect my business, I'll do it myself!"

Now that Seba knew what Stavros did to his silkworms—both the caterpillars and the employees—Stavros's statement made him feel sick. He had no more regard for the people who worked for him than he did for the silkworms that he boiled alive. He was going mad only because he couldn't control them.

Nasir took a step toward Stavros and said, "Those are bold accusations, my friend. Why don't we go to my uncle's offices, and you can make a complaint? Then the kadis will hear from Dr. Turnbull and will mete out justice in accordance with the law."

"My silks and silkworms will be gone by then. I need justice now!" Stavros rushed to the door behind which Seba stood, yelling, "Turnbull, I know you're in there—I'll kill you myself!"

As Stavros lunged toward the door, Seba pushed the door outward with all the force he could muster, and it clocked Stavros in the head, knocking him backward several steps. Stavros's eyes turned to fire as the recognition dawned on him, and he screamed at Seba while advancing, the knife pointed at Seba's heart, "You traitor, you thief—I knew you would betray me! You have no loyalty!"

Seba stepped out of Turnbull's dining quarters. He had retrieved the carpenter's knife from the table, and he now held it up defensively, daring Stavros to attack him.

Seba called, "No, you're a thief and a murderer! I should have never listened to you."

"How dare you, after all I've done for you!" Stavros lunged toward Seba, who was too quick; he jumped out of the way, barely avoiding Stavros's large knife.

Nasir ran toward Stavros, and knocked him on the back of the head with the butt of his flintlock. It slowed Stavros, but also enraged him, such that he was like a wild donkey, kicking and biting, and swinging the knife. Stavros wheeled on Nasir, and the two were engaged in a standoff.

"Stavros, if you go too far, you will never be able to return. Please, put down the knife."

"Those are just words, Nasir, and I've had enough of words. I need action."

The pirates and Turnbull's crew stood frozen, staring at the spectacle. They all looked as surprised as Seba at the turn of events, even Hector and Marco, who stood side-by-side, their faces a muddle of confusion. If there had been a plan, either to raid Turnbull's ship, or to retrieve the crates missing the tughras to resell them, or to send Ottoman officials to the ship to search for fraud, Stavros's appearance on the ship must not have been part of the plan.

In a flash, Nasir tackled Stavros, knocking him to the ground, and Seba saw the knife glint in the early morning light. They rolled on the ground, kicking and stabbing at each other, and Seba was again reminded of the brawl at the Aigokeros. Dr. Robin was right; Nasir never wanted to start a fight, but he certainly never backed down from one, either. Stavros was bigger, but Nasir was faster, and they were evenly matched for a time. However, at some point while they were tussling on the deck, Nasir stopped moving. Stavros jumped up and looked around wildly. Seba observed from the expression on Stavros's face that he was becoming aware of the gravity of his situation. *Stavros looks scared.*

Stavros turned and ran down the gangplank, the bloody knife hanging from his thumb and forefinger. Hector and Marco knew that their boss had mortally injured the nephew of Captain Paşa. They looked at each other, and ran down the gangplank behind Stavros. When Stavros had almost reached the dock, he turned and flung the knife into the water with a scream of rage and defiance. Seba watched the knife sink below the water's surface, and then he heard himself yelling, "No!" as he ran to Nasir. Seba gently flipped Nasir onto his back, but he was not prepared for what he saw.

Seba's hand flew to his mouth as he reached out with his other hand toward Nasir. Blood was pouring out of a knife wound in Nasir's chest, as well as several other gashes on his neck and upper arms.

Seba screamed, "Dr. Turnbull, help! Nasir's been stabbed! Stavros and his henchmen are getting away!"

Hearing those words, Turnbull's crew followed the pirates down the gangplank onto dry land, brandishing their knives triumphantly and shouting after the attackers.

"Good riddance, you scurvy rats!"

"Don't ever think of raiding a Greek ship again!"

"Stay away, you thieving scoundrels!"

"Keep running, you yellow-bellied cowards!"

As the crew continued to chase Stavros, Marco, Hector, and the pirates down the length of the waterfront, Captain Alexiano and Dr. Turnbull emerged from the captain's quarters and sprang into action, running to Nasir and holding both hands over Nasir's chest, where the blood was already pooling.

"Sebastian, bring me the leather physician's bag from my quarters! Pierce, go after that criminal who stabbed Nasir! Catch him before he gets away! Hendricks, fetch Dr. Robin, and tell her it's an emergency! Nasir has been injured, and I'm afraid he's already lost too much blood!"

21 FOLLOW THE DOLPHINS

Seba sat on a cask, stunned by Stavros's violent attack and feeling nauseous as he watched Dr. Turnbull's attempts to stem the blood pouring from Nasir's wounds. There were others on deck who had been injured by the pirates, and their mates were helping them to their feet and cleaning their wounds as well. It reminded Seba of the aftermath he and Paolo found when they returned to the Aigokeros after the brawl. Nasir's eyes were closed, and although Seba could see his chest moving up and down, Nasir's breathing was so labored that Seba thought each exhale would be his last. *No, no, no, you can't die, Nasir.*

"Dr. Turnbull, is there anything I can do?"

He didn't look up from his patient, but Dr. Turnbull replied, "I'm going to need more bandages. They're in the chest in my dining quarters. I haven't seen wounds so deep since the Seven Years' War. It's barbaric, I tell you."

Seba opened the door, chagrined by the sight of his father hiding in Turnbull's liquor cabinet. "Papa, they're gone, but

275

Nasir's been injured. We have to help him. Dr. Turnbull says there's a chest with bandages in it, and we need them right away."

Kostas climbed out from the cabinet and pointed to the opposite corner of the room, where there was a chest with a tapestry on it. Seba felt nauseated by the sight of the tapestry. He would be fine if he never saw another embroidered fabric as long as he lived. Seba slid the tapestry onto the floor, pulled a pile of cotton cloths from the chest, and turned and ran out the door with them.

Seba placed the cloths next to Dr. Turnbull, who was now covered in Nasir's blood and working feverishly to staunch the bleeding.

Seba heard footsteps on the gangplank and looked up to see none other than Paolo, whose eyebrows went sky-high as he gazed at Nasir, unconscious on the deck of Dr. Turnbull's ship, with the doctor leaning over him and applying tourniquets on both of his arms as his knee pressed into Nasir's chest.

Paolo was out of breath, and looked as if he'd run all the way from the workshop to the wharf. "Linus thought I would find you here. He said Eleni told him everything, and I should come here and try to stop Stavros from boarding Dr. Turnbull's ship. He had everything written down in that little journal he carries with him. It must be like a book of Alkeidis factory secrets or something."

Seba was incredulous. "Eleni and Linus knew that Stavros was going to come here?"

Paolo said, "I don't know what they knew, Seba, but Eleni said that the more time Stavros spent with Hector and Marco, the more volatile he became. Linus told me that she found wood shavings bearing the sultan's tughras in the desk in his office, and when she confided to Linus her concerns, he told her that Stavros asked to meet you in the silk room and sent everyone else away last night. They must have surmised what Stavros was doing, and they implored me to stop him before it was too late."

Seba's shoulders sagged. "It *is* too late. He stabbed Nasir, and then he ran off. We don't know where he went, but Hector and Marco and their pirate gang followed behind him. I don't know if Nasir's going to live."

Paolo looked down at Nasir, and the color drained from his face. "That poor fellow—he attracts violence like a moth to a flame."

Seba wanted to laugh at the irony of Paolo's statement, but the attack on Nasir had sucked all the mirth from his body.

Dr. Robin arrived not long after Paolo, carrying a bag full of bandages as well as her suture kit. She knelt down on the other side of Nasir, facing Dr. Turnbull, who explained the injuries using medical jargon that Seba did not understand. Dr. Robin looked pale and asked several questions, which Dr. Turnbull answered in the affirmative. The two of them used a glass tube in water that Dr. Robin placed into the wound, and Dr. Turnbull then sucked the air from it, like a pump to clear the blood from Nasir's chest. Then Dr. Robin took one of her glass bottles and poured its contents onto cotton rags that they used to clean the area around the chest. Seba heard them say that Nasir's lung had collapsed, and they pressed on his chest, as if trying to pump up a bladder. They worked for a long time until, satisfied with their work, they put a cotton patch over the wound and cleaned up the other cuts.

Paolo asked, "Is he going to live?"

Dr. Robin and Dr. Turnbull said simultaneously, "I hope so."

Dr. Robin continued, "My friend has healed from past wounds that would have killed a lesser person. It was only a few weeks ago that I treated him for broken ribs. His body probably has not completely healed from the injuries he suffered in that fracas at the Aigokeros."

Dr. Turnbull said, "He's a military man, like myself, who was once in the foreign service for His Majesty King George II, God rest his soul. Nasir has a strong constitution, and there is no more honorable man in Smyrna. I pray that God will protect him."

The two physicians asked the crew to bring a cot to transfer Nasir to Dr. Turnbull's dining quarters, to enable him to rest peacefully in a central location where his recovery could be easily monitored. After they were satisfied that Nasir was convalescing as comfortably as could be expected, Dr. Turnbull turned to Dr. Robin and said, "I believe I'm in need of a nice glass of Madeira after all this excitement. I've brought a few bottles with me from our travels in Portugal. Would you like to join me?"

Dr. Robin pulled a pocket watch from her skirts and looked at it quizzically. Seba could tell from the angle of the sun that it was early, and he imagined that Dr. Robin was thinking the same thing. However, she returned her pocket watch to her skirts and said kindly, "I couldn't possibly refuse such a generous offer, cousin. Lead the way."

Seba and Paolo sat down on two barrels of tar that were kept on the main deck for waterproofing. Seba whispered to Paolo, "I've found my father."

Paolo yelled, "Wha—" but Seba clapped his hand over Paolo's mouth so quickly that it made a slapping sound. He pulled Paolo inside the doorway of Dr. Turnbull's dining quarters.

"Shhh, he's escaped from Constantinople, and he's in

danger. No one can know that he's on board. We're leaving with Dr. Turnbull as soon as we can, but now I guess we can't leave until Nasir is recovered. I'm afraid Stavros is going to come back to the ship and do something crazy. He stole something important from me, and I know he's going to try to use it against me. If he alerts Governor Paşa's military guards, they'll find out who my father is and turn him over to the janissaries. We won't be able to rest until Stavros is caught, or until we sail from this port, whichever occurs first."

Paolo looked over at Nasir, bandaged and lying on a cot, then his eyes grew wide as he viewed the other man in the room. He pointed to Kostas and mouthed, "Is that your father?"

Seba nodded, and his heart filled with pride. Before Seba had a chance to introduce Paolo to his father, they heard a commotion outside on the deck. The crew was calling for Dr. Turnbull and haranguing their fellow crew member named Pierce.

"Picaroon Pierce is back!"

"He looks like a boiled langostine!"

"You're going soft, Pierce! A bit of running has you worn out!"

"He can't take the heat in this climate!"

"Shut up, you old sea crabs, and get him some water so he can give us the news!"

Seba and Paolo ran for the door, each pushing the other to get past the threshold first. The man called Pierce was indeed winded, his chest heaving in and out and his face ruddy with exertion. He leaned on the mainsail's halyard as he caught his breath. Dr. Turnbull, Dr. Robin, and Captain Alexiano alighted from the captain's quarters as one of the crew members dipped a mug into a water barrel and handed it to Pierce.

Dr. Turnbull said, "Take a moment, Pierce. Dr. Robin and I don't need any other patients on this ship today."

Pierce gulped down the whole mug of water and said, "Stavros Alkeidis has been arrested for the stabbing of Nasir Beyzade Paşa. He tried to resist the Ottoman guards, and during the struggle, a pouch of mastiha and a gold ring bearing the sultan's tughra fell from his pockets. No one but the sultan and his officials are permitted to possess those rings, and no one but the sultan himself carries such a large quantity of mastiha on his person. The Governor's guards told Alkeidis that in light of the contraband, he would be tried for theft and treason, in addition to the stabbing. They took him away in chains, and he was yelling the whole time that Dr. Turnbull was harboring a mastiha thief, and that the ring and pouch of mastiha belonged to the thief. Of course, no one believed him, and he became more violent. By all accounts, it took three guards to subdue him, and one of them may have suffered a broken jaw in the process. Nearly all of the inhabitants of Frank Street were standing in front of their homes and shops, gawking at the spectacle. It will be the talk of every taverna in town tonight, I'm certain. One of the kadis met the guards at the Governor's office, and a clerk named Buğra said that Captain Paşa would take care of Alkeidis himself. He said that a man named Linus has been working with Captain Paşa for many months now, compiling and investigating allegations of piracy and fraud against Stavros Alkeidis. They were waiting until they had more information, but now that Alkeidis has attacked Captain Paşa's nephew, they have more than enough evidence to convict him of multiple crimes. Oh yes, and two rather large men with Stavros Alkeidis were also arrested on charges of piracy."

Seba walked back into Dr. Turnbull's dining quarters and said quietly to his father, "It's over. We're safe."

Paolo, who had followed Seba inside, clapped him on the back said, "Did you know that Linus was a spy for Captain Paşa? I wouldn't believe it if I hadn't heard it with my own ears."

Seba shook his head. "I would have wagered an entire pouch of mastiha that he was not a spy, but maybe that's what makes a spy good at his job. No one would ever guess. He seemed to really love working at the silk factory. I hope that he continues there, because Eleni will need his assistance to clean up everything that Stavros has tainted."

Paolo laughed. "Well, I guess this makes my decision about who to work for a bit easier. I was contemplating whether I should volunteer for this East Florida venture, and now that Stavros will be in trial and then likely in prison for many years, I think my decision's been made for me. I'm going to ask Dr. Turnbull if he has room for another recruit."

Seba chuckled, along with his father, who appeared to have returned to his old self. Then Paolo spied Dr. Turnbull's dining table, which was filled with the crock of avgolemono, as well as pastries, savory breakfast dishes, and fruit. "But I can't ask him on an empty stomach, can I? Do you think Mr. Florida will mind if I have some breakfast first? I'm sure he wants his recruits to be well fed."

Kostas said, "He's been feeding me at least three meals a day since I met him, and he seems to enjoy eating as much, if not more, than the next man. I don't think he'd deprive anyone of a full belly."

With a mouth full of baklava, Paolo said, "I knew I liked that Englishman."

Seba and Kostas laughed heartily as they drank Turkish

coffee from the little ceramic cups that Dmitri had brought them.

Seba, Paolo, and Kostas waited in Dr. Turnbull's dining quarters for news of Nasir's condition, and the Krizomatis men shared what they knew with Paolo, including Kostas's treatment at the hands of the brutal Ottoman guards in Constantinople.

Paolo, stuffing his face full of breakfast cakes, said, "And what of your colleagues? Did the other shipbuilders escape as well?"

Seba had been so concerned about his father that he forgot to ask about the other men from the shipyard—Samos, Ionnis, and Antonio.

Kostas answered, "Yes, we were a team, and we still are. The Danish captain vouched for us, and promised the overseer that he would personally bring us back as we rowed out from the dock to where the *New Fortuna* was anchored. We were so happy to be out of the irons. I had forgotten what freedom felt like, and as I walked the decks, feeling the salt spray on my face, I almost believed I was Odysseus himself, returning from the Trojan War."

Kostas closed his eyes and blew air slowly through his cheeks. "We were on this very ship, sailing around the Sea of Marmara, when the earthquake hit. The tsunami was merely a mild swell out at sea, several miles from the Constantinople harbor, but we all watched in horror as the wave grew taller than a mountain as it approached the port. The Danish captain was grateful for the invitation to demonstrate his design, and he said it was the reason we were still alive. He told us not to worry about his promise to the overseer. We were given the gift of freedom, and he encouraged us to make the most of it. He had seen the effects of these walls of water in the past, and said it was unlikely that anyone who worked on the docks had survived. Dr. Turnbull called together all the crew that evening, and we prayed together for the souls who had been lost at Constantinople. Ionnis, Samos, Antonio, and I thank God every day for delivering us from evil. We are blessed to have been rescued, and are interested to learn more about Dr. Turnbull's East Florida venture."

Seba cocked his head, the wheels in his mind turning. "You mean Antonio is going to see his child for the first time?"

Kostas put his hand on Seba's arm. "If all goes well, then yes, we'll reunite with your mother, and Antonio will reunite with his wife. He'll also see his baby, who is no longer a baby, for the first time in his life."

Paolo looked as if tears were beginning to form behind his lashes. When Seba looked at him questioningly, he said, "I'm so happy for him, and I'm happy for us. I have feelings, too, Seba! We're Greek, for heaven's sake, aren't we?"

Seba and his father guffawed loudly. They *were* Greek, for heaven's sake.

A few hours later, Nasir gained consciousness long enough for Dr. Robin to declare that he could be transported to Dr. Robin's home, where he could be monitored and fed Claudine's delicious broth, which, according to Dr. Robin, was as good a medicine as anything in her surgical room.

Dr. Robin and Dr. Turnbull embraced, and the Englishman said, "Thank you, cousin. I know my time in Smyrna was cut short, but I believe that it would have been even shorter if you had not intervened to protect me. If you ever venture west to the New World, please know that you will always have a place in my home—New Smyrna."

Dr. Robin was beaming, and she tapped her cousin on the back. "We are family, Andrew. Maybe not by blood, but we are family, nonetheless. You are always welcome here."

Hearing those words about family, Seba thought of Buğra. It didn't matter that Buğra was a Turkish Muslim and Seba was a Greek Christian; Buğra had treated Seba like a brother during Seba's entire time in Smyrna. Buğra had given him a comfortable place to stay, had introduced him to Meleia, had provided him with food, clothes, and sage advice, all with a gentle smile and genuine joy for living. Seba couldn't bear the thought of leaving without saying goodbye to Buğra.

Seba placed a hand on Dr. Robin's shoulder and said, "Dr. Robin, may I ask a favor?"

She turned and smiled at Seba. "Of course, young man. What is it that you require?"

"I have a friend, Buğra, who works in the clerk's office for Governor Paşa, and he has been like a brother to me during my short stay in Smyrna. I won't have time to visit him and thank him properly, so I'd like to write him a note. Would you be able to have someone deliver it to him at the clerk's office?"

Dr. Robin reached for her doctor's bag as she spoke. "That is very kind of you, Sebastian. I've known Buğra his whole life—in fact, I delivered him into this world. It would be my pleasure to relay your message of appreciation." She retrieved a sheet of paper from her bag and handed it to Seba. "Here, take this into Dr. Turnbull's dining quarters— he has ink and a quill on the desk next to his liquor cabinet. Please hurry, because I need to transport Nasir back to my home as soon as possible so he can recover in peace."

Seba replied, "Thank you so much!" He took the paper from her and ran to Dr. Turnbull's desk, where he penned a note to Buğra:

Dear Buğra, I'm sorry that I cannot say goodbye to you in

person over a mug of barley ale at the Aigokeros. I am truly grateful for the hospitality you've shown me here in your home of Smyrna. Sleeping in your loft made me feel like I was back in Sessera, and the sounds of your horses and donkeys below gave me comfort when I felt alone in this big city. I never would have believed that one of my best friends in Smyrna would have been an employee of the Ottoman government, but you showed me that it is what is inside people's hearts that is important, much more so than any political affiliations. You are kind, caring, and generous, and I wish that I had more time to laugh with, talk to, and learn from you. Thank you for teaching me that Muslims and Christians have much more in common than most people know, and thank you for treating me like a member of your family. I'll never forget you, and I wish you many blessings. Your friend and brother, Seba.

Seba folded up the paper, and ran back out to the deck as Nasir was carried gently toward the gangplank by several sailors whom Dr. Robin had haled from the docks.

Handing the paper to Dr. Robin, Seba asked, "Can I say goodbye to Nasir?"

She put the note in the pocket of her skirts and nodded, saying "I'm not sure that he will hear you, Sebastian, but he may feel your presence. Any goodwill you may extend to him, in person or in prayer, will benefit him, I'm certain."

Seba knelt by Nasir's cot, held his hand, and said, "Thank you for everything, Nasir. You showed me what it means to be honorable in the worst of circumstances, when the temptation to follow the wrong path is overwhelming. You are one of the bravest people I've ever met. I'll never forget you. No other scion of Smyrna can compare to you."

Nasir's eyes did not open, and he didn't make a sound, but Seba felt the most infinitesimal squeeze of his fingers. It was a simple message, and Seba knew then that Nasir would be fine.

After Nasir was carefully transported to the docks and was on his way slowly to Dr. Robin's office, and Paolo (who had wiped the breakfast crumbs from his face) had implored Dr. Turnbull to accept him as a recruit, Dr. Turnbull told Captain Alexanio that it was time to depart.

The captain barked out orders at a furious pace, and the crew bounded into action, pulling up the anchors, letting out the sails, and drawing in the mooring lines.

"We're bound for Chios, you sea dogs! We'll be there tomorrow, but we won't stay there long! We'll be sailing the wide Aegean Sea within the week!"

The sailors shouted their appreciation to be heading to open waters, and they worked cheerfully, calling out and teasing each other, which Seba well knew was a requirement of being a mariner.

As the ship began to turn toward the west, a few of Mr. Florida's other recruits made their appearances on deck. Seba was surprised to see Michalis and Mattheios, the twin boys who had previously worked for Stavros, the former with the stump of one arm covered in a leather strap, as well as Samos, Ionnis, and Antonio, whom Seba now recognized from his childhood visiting the shipyard.

Seba walked to the bow of the ship, feeling the brisk Aegean Sea breeze in his face. He was heading west with his father toward a new adventure, a new journey on the way to reclaim his legacy. The warm July sun was behind them to the east, illuminating the blue waters of the Gulf of Smyrna. To the north, Seba watched a pair of dolphins playing in the harbor. His father came behind him and put his hands on Seba's shoulders. "It's as I told you, Seba. You can't go wrong when you follow the dolphins."

AUTHOR'S NOTE

I'm grateful for the opportunity to continue Sebastian Krizomatis's journey in the Merchant Tides series. Visiting Izmir (formerly Smyrna) was a highlight of writing Scions of Smyrna, and I have my daughter Jane, her friend Alara, and Alara's mom, Beril to thank for making the trip so special. To say that they hooked us up would be an understatement.

I was as awestruck and wide-eyed as Seba when our plane landed in this gorgeous metropolis. The waters of the Bay of Izmir are deep blue and beautiful, and the crescent shaped coast and mountains rise up to surround the harbor exactly as it was described in the 18th century accounts of travelers I read while researching this book. Izmir is a vibrant cosmopolitan city full of the most kind and generous people I've ever met.

Thanks to Alara, Maryam, and Beril for giving us the insider's guide to Izmir (including fresh figs!), and to Parya, Turker, Nizam, and Ali for the wonderful hospitality during our stay. The music, the food, the salt spray, the daily calls to prayer, the history, the tea served in tulip glasses, the Turkish sand coffee, the breeze off the Aegean Sea–it was all magical. Jane and I felt so welcome that we didn't want to leave.

It's not hard to imagine what this bustling city was like in the 18th century, because today it truly exemplifies how people from east, west, and all over the world, can celebrate their differences while living together harmoniously.

I hope you enjoyed reading this book as much as I enjoyed writing it. If you liked it, please consider leaving a review. Honest reviews help authors find their readers and enable authors to continue writing what they love. If you would like to read more about Sebastian's adventures, sign up for my mailing list at www.kpearsonbradley.com and receive updates on upcoming books in the Merchant Tides series.

ABOUT THE AUTHOR

K. Pearson Bradley is an American writer. Scions of Smyrna is the second book in her Merchant Tides series, following the first book, entitled Tears of Chios. She lives in Saint Augustine with her husband.

Made in the USA
Columbia, SC
08 April 2024

33893848R00166